An

An Inconvenient Friend

Rhonda McKnight

www.urbanchristianonline.net

Urban Books, LLC
78 East Industry Court
Deer Park, NY 11729

An Inconvenient Friend Copyright © 2010 Rhonda McKnight

ISBN 13: 978-1-60162-864-0
ISBN 10: 1-60162-864-1

First Printing August 2010
Printed in the United States of America

10 9 8 7 6 5 4 3 2 1

*This is a work of fiction. Any references or similarities to actual
events, real people, living, or dead, or to real locales are intended to
give the novel a sense of reality. Any similarity in other names, characters, places, and incidents is entirely coincidental.*

Distributed by Kensington Corp.
Submit Wholesale Orders to:
Kensington Publishing Corp.
C/O Penguin Group (USA) Inc.
Attention: Order Processing
405 Murray Hill Parkway
East Rutherford, NJ 07073-2316
Phone: 1-800-526-0275
Fax: 1-800-227-9604

An Inconvenient Friend

Dedication

For my mother, Bessie McKnight . . . thanks for the love, wisdom, and being my best friend.

Acknowledgments

It's so hard to write acknowledgments for my second book when, at the time of this writing, my first book hasn't come out yet. I'm sure by the time this book hits the stores I will be indebted to so many people for helping me get the word out about *Secrets and Lies*, but I guess those thanks will have to be in book number three.

Always first—My Lord and Savior, Jesus Christ, for blessing me with the gift, time, and mind to use all wisely.

My sons, Aaron and Micah—I love you madly, and I pray my writing and traveling is never a burden.

Mom—In addition to being the best mother in the entire world, you are the best grass roots publicist on the earth. Thank you so much for believing in me and pushing the book to and on everyone in South Carolina. You are such a marketing queen. I love you. Love you too, Daddy!

Sherri Lewis—You know you are seriously "The Truth." I don't know what I would do if I couldn't e-mail, text, and call you (Please don't move to Africa). Thanks for getting behind this crazy story and helping me see it through to the end. 'Preciate your sharp eye.

Tiffany Warren—My new best friend, thanks for the wisdom, the funny e-mails, and long phone chats. You've been a bigger blessing than you can imagine.

Sharon Oliver—Your grace, persistence, and marketing savvy inspire me. You pack a big punch, but remain prayerful and humble. I admire your spirit and determination.

Acknowledgments

Tia McCollors—The voice of reason when I'm having a freak out moment. How do you stay so cool? Thanks for always being there when I need you for the mommy stuff and the writing stuff. Thanks also for introducing me to some of your book clubs. I appreciate the support.

Victoria Christopher Murray—My literary mentor, words cannot express the level of appreciation I have for your guidance. Just know I appreciate you from the bottom of my heart.

Other mentors and awesome sisters that continue to pave the way for newbies like me—Jacquelin Thomas, ReShonda Tate Billingsley, Angela Benson, Stacy Hawkins Adams, Kimberla Lawson Roby—thank you ladies for always taking the time to share and encourage me and others.

My girls, near and far—Janice Ingle, Margaret Brown, Jacqueline Carter, Tracey Boyd, Jenenne Young, Dee Stewart, Maria Caraballo, Marletta Elliot, Felesia Bowen, and the ladies of *Faith Based Fiction Writers of Atlanta*—thanks for the love, support, and encouraging words.

My South Carolina family—Sherri Smiling, Aunt Willie Mae McKnight, Elma McKnight, Tyra Johnson—Thanks to y'all for wearing those *Secrets and Lies* T-shirts all over Manning.

Facebook friends—I am not getting myself into trouble calling out names. So thanks all 1,600 of y'all!

Much love to my sister-circle at Urban Books (Urban Christian imprint)—Zaria Garrison, Monique Miller, Sherryle K. Jackson, Nikita Nichols, T.N. Williams, and Pat Simmons.

My editor at Urban Books, Joylynn Jossel, for continuing to believe in my work and letting me be me. Thanks to Carol Mackey at Black Expressions Book Club for selecting *Secrets and Lies* and putting me in hardcover. Thanks again to my agent, Shana Crichton, for her support and sound advice.

To every reader, book club, bookstore, and librarian who

Acknowledgments

have already purchased *Secret and Lies*—Thanks so much for taking a chance on a newbie author. Words cannot express my gratitude. A little extra love to Tanisha Webb of *K.C. Girl-friends*, Tifany Jones of *Sistah Confessions*, and Ella Curry of the *Black Author Network* for teaching me so much along the way.

To all the bloggers, website administrators, and Internet radio hosts who supported my virtual tours—I'm forever in your debt.

To all the reviewers who took the time to review *Secrets and Lies*—Thank you for your support and love of African American fiction. Your service is invaluable.

Lisa Zachery at PaperedWonders.com—No one designs better bookmarks and postcards than you. I'm amazed that you manage to top yourself with every project.

Big thanks to my virtual assistant, Kym Fisher, for keeping me grounded, organized, and together.

And last but not least, thanks to Tyora Moody of *TyWebbin Creations* for the best website, blog tours, press kits, logo, ad designs . . . you do it all, and you do it well. You are incredible. Thanks so much for establishing my visual brand!

Now let's get to the good stuff—Samaria Jacobs is back with more drama. Her creed is "If at first you don't succeed—try, try again." Can we get this chick redeemed? Turn the page and find out!

What People Are Saying about

An Inconvenient Friend

"Rhonda McKnight has written a sizzling novel full of jaw dropping, sexy drama and unexpected plot twists. I was captivated by this fresh, original story from page one."
—Victoria Christopher Murray, *Essence*® bestselling author of *Lady Jasmine* and *Too Little, Too Late*

"Talk about scandalous! *An Inconvenient Friend* is full of drama and deception, but God's message of forgiveness and redemption are powerfully delivered. Rhonda McKnight has quickly earned her place as a favorite in Christian fiction.
—Sherri Lewis, Essence® bestselling author of *Selling My Soul* and *The List*

"Rhonda McKnight really shines in her sophomore release! She combines the perfect mix of inspiration and drama; friendship and betrayal. I was engaged from the very first page. I am definitely a fan!"
—Tiffany L. Warren National bestselling author of *In the Midst of it All* and *The Bishop's Daughter*

Praise for Secrets and Lies

"Through memorable characters and a plot that keeps you turning the pages, Rhonda McKnight takes you on an emotional roller coaster ride that holds you hostage until the end!"
—Victoria Christopher Murray, Essence® bestselling author of *Lady Jasmine* and *Too Little, Too Late*

"Rhonda McKnight has written an emotional but inspiring story of faith, trust and forgiveness as well as the importance of having God in our lives."
—Jacquelin Thomas, Essence® bestselling author of *The Ideal Wife* and *Jezebel*

"Rhonda McKnight is a fresh new voice in Christian fiction who writes with the skill and grace of a seasoned pro. Her characters seem like friends and her prose flows effortlessly."
—Stacy Hawkins Adams, Essence® bestselling author of *The Someday List* and *Watercolored Pearls*

"Rhonda McKnight's debut novel doesn't disappoint. It mixes appealing and relatable characters with doses of drama and mischief that kept me hooked until the last page."
—Tia McCollors, Essence® bestselling author of *The Last Woman Standing* and *A Heart of Devotion*

". . . If a man has a hundred sheep, and one of them has gone astray, does he not leave the ninety-nine on the hills and go in search of the one that went astray?"
— Matthew 18:12

Chapter 1

I stepped into the classroom marked "Women's Bible Study" with a mission in mind that had nothing to do with Jesus. I was going to get to know more about my man's wife and use what I learned to steal her husband. This place they called holy ground was about to become a battleground. The plan—*Operation Steal Greg.*

"Is this classroom C?" I made sure to add just the right mix of airhead and sweet church girl to my voice. The door was clearly marked, but I had to say something because I was late, and all the real church sisters were already seated and staring.

A plump chick in her late thirties jumped to her feet like someone yelled happy birthday and she was popping out of a cake. "Yes, sister, come in. Have a seat." She swayed an open palm in the direction of the chair she'd vacated.

I smiled tight, then took two steps to the left and away from the over eager beaver. "Thanks." I crinkled my nose and pointed. "I'll take something over there."

Big girl looked disappointed, but my choice of seating was strategic, so I wasn't giving in to sad puppy eyes. I flicked a lock of my hair over my shoulder and did a visual sweep of the occupants. Thirty or so women were dispersed throughout the room in small groups that reminded me of cliques in the high school cafeteria. I could tell they were the kind that chewed you up and spit you out like the mystery meat that followed Tuesday's spaghetti.

Since they were staring, I put a little extra motion into my well practiced jig. Sixty eyeballs followed the rhythmic gliding of my hips as I made my way to what I thought would be the perfect seat to make observations; the vacant back row. I rested my Dolce Gabana handbag on an empty seat, picked up the Bible that lay in wait for me, and as a final gesture for the royal nosies, wiggled down into the chair and crossed one leg over the other.

Try that, I thought, noticing more than half the occupants in the room were overweight and hard pressed to cross any extremity over the other.

I turned my attention to the woman behind the podium who I figured must be the Bible Study teacher, if that's what you called the presenter at a thing like this. The only study groups I'd attended were for school. Church wasn't my thing. I had never quite figured out the purpose for it all, and as far as I could see, most of the hypocritical, nasty, backbiting Christians I worked with hadn't either. Nah, I'd taken a pass on the church thing—until now.

"Hello." The teacher met my gaze. "I'm Sister Green. Welcome to women's Bible Study." Then, with an uncomfortable cough, she dropped her eyes to the book she was holding.

So much for introductions.

"Let's go to the sixteenth verse, and if you would, Sister Hawkins, read down to verse twenty-one for us," Sister Green continued.

A wiry woman not too far from me stood to her feet and began reading, "So I say, live by the Spirit, and you will not gratify the desires of the sinful nature. For the sinful . . ."

I tuned her out, after all, that wasn't the reason I was here. I craned my neck left, and then right, looking for the person I'd come to see, but she wasn't here. I'd only seen Greg's wife once, from a distance, when I'd lurked outside a charity event he'd slipped and told me they were attending.

Angelina Preston had long hair that fell in an angled bob down her back. No one's do fit the bill from where I sat, and because I was in the back, I couldn't see any of their faces. I hoped I hadn't wasted an evening coming to this gathering of stuck up, sanctimonious, women for nothing. I snapped the Bible closed I'd had open across my knee and began tapping my heel impatiently. Just when I was about to call it a wrap, the door opened.

Angelina Preston swept into the room looking like an African American corporate *Barbie* doll in a chocolate St. John suit, Jimmy Choo slingbacks, and matching handbag. I let my mental calculator go to work. The woman was wearing close to a thousand dollars worth of gear, and that didn't include the rocks in her ears or the one that for sure was weighing down her left hand.

I squirmed in my seat. I wanted to curse, but remembered I was in a church, so I bit my tongue. Talk about a bad sister. I uncrossed my legs and watched Angelina glide across the short space and slide effortlessly into a seat. Her featherweight hair billowed like smoke behind her. She turned to the women on her left and right, offered them a few words and a quick smile through perfect teeth, and looked to Sister Green.

"Sister Preston, we're glad you're here. I'll turn the lesson over to you." Sister Green moved away from the podium like someone had told her there was a bomb underneath it. From the awkward way she had been conducting herself before Angelina showed up, I could tell she wasn't one for public speaking. Her role as teacher really had me wondering about the church thing already.

Angelina stood and peeled off her jacket as she made her way to the front of the room. "Good evening, ladies."

Her voice matched her corporate persona. It had that Demi

Moore husky quality that was great for business, but also sexy to a lot of men in the bedroom. "Hmmm, something else to hate about her," I murmured under my breath.

"Thank you for excusing my tardiness. It couldn't be helped. As most of you know, I'm on the board for the Department of Youth and Family Services, and thanks to the media, you're probably also aware that we had a child death last night that necessitated an emergency board meeting."

"How is the family, Sister Preston?" one of the women asked. A solemn pallor had fallen over the room. I vaguely remembered hearing something about a four-year-old foster child dying from an unexplained fall. I shuddered at the thought.

"The family is outraged, understandably, but I'm not really able to discuss the case."

The women seemed to understand that. I had no idea Angelina was affiliated with child welfare. What thankless work for someone who—well—didn't have to work at all.

"We can pray for the family after the meeting." She closed the subject neatly. "Let's pick up where we left off last week."

"Sister Preston." Big Girl stood and careened her neck in my direction. "We have a guest."

Darn, I didn't need anyone pointing me out. I was trying to be incognegro, but it was not to be so. Angelina wasn't going to be rude and ignore a sista like her predecessor had.

She tilted her head ever so slightly, and her mouth eased into a smile that was full of sincerity. "I apologize for not noticing. I'm Angelina Preston, the women's adult education coordinator for Greater Christian Life. Welcome. Please tell us your name and anything else you'd like to share with the group."

I wasn't sure how introductions were handled in church. I stood to my feet and stated the lie I'd prepared for this moment. I hesitated for a second, wondering if I were supposed to call myself sister, but then I realized Angelina hadn't put sister in front of her name, so I nixed it.

"Good evening, ladies. My name is Rae Burns. I've been coming to the church for a few weeks now. I live in Roswell. I'm single, and I work as a healthcare consultant." I plopped down in my seat, shocked that perspiration had dotted my top lip and pleased that I hadn't messed up and said my real name.

That coming to the church a few weeks part was not true either. Except to attend a wedding or funeral, tonight was the first time I'd stepped foot in this church or any church. I was thinking with nearly two thousand members that no one would know this was my first visit. I was obviously wrong. A few of them looked between each other, comparing mental notes, shaking their heads that they had not seen me at their service. I ignored them. I only cared what one woman thought, and that was the one who was looking directly at me.

"We're glad to have you with us, Rae." Angelina's delivery was warm and sincere. "We hope that this evening is the first of many journeys into the Bible with us." After an appropriate pause for welcomes and nods from other women in the room, Angelina resumed her discussion of the lesson.

I resumed my studies also. From her appearance to her public speaking skills, the way she threw her hair over her shoulder and the classy way she held her swan-like neck; every word, every movement, everything about her was polished. Her persona seemed to be perfected to convey one resounding message. *I am the hotness with a capital H. Don't mess with me.*

It was starting to get on my nerves because I was going to mess with her, and I hated the fact that I was starting to feel intimidated. I mean as far as looks, she was predictably what I expected. A doctor's wife—classy. A handsome doctor's wife—

beautiful. I did notice one thing that I wouldn't have guessed, not based on Greg's old southern money, Louisiana upbringing. Angelina wasn't from the south. This surprised me because the southern gentlemen usually married the belles who understood them, but northern she was.

I had studied a lot of accents. She spoke that clipped English that well-to-do black folks from up north chirped in their superior, northernly way. My guess was this diva was from Jersey or Connecticut. Greg and I had never talked about it. With the exception of the few times he let me know Wednesday evenings were a good night for us to be together, because his wife taught Bible Study, he never mentioned her. The only reason I knew where to come tonight was because he'd been talking on the phone to her, and I overheard him sarcastically say something about her undying allegiance to Greater Christian. I had heard that name, Greater Christian, before, on radio advertisements. One trip to Google had me in the complete know.

I covertly tried to learn more about Mrs. Preston from Greg. A girl likes to know a little about her competition, but he was unwilling to share. That was a big why for me. Why no complaints like most married men? The complaints were what usually soothed their dogged guilt. His lack of flack about the Mrs. made me wonder how Greg soothed his. Surely he had some. I knew he wasn't absolving it in church because he laughed when he told me he hadn't been to church in years. "That's my wife's bag." His tone was full of venom. The good doctor and Jesus had fallen out over something, so I felt sure I wouldn't be running into him here.

Angelina Preston was attractive, well bred, and my guess would be educated, but obviously, as my mama always told me, all that glittered wasn't gold. Her husband was in my bed.

I let out a long sigh. I was no fool. I understood how the cheating husband thing worked. Most men didn't leave their wives because they actually loved them or something like that. Chicks on the side, I had learned early on, fell into one or two categories. The first was what I called "something different." This would be a woman that was completely different from the wife; usually a real freaky-deak who probably traveled with handcuffs and a portable pole. She was willing to do the things wifey had never done or didn't respect the Negro enough to do anymore. But she was a distraction, a way to make the man feel better about his boring home life.

The second category, and the one I preferred to be, was the new model. That was simply a younger version of the current wife. From my experience, more often than not, the younger version was more common, at least amongst the upper middle class men I spent my time with. Their wives didn't stroke them in the right places anymore. First and foremost, the ego and then . . . well, let's say most of the married men I'd dated didn't think they were getting enough sex. I liked being the new model. It held more promise. After all, who was going to actually leave their wife for a freak? You couldn't take a freak to a business dinner or a charity affair, but you could take the new model anywhere and everywhere, and that's what I had in mind. My future.

I squinted for a better view. Now that Angelina was really close up I could see the similarity; same complexion, bone structure, height—heck, *did we get our hair wrapped at the same salon?* I thought, patting my shoulder length tresses. Add ten years and fifteen pounds and I was already Mrs. Gregory Preston. I clucked my teeth. I didn't like what I saw. The woman was darn near perfect, which meant this might be more difficult than I'd originally thought. But I was up to the challenge. Nothing in life that was worth having came easy, and getting my claws into a successful surgeon like Dr. Gregory Preston would be worth whatever I had to go through, including this boring study lesson. Besides, starting over with another man was out of the question. I needed big money soon, or I was going to lose everything I had.

Chapter 2

"You know the church used to be a place you could go to get away from the world." Carol Wright fingered the strand of pearls that hung around her neck. The sour expression on her face made Angelina think the crème puffs she'd eaten were bad.

Angelina followed Carol's eyes to find her staring at the young woman who had introduced herself as Rae Burns earlier. She could see what Carol found so distasteful. The dress was way too tight and much too short for anything other than a cathouse or a nightclub. Her makeup was so heavy Angelina thought if she stuck a finger in her cheek it would leave a hole. And those breasts, bad implants that stuck out from the woman's small frame like full water balloons at a carnival shooting gallery. Still, that was no reason to stare at her like she was from Mars.

"I don't think getting away from the world was ever the intent." Angelina pulled her eyes from Rae who had moved from the refreshment table that was set up at the back of the Bible Study classroom. Most of the women were avoiding her. The women at Greater Christian Life always shunned outsiders. Angelina knew that needed to change. She'd talked to them many times about welcoming others into the fold, but everyone at this church was so cliquish. That was one of the reasons the Bible Study wouldn't grow beyond its current attendance. People flocked to the services on Sundays to hear

pastor's messages, but that was the extent of it. Once they attended a Bible Study or other ministry meeting and met with
the cold reception, they didn't come back. She was trying to
change that. At least, in her class.

"I don't mean people shouldn't be saved. I mean they need
to assimilate. When in Rome, do as the Romans," Carol continued. "She can't do anything about those ridiculous boobs,
but she can dress more appropriately."

Angelina pursed her lips. "Don't do that."

Carol gave her a look that said, *what?* Then she pushed her
shoulders back. "I can't help it. When you buy them they're
no longer breasts."

"Oh, and I suppose when you paid for your weave it was
no longer hair?"

"Ha-ha." Carol took a finger and swept back a stray strand
that hadn't moved with the rest of it. "Since you're in a funny
mood, the joke can be on you. She can be *your* mentee."

Angelina's shoulders dropped. She didn't have time for another project. She was busy at work and now this child death
situation.

"I know it's my turn," Carol said, "but I don't have the
patience for all the ghetto fabulous drama." Angelina eyed
Carol suspiciously. "Besides this Mentor-a-Sister thing was
your idea, so you can take the lead on that messy job."

Angelina looked at Rae again. Carol was right. Mentor a
Sister was one of many ideas that she'd had for the women's
group. The older women were supposed to teach the younger
women. That was the scriptural reference for the project's
purpose. Others with similar purposes always ended due to
lack of participation. Deep down inside Angelina knew why.
The women of Greater Christian Life were a bunch of snobs.
Doctors' and lawyers' wives who lacked the patience for anyone who wasn't just like them. But she was determined that

they were not going to sit around and do nothing to help other people. That's what the church was for. She would resign her membership before she continued to worship in a house that wasn't relevant.

She let her eyes slide in Rae's direction and wondered what had attracted her to Greater Christian in the first place. Angelina didn't see a wedding band or an engagement ring. Then she remembered Rae said she was single. They didn't often have young, single women. Not for more than one or two sessions anyway, and they'd never have any if they couldn't manage to keep one.

"You're right. I'll lead by example," Angelina said with enthusiasm she wasn't sure she felt. "You'll see in no time, she'll be all that God wants her to be."

"You don't have to shoot for God. If you can get her out of those tight clothes, I'll give you twenty bucks." Carol walked away and joined a small group of women across the room.

Angelina rolled her eyes. Somebody needed to mentor Carol. She put the cup she'd been holding to her mouth and drained it. She was tired and hungry. It had been an awful day, beginning with a call at five in the morning that one of their foster children had fallen from the landing of a staircase and broken her neck. The child was only four, and no matter how many times the social workers and supervisors tried to explain it, she couldn't understand why they'd placed the child and her three-year-old sister in that home in the first place. There were too many accidents in the foster parents' history.

Angelina had been on the board for four years, rising from the ranks of caseworker to supervisor to county director. Greg had pinned her inability to conceive children on the stress and aggravation from her work. Her friends agreed with solemn statements like, "That could be it, girl," and "Maybe you should quit and see what happens." So she did, but not working at all was out of the question. She started Something Extra, a non-profit that raised funds to help foster children with the extras in life that foster care subsidy monies didn't always stretch far enough to cover. That included money for Christmas presents, back-to-school clothing and supplies, cheerleading and football team fees, graduation dues, vacations; even vehicles and college scholarships when she could finagle them. She and her volunteers were busy all day every day, setting up fundraising events and begging for money to pay for them.

Angelina felt she had a special kinship with foster kids. Even though she'd grown up with her mother, she did understand the idea of not having parents. Her father had left right before her seventh birthday, and her mother worked two jobs. She was alone a lot. Even when her mother was there, she was being critical about something. Angelina knew it wasn't the same as being completely abandoned by one's family, but she did know about the ache of loneliness, and it hadn't ended with childhood. She was lonely now.

Her BlackBerry vibrated. There was a text message from the board secretary.

The caseworker has resigned.

Of course. The resignation was expected. The caseworker had done her job irresponsibly, and the threat of a civil lawsuit was looming. The deceased child's mother, a twenty-year-old heroin addict who'd never had custody of her daughter from birth due to her active drug habit, came running into the board meeting sobbing and screaming about how the agency was going to pay for what happened to her daughter. Of course an attorney was on her heels handing her the much needed Kleenex for the show. Angelina was certain her only concern was that they pay in dollars, since she'd never attended visitation sessions with either of her daughters. And even through all her screaming during the meeting, she hadn't once asked for custody of her three-year-old, Katrice.

Angelina had been at the county office when they'd taken custody of Katrice from the foster parents. That baby's big brown eyes haunted her. Tears spilled from them. She cried for Bobin, the mispronunciation of her sister, Robin's, name and Aunt Ma, her foster mother. If her own mother would go to rehab and get clean. . . .

She swallowed against her disgust. No point doing the if only game. That had been the downside of the job, learning how many people actually didn't give two flips about their own children. It made Angelina sick as she thought of her own empty womb. Her hand self-consciously fell to her abdomen. That woman's baby was dead, and she'd never given her the time of day. All Angelina could think about was how much she'd give to have a child of her own. If only . . .

Now is not the time, she thought, fighting the depression that always engulfed her when she thought about children. There was a child's death to deal with. Now she had to meet their visitor and focus on the ministry God had given her; encouraging other women. She was good at that. She took a deep breath, smoothed her hair, and walked toward Rae Burns who, to her surprise, was staring right at her.

Chapter 3

"Hi. I don't know if you remember my name from earlier—Angelina Preston."

I chortled as I shook her hand. I couldn't believe my luck. Here I had been trying to think of a way to talk to Angelina, and now she was introducing herself. "A pleasure to meet you. That was a great lesson you taught."

Now that she was closer, I could see she was a little younger than she looked from a distance. I knew Greg was forty-four. I'd stolen a look at his driver's license. This woman couldn't be a day over thirty-eight. I was sure Greg told me he'd married his college sweetheart. He had lied. I was hoping for more of an age difference. After all, the younger model needed to be noticeably younger.

"Thanks. I appreciate that. I don't always get impartial feedback. As you may be able to tell by the little clusters around the room, some of us have known each other for a long time. It's nice to have an opinion from an . . ." She paused looking for a word.

Outsider, I thought, mentally finishing her sentence; because I definitely wasn't in with this frosty crowd.

"It's nice to have an objective opinion." Angelina found her word. I nodded. "So Rae, tell me when you joined the church. I don't think I remember seeing you at the altar."

The altar. What was she talking about? Was it a sin to come to Bible Study before you went to the altar? I'd have to Google it when I got home. "I didn't come to the altar. I mean, I haven't joined yet. I wanted to see what the church had to offer first."

Angelina was unphased by my confession. She simply nodded. "Well, I hope we've impressed you this evening. At least enough to come back." She leaned forward and smiled. Her luminous, healthy hair moved like silk. She had a fine grade of hair. Chemicals and heat couldn't do all that. I was instantly jealous of that too.

"I will." I finished my cup of punch and tossed it in a nearby trash basket.

"Glad to hear it." Angelina gave my forearm a friendly pat. "Since you haven't joined the church yet, would you mind sharing your contact information with me? Maybe we could talk from time to time. I like for everyone who attends the meeting to feel welcome. I can also answer any questions you may think of later in the week."

"Sure." I reached into my purse, careful to get the clip of phony business cards I'd made earlier in the day that had RAE BURNS, HEALTHCARE CONSULTANT and my cell phone number printed on them. I made a mental note to change my voicemail message to one of the generic ones. It wouldn't do for Angelina to call me and get the greeting from Samaria Jacobs, my alter ego.

I removed two cards and a pen. "That will work both ways right?" Angelina's eyebrows rose. "I'll share. If you'll share." I handed her the back of the second card and a pen.

She paused, and then walked to the refreshment table to use it as a desk. I followed. Angelina returned my card. "Please, feel free to call anytime."

I looked at the information Angelina had shared. Then like the prize it was, I tucked it into the pocket of my handbag. "So I can call during the day? Do you work full-time?" I was dying of curiosity. "I won't be a bother, but if I think of something . . ."

"I do work, but I can usually take a phone call. Don't hesitate," Angelina replied. "Now let me introduce you to a few of the other women."

No way, no thanks. "Actually, I really need to get going." I looked at my watch like I was checking the time. "I have a proposal to complete for a client, and it's due first thing in the morning."

"Okay, next time."

I thought she looked relieved. She knew good and well those stuck up women didn't want to meet me, and I darn sure didn't want to meet any of them. "I'll be going, but before I do, would you mind telling me the name of the perfume you're wearing? You smell like an angel."

Chapter 4

Angelina's breath caught in her throat. Her heart raced, and even in the cool of the room, she felt perspiration break out all over her body. It always amazed her that making love with her husband still had this effect on her, even after thirteen years. After everything they'd been through.

Greg kissed her lips, slid to his side of the bed and whispered, "This is going to be a good day."

Angelina pulled the sheet around her body and rolled on her side to face him. "I was thinking the same thing." But in actuality she thought, *I hope I get pregnant.*

"So what's going on with that investigation?" Greg asked the question as if she hadn't filled him in on every detail last night when they were lying in these exact same positions.

Angelina fought to keep in the wind of frustration that filled her lungs. She rolled back over to her side of the bed, picked up her BlackBerry, and pushed the power button. It was almost six A.M. She was bound to have a message from someone by now. "I told you, the stairwell was in disrepair. We shouldn't have had a child in the home until they fixed the landing."

Greg shook his head like it was the first time he'd heard it. She supposed it was since he apparently had not listened to a single word she'd said last night. "I don't know how you do that work." He reached for his own phone and turned it on.

That work. Her work. Always reduced to a bitter pill on his

tongue. "It's difficult for everyone, but someone has to or it won't be done."

Greg swung his legs over the side of the bed, then reached back and gave her thigh a vigorous pat. "I wonder why the someone has to be you." He stood, walked his nude body into the bathroom, and seconds later, Angelina heard water spray in the shower.

She thought about the love they'd made and wondered how they could make music so wonderfully one moment and make war the next. Or at least it could have been war if she'd decided it was worth the fight. She threw her feet over her side of the bed and reached for her discarded nightgown and slid it back over her head. *I hate him*, she thought, but she knew that was a lie. She walked around to his side of the bed and picked up his underwear that lay on the floor. She didn't hate him at all. The problem was she loved his dirty drawers. She realized she was holding them a little too tightly. *Okay, not literally.*

Angelina walked to the closet and dropped them in the hamper, pulled clean underwear from his bureau and a suit from the closet and laid them on the bed for him. He came out of the bathroom drying his head with a towel.

"That was quick." She couldn't help but acknowledge the rare three minute shower.

"I have an early procedure."

Angelina knew she had to be careful about how she stepped into the next mine field. "Early procedures, late procedures. I never know when I can expect you to be home."

He stopped for a few seconds and looked at her like she'd cursed at him.

"I mean, I'm trying to set something up. I called Dr. Luke yesterday. I think we should talk to him about trying again."

Greg shook his head, picked up the underwear, and began

to dress. Angelina noticed the angry vein pop out in the center of his forehead, the one that always presented itself when
she bought up a topic he didn't want to discuss.

"I don't know if I'm ready for that yet." Greg looked her in
the eyes. "As a matter of fact, I'm sure I'm not ready."

Angelina felt like she'd sucked in a room full of bad air. *He
wasn't ready.* This wasn't the right time for the conversation,
but they were here. He'd put his thoughts out there, and waiting to hear all that was on his mind was not an option. So
with fear clenching her stomach with the grip of a vice, she
pressed on. "It's been two years. I'm not getting any younger.
Neither are you. If we're going to have children—"

Greg threw up a hand and silenced her. He seemed to be
measuring his words. "Maybe we shouldn't. I mean, maybe we
should leave it the way it is with us."

He couldn't have shocked her more if he'd punched her
in the face. *Not have children? Where had this come from?* "You
wanted children, Greg. You wanted—"

"I wanted our Danielle, but now she's gone, so I don't
know that I can really put my heart back out there to do this
again." He picked up his towel and ran it over his damp hair
like he was talking about the weather or sports.

"We can't give up on everything we ever wanted and planned
because of what happened."

"Well, maybe what happened has changed what I want."
He paused. His eyes bore into hers, and she was sure he could
see her heart ripping in two, but it didn't stop him. "Look,
I'm running late. I've got to get out of here. Can you get a
shirt for me?"

Angelina didn't move. He had never said that before. Never
said they shouldn't try. Greg walked around her frozen frame
and reached into the closet for a dress shirt. He stared into
her eyes when he removed it from the hanger, continued to

stare as he did the final buttons, and after he pulled on his slacks and fastened his tie. Angelina had not moved. She was frozen in time by his words. *He couldn't put his heart back out there. What child had he carried for nine months and nursed for six?*

Greg's phone began to hum a familiar beep. He swiped it from his night table and shoved it into his pocket without looking at the screen. "Lena, don't freak on me. I just think we should talk about it."

"I'm trying to talk about *it*." Her lips trembled as she spoke.

"When both of us have time."

He came to stand in front of her, smelling like a mix of warm musk and mango shampoo. Looking like every black woman's dream with his Adonis features, chiseled body, and perfect height. Who picks up a ringing phone without looking at? She wanted to rip the BlackBerry from his slacks and smash it into his face. "You're beeping," she said.

He looked confused, like he couldn't hear the insistent chirp in the quiet of the room.

"Your phone is beeping." She pointed at his jacket pocket. "Don't you need to see who it is?"

"I know who it is."

That much is true, she thought.

"It's the hospital. My patient is probably there."

Angelina nodded and took the kiss he placed on her cheek. He really thought she was stupid. That particular beep was not the hospital.

"Don't hold dinner. I've got a long day." He threw the words over his shoulder as he left the room. He'd been tossing them way too much.

A long day—there were too many of those lately. Late evenings, strange phone calls, special beeps on his pager. She sat on the side of the bed and let the tears she'd been holding cascade down her cheeks. Her life was a mess. Her husband was probably cheating, and now as the final act of betrayal, he wanted to take her babies.

Greg's going to break my heart. Angelina didn't know when the other shoe would drop, but she knew it was falling. She closed her eyes and shut out the voice in her head that said leave him now because she wasn't going to do it. She needed to get something out of the thirteen years she'd sacrificed in the marriage. She wouldn't let him steal her dream of being a mother. She had lost Danielle right before she was to turn six months, and she'd accepted that. She had no choice. That had been God's will. Her choices were to accept it or lose her mind. But to give up what she wanted to a man who walked around in a flesh and blood suit. *No way.* She was going to get pregnant and Gregory Preston was not going to stop her.

Chapter 5

I pulled my BMW Z4 convertible into traffic on Hammond Drive. The perfume counter at Saks had been pretty crowded for a Thursday morning, but I'd gotten what I wanted, or at least what I needed. I hadn't expected to run into a one day sale. All the happy little, stay-at-home moms were out today spending their husband's money like I would be doing one day soon. I glanced at the clock on the dashboard. I was going to be a few minutes late for my lunch with Greg, but that was a good thing. He needed to wait for me for a change, especially since I had to wait so long for him to get up the nerve to actually take me to lunch. It hadn't come without persuasion.

"Come on, you know I can't go out with you in public." Greg had protested as he moved his body higher on the pillows I'd propped behind him.

I was ready for that lame excuse. I already knew how to work around that one. "You can explain me if you have to. I'm a consultant, remember? It would be a business lunch." That was somewhat true. I had a consulting business, back office practice administration stuff, but it wasn't doing well. I'd had very few clients. A nursing background wasn't enough of a credential these days. Everyone wanted an MBA, which I'd failed miserably at getting after I'd flunked out of the advance practice nurse program. Higher, higher education wasn't for me.

Greg hemmed and hawed for a moment. I pulled back the sheet that covered our bodies and climbed on top of him. After leaning forward and kissing him on the forehead and then the lips, I applied the pressure. "Look, I really like you, baby, and like you said, I knew you were married before I got into this, but baby, I can't stay cooped up in this condo every day waiting for you. I'm young. I've got to get out." I played with the hair on his chest.

After a moment of the pleasure, he weakened. "Okay. We can have lunch."

I clapped my hands victoriously and squealed.

"But no touching and acting like lovers. The last thing I need is for my wife to find out about you. I'd be finished."

Finished indeed, I thought.

I pulled in front of Moreland's Fine Dining. I opened the small bottle of perfume I'd purchased and covered myself in a fresh spray of the scent. It wasn't exactly something I would wear, but it was appealing enough, and obviously if Mrs. Preston wore it, Mr. Preston liked it. The parking attendant pulled the door open and offered me his hand. I accepted his assistance and reached in for my briefcase. I loved first class service. Nothing topped it.

I strolled into Moreland's like I had been here a thousand times. Although I had many occasions to dine in fine restaurants with the various men I'd dated in the past, the bourgeois interior of this particular establishment took my breath away. I'd read about it in *Upscale* magazine and saw clips on the Fine Dining Network channel, but I'd never expected it to be so posh. A tingling sensation traveled down my spine as I made purposeful strides through the restaurant atrium. I loved when men spent money on me. It was the perfect foreplay, and most of them knew it.

"Madame, may I assist you?" A man stepped into my path.

I assumed he was the maitre'd judging by his snooty tone and penguin attire.

I was stunned at his swiftness. I'd almost banged right into him. I wanted to let him know how annoyed I was at how he'd cut me off mid-stride, but instead I put on my brightest smile and used my well-rehearsed business voice. "Samaria Jacobs with Jacobs Better Health. I'm dining with Dr. Preston."

The maitre'd took a few steps to a waist high podium at his left, looked over his glasses and down his nose at the reservation log, and then back at me. I was rewarded with a crisp smile. "Yes, Dr. Preston is waiting. Allow me to show you to the table."

We walked a short distance, turned a corner, and I spotted Greg sitting at the end of a row of round tables near a window in the rear. He was doing something with his BlackBerry and was so distracted that he hadn't seen my approach. Which was a shame; I'd purposely worn a skirt that accentuated my long legs.

The maitre'd cleared his throat to get Greg's attention. "Dr. Preston, Ms. Jacobs."

Greg stood. He took my elbow and guided me to the chair across from him. The maitre'd nodded and walked away. I didn't get the kiss I was used to receiving every time he greeted me. I hadn't expected that—not today. I took my seat and placed my briefcase in the space next to me. Greg put his tall frame back into the seat he'd risen from. I took in a breath, and my stomach did the same flip it did whenever I set eyes on him.

Greg was fine. His skin was the color of an espresso bean, but his eyes a lighter, hazel color that contrasted so much with his complexion that it almost looked eerie. His short, curly hair had a part cut in front which gave him a boyish quality that I found very sexy for a man his age. His DNA would make some beautiful babies. Of course my perfect genes would help.

I met Greg at a downtown sports bar near one of the hospitals. At first he was standoffish. I could tell Dr. Preston wasn't interested in a woman on the side, which made him even more appealing. Then one Wednesday afternoon he came into the bar visibly upset. After much prodding, he shared that he was grieving over a young patient that died in surgery. He was vulnerable and ripe for my advances. So I pushed and got him. I'd had him for six months, but being the woman on the side wasn't good enough. I wasn't getting any younger. I wanted more. I wanted financial security.

"Waiting long?" I asked, cupping my hands together on the table.

"You know exactly how long I've been waiting because you're late." Greg pushed away from the table and adjusted his tie.

"I'm worth it," I replied, batting my eyelashes. I pulled my legs under the table and stroked his upper thigh with the tip of my shoe to remind him of why he was here in the first place.

Greg shifted in his seat, and I sensed I'd gotten my message across. I opened my briefcase and removed a small notebook computer.

"What's that for?"

"This is a business lunch, isn't it?" I raised an eyebrow. "I'm helping with the presentation, Doctor."

He laughed deeply and seemed to relax instantly. "You're something else."

"You know it." I winked.

Greg and I chatted a bit. I ordered the most expensive steak on the menu and started a good bottle of wine. The good doctor couldn't drink on the job, but I managed to get him drunk with lust. I teased him more than he could bear, so after lunch, we checked into a room down the street at the J.W. Marriott Hotel. Sex hadn't been in the plan for today, but I figured after paying over ninety dollars for lunch, if he was willing to spend another buck and a half for a hotel room, I'd let him. After all, the whole point of the outing was to remind him that I was no cheap trick he had on the side.

Not that he wasn't already doing things for me. He had begun giving me a small stipend a few months ago to help out with my bills. I'd let him know how much I was struggling with the new business and he, of course, was more than happy to keep my stress to a minimum. I presented a monthly invoice to his office for consulting services, and by the tenth of every month, I had a check that covered half the cost of my condo and my entire car payment. Plus there was jewelry and other little things he would buy me from time to time. But even with his help, I had a cash flow problem. My paycheck was gobbled up in student loan debt and credit card bills. The two totaled more than sixteen-hundred dollars a month. The messed up grad school attempts and extra money I borrowed from the Department of Education had me sunk. A person couldn't escape student loan debt, not even in bankruptcy. I'd already explored that option. My ninety thousand dollar tab to Uncle Sam's higher education department wasn't going anywhere.

Greg stepped out of the bathroom, freshly showered and fully dressed. "I had a great time." He came closer to the bed. I let the sheet fall from my shoulders. He got that gleam in his eyes again and leaned forward to kiss me.

"You're something else you know." He pulled away. "I've got to go. I have to be in surgery in an hour."

"Too bad." I lay back on the mattress and rolled onto my stomach, revealing the rest of my banging, naked body.

"Yes, too bad. But somebody has to work around here." Greg leaned down and kissed me one more time on the forehead. "I'll call you later."

I grabbed his tie, tugged until he came closer to me and whispered, "You sure you don't have twenty more minutes?"

He growled low and deep. "I'm certain." He removed my hand from his tie, smiled again, and pulled on his jacket.

"Don't forget to call me." I worked my body deeper into the mattress.

"I won't," he said. "Oh, and by the way, I like the new perfume." He disappeared through the door.

"I bet you do." I turned over on my back and pulled the sheet around my body. I reached for my cell phone, pushed the buttons, and waited for an answer on the other end.

"Hello, Angelina. This is Rae Burns. I was wondering if we could have a cup of coffee."

Like a clip out of a runway fashion show, I watched as Angelina pushed the door open and glided into the Caribou Coffee Shop where I was waiting for her. The spot was almost empty, so she saw me right away. She nodded a hello, went to the counter to order something, and then joined me. I jumped up from my seat and gave her a hearty hug like I'd learned from watching the church sisters the other night. "Thanks so much for meeting me."

"No problem. I told you, I've love to help if I can."

"Most people don't make time for strangers."

"Actually, I have to let you in on a little secret," Angelina replied, hanging her bag on the back of her chair. "Our women's group has a formal mentoring program for new Christians. It's called Mentor-a-Sister. Once a woman joins, she's assigned a mentor to acclimate her to the church."

I took a sip of my latte and considered what this might mean. "That's interesting," I said, although I didn't quite know how interesting it actually would be.

"It's a good program. The person who's assigned to mentor is a spiritually mature woman who can answer questions about the Bible or pastor's message. We pray with each other, talk to each other—share anything that needs to be shared. It's kind of like a fast friendship. It really helps because people usually feel all alone when they join a new church, especially one as large as Greater Christian."

I didn't say anything, just moved my cup around on the table. I couldn't believe my luck.

Angelina continued. "It's not meant to be intrusive. It's strictly on an as needed basis. You call, and your mentor is there for you. You don't want to be bothered, and I go away."

I sat back. "By '*I go away*,' do you mean, you? Would *you* be my mentor?"

"If you'd like me to be. I'm only working with one other woman right now, and she's already made some new friends."

Bingo. I nodded noncommittally. I didn't want to seem too eager.

Angelina looked puzzled, and when she made the next statement I knew why. "Don't let me scare you off. I won't be a pest, and I can certainly assign you to someone else if you'd like."

"I think it's a great idea. I could use someone to talk to about spiritual stuff from time to time." Shoot I didn't want to play it so cool that I lost her.

Angelina's face relaxed. The cashier delivered her coffee. She thanked her and took a hungry sip like she needed the jolt of caffeine. "So you said you hadn't joined the church yet?"

"No." I played with my cup. "I don't think the women like me. They were pretty chilly at Bible Study."

"Well, you can't let other people run you off from a good church."

I raised my cup, took a sip, and held it to my lips to buffer my statement. "There are so many snobs."

"There's a reason you keep coming back."

I put my cup down and looked her in the eye. "I try to surround myself with people who are where I want to be."

Angelina nodded. "That's admirable."

I shrugged. "It can be lonely too; always being the outsider." A beat of silence passed between us. I couldn't believe I'd said that. "Maybe you can unofficially mentor me. Convince me it's the right church."

Angelina pursed her lips. She was amused, but nodded her head. "We can give it a try."

"Okay." I raised my cup and took a sip. "Now that we have that bit of business out of the way, let's talk about why I asked you here." I returned my cup to the table, crossed my legs, and locked my hands together atop my knees. It was time to find out if this diva knew her husband was creepin'. In the coolest and calmest voice I could muster, I said, "Angelina, your husband is cheating."

Chapter 6

Angelina felt like someone had kicked her, and she was actually having trouble seeing straight because Rae Burns had morphed into Satan. She was sitting there as cool as you please with her legs crossed liked she'd just said they're having a secret sale at Neiman Marcus instead of, "your husband is cheating."

A bead of perspiration formed over Angelina's top lip, and she struggled to find her voice. The kick to her gut had been so hard. *Who was this woman?* She looked down through double vision and saw that her hand was trembling, so she released her coffee cup and clasped it with the other underneath the table. That would also ensure that she'd have a delay in snatching this heifer's weave out of her head if she answered her the wrong way. She cleared her throat. "What did you say?"

"Oooh, girl. Calm down. It's a hypothetical question." Rae waved a hand. Then she picked her cup up off the table.

Angelina felt her heart slow it's beating, but she still wanted to smack the stew out of her. What kind of stupid game was she playing? Why would she . . .?

"I have a friend, and her husband's cheating on her, or at least it looks like it. I need to give her some advice."

Angelina reached for a napkin and began to pat the sweat above her upper lip.

"Are you okay?" Rae frowned.

Angelina picked up her now bitter coffee, took a sip, and put the cup on the table. "I'm okay. I'm just tired. A lot's going on at work."

"Oh yeah, it must be with that child's death and all. They won't stop talking about it on the news." Rae was glaring at her. "And the poor little sister. What's to become of her?"

What was to become of Katrice indeed? Angelina had spent the day with the foster home assignment unit at Youth Services' downtown office trying to find the right home for the little girl. They needed someone who wanted to foster-to-adopt, so when Katrice's mother's parental rights were severed in a few months, she wouldn't have to move again, but they hadn't found anyone. They searched in an antiquated database that hadn't been updated, and then went through manual files, but no one in their entire roster was a right fit. None of their adoption-ready foster parents were looking for a little black girl. It broke Angelina's heart.

"The news reported she's in a new foster home."

"I can't talk about the case," Angelina responded. Rae shrugged, and Angelina was glad she was moving on, but no sooner than she thought it, she regretted the boomerang in the conversation.

"So now, your husband's cheating," Rae continued. "What's the first thing that goes through your mind? Besides who is she?"

Angelina reached up and smoothed her hair. She really, truly didn't want to go there. So she stalled. "Tell me about your friend."

Rae rolled her eyes up. "She's a good friend, one of my best since high school, and she's been married to this clown for five years. He's a college professor, and he's been working late and leaving early a lot, getting phone calls, coming home showered . . ."

Rae's voice began to fade as a mental picture of Angelina's own husband came to mind. His late nights and early mornings. He had a lipstick stain on a shirt last week and the unmistakable scent of a woman's perfume hummed from the cotton fabric.

"So what do you think?" Rae's voice sliced through her thoughts. "This man is a college professor. Working late? What's he doing—grading papers?"

Angelina picked up her coffee cup again. It was cold, but she took a sip anyway. It couldn't make the nausea she was feeling any worse.

"I just don't know why she doesn't do something about it." Rae paused. "I mean, I didn't mean to shock you earlier, but what would you do?"

Rae's eyes were wide with anticipation. She looked like she was enjoying the conversation. Angelina didn't know quite how to take what seemed like a lack of empathy for her anonymous friend, but she indulged her anyway. "I don't know. It's hard to know what to do. It's not cut and dry. It depends."

"On what?" Rae looked exasperated.

"On lots of things. The couple, the woman, the marriage itself." Rae crossed her arms and waggled her foot at the ankle. Angelina continued. "Kids, family commitments, money. . . ."

"Angelina, that's sounding pretty weak." Rae dropped her arms.

Angelina shook her head. "There are things that keep people together. Lots of couples survive infidelity."

"But even God said a woman doesn't have to stay with a cheating husband. I heard one of the TV ministers talking about that."

"The Bible says if you can forgive, you can stay and work it out."

"I think it's dumb to put up with a cheating man. If he's

done it once, he'll do it again. I think she should leave. She's setting herself up for more heartache."

Angelina wanted to tell her to shut up. To stop being the voice of reason in her head. But instead she told her the same things she told herself. "People . . . men, make mistakes. None of us are perfect."

"A mistake." Rae crossed her arms in front of her again and let out a snort. "You make a mistake and mess up your checkbook or step in dog poop on the curb. We don't accidentally get into bed with someone. That's intentional."

Angelina knew she was frowning. "I didn't mean it that way."

Rae sat there waiting for her to say something deep she supposed. But she didn't have anything deep to say because her husband was probably cheating, and she hadn't done anything. Hadn't said a word. "Look, why are we talking about your friend? We're supposed to be talking about you."

"I know, but my friend's thing is major for me right now. She's a new Christian, and she needs some help with this."

Angelina couldn't believe how tenacious Rae was. She was like a pit bull. "Does she have a church? She should talk to her pastor."

"No, she won't do that. She's embarrassed. Don't you think it's embarrassing to tell someone, anyone, that your husband is hittin' it somewhere else?"

I don't need this today. "I think the embarrassment is a small part of it."

Rae's cell phone rang a Beyoncè song in her purse, and she grabbed her bag and reached for it. Her eyes rolled upward, and she threw up a manicured index finger. "One sec, okay?" She flipped the shell open, and Angelina was glad for the reprieve.

"This is not a good time . . . I know, but . . . Ma, I'm

in the . . . okay . . . okay, yes!" She snapped the phone shut. "I have to go." She plastered a grin on her face and forced a smile into her voice, but clearly was not happy about the phone call. "Family matter. Kind of pressing." Rae stood and smoothed her linen suit.

"Yes, I heard you mention your mom." Angelina stood also.

"Something like that." Rae tossed her empty cup in a near-by trash basket.

Angelina thought she looked more disappointed than she should have, or maybe the call had been that upsetting. Angelina wasn't sure. "Well, I really said all I can say without knowing your friend better. If she's a Christian, she should pray and consider talking to her pastor about her problem." Angelina could tell Rae was no longer interested in what she had to say. "Call again if you need to talk."

Rae nodded and retrieved her handbag from the chair. "I will. Thanks for meeting me."

Rae walked away from the table and out of the restaurant, but not before Angelina saw the sheen of unshed tears in the woman's eyes.

Chapter 7

I pulled away from the curb. My mother's timing couldn't have been worse. I had Mrs. Preston rattled, but I couldn't tell if it were because I implied her precious husband was cheating, or if I'd pushed on a sore spot because she knew he was cheating. I needed more time to figure that out, and I would have if I hadn't been interrupted.

I pressed the call log in my phone and pushed to redial. Seconds later I heard my mother's grumpy voice growl hello on the other end. "What were you saying about your lights?" I asked.

"They gonna turn 'em off. I need you to get over here."

I bit back disgust. "Mama, I was in a meeting. Didn't you know they were going to turn off your lights before today?" Rhetorical question, one that I had asked many times, but what else could I say? I had to complain. I had a right to.

"Ya' cousin said he was gonna have the money, but they shorted his check."

Cousin June had the shortest check in the history of payroll. Only a fool would keep working for someone who 'shorted' them as much as his employer did. So the long of it was June was lying.

I could almost feel the steam coming out my nose. This was always the way it happened. Last minute—no, last second calls for money to save a necessary utility. I couldn't let my mother sit in the dark, so there was no point in the discussion. "Where can I go to pay it without having to come all the way over there?"

"It wouldn't be all the way if you didn't live darn near in Tennessee," my mother grumbled. "I need some cash too for a personal bill, so bring me an extra fifty."

I bit back the protest that wanted to escape my lips. "An extra fifty over what?" I asked, through gritted teeth.

"The bill is two hundred and ninety dollars."

"Two-ninety! How many months is that?" I wanted to leap through the phone and shake her.

"Samaria, don't start asking me about the bill. I paid some on it every month, but it wasn't enough. I done told you June was going to pay it, but he ain't coming through, so get your little fast tail over here." Dial tone.

I exited I-20 onto Boulevard and was instantly transported to a place that existed in the recesses of my memory where I hid all the visions I didn't want to revisit in my conscious mind. White Gardens was the last of the crumbling public housing projects in Atlanta, and it was scheduled for demolition in the next few months. It was, however, already a hot mess. It got more tore up every time I came here. If the rotten, rusted bars at the entrance didn't warn a person that they were driving or walking into the gates of purgatory, then the broken glass, trash, and homeless crackheads sleeping on the old benches would do it. Who decides to be homeless in the projects? I mean, if you gonna sleep in the streets, at least do it where you got a better view.

I pulled in front of my mother's dilapidated building, turned off the engine, and checked out my surroundings. A small group of teenage boys were standing near the light pole across the street, hovering around a CD player, their nods and movements in rhythm with the beat.

I opened my door. Boom . . . boom . . . boom . . . The vibra-
tion met my ears, the volume jostled my heart. The boldest of
the crew turned to look me directly in the eyes. He was wearing a T-shirt that hung darn near to his knees. I could make
out the words "Pac Lives" and recognized the nearly life-size
picture of the slain rapper embossed across the front. Pac was
darn near synonymous with Jesus Christ in this place. Definitely God to kids like these who didn't have anything else to
believe in.

The man child looked me up and down as he pressed his
fist into his free hand. I raised my arm and pushed the key fob
to set the Beamer's alarm, after which I put a tight fist at my
waist, dropped my hip, and raised an eyebrow. He knew what
I was saying. "Don't mess with my ride." And since young
blood's fear-detector didn't pick up any waves of terror coming from me, he turned his back and continued to belt out
rhymes with his boys.

I took the twenty or so steps necessary to reach my mother's
door. Before I could knock, the squeaking hunk of wood was
pulled open by my mother. Bottom lip jiggling, she stared like
I'd arrived in a pumpkin carriage pulled by mice. "Whatcha
done did to get that car?"

I looked back at the Beamer. I'd actually had it for months,
but chose to drive my old Honda to the hood. Mama didn't
need to know my business, and I didn't need my ride stolen.
But I'd sold the Honda last month to catch up on student
loan payments before they went into default. The last thing
I needed was the federal government coming after my paycheck. I did not mess with Uncle Sam. "My consulting thing
is starting to come together." I stepped through the door.

"Consultant?" She snorted. "Girl, please. I may seem ignorant, but I know what it cost to live in Roswell and drive that
car. You got a hustle, and it ain't no consultin'."

"Sometimes you have to look the part before you're actually there or people won't give you business." I scanned the sparsely furnished, dirty apartment. White Gardens was a dump, but nothing said dump like my mother's unit. The walls were a dusty mustard that was yellow before they stopped being washed. The carpet I'd replaced a couple of years ago looked like it saw more foot traffic than a bus station. And the stench; I could smell the roaches teeming under the floorboards. I shuddered.

My mother looked unconvinced about the consulting thing. She walked across the room and dropped her oversized body into the extra-large leather recliner I bought her last year for her birthday. "Samaria Ann. I raised you."

Like I could forget that. Her tone got on my last nerve.

"I know you, and you ain't nothing but a conniving little trick. You just like me when I was your age and all the women before you in this family." She grunted and smiled with pride. "I'm just curious 'bout what you pulling off."

I shifted my weight from one foot to the other. I never told her my business, and she knew it. "I've been working a lot of hours, and I've got a lot of debt, which makes it hard for me to come over here handing over money at the last minute."

A string of cuss words that could have wrapped around Atlanta like I-285 came flying out of her mouth like she'd been saving them up for me. "Don't you bring yo' stuck up . . . been told you 'bout sassin' me ya' little. . . . if it wasn't for me, you wouldn't be standing there with all that expensive . . ."

I tuned out her rant. It would stop five seconds after I handed her the money. I slipped my hands into my purse, pulled out the wad I'd gotten from an ATM, and handed it to her. "Okay, okay, you ain't got to be cussing at me like that."

"I wouldn't have to be cussin' if you wasn't so—"

As predicted, she stopped mid sentence when she saw I'd

given her an extra hundred. She looked me up and down and cut her eyes. I could literally see the words going back down her throat. "'Preciate you, baby. It's just that I ain't ever complained when I had to do a lap dance to put food on the table."

I sighed remembering it was food stamps that put the meals on the table. But I also remembered all the black eyes and busted lips my mother had over the years asking broke down men for money to pay the light bill. She did sacrifice her body, her soul sometimes. So I wasn't gonna dis her. Ever.

"It's your turn to return the favor. If you need to take your hot little behind somewhere and get some money, then you do it. I'm too old to pull my own hustle. I expect my daughter to take care of me the same way I took care of her."

I nodded. "You took the words right out of my thoughts, Mama. That's why I'm here."

My mother reached into a bowl of pecans and stuck one in her mouth. She cracked the shell with one of her few remaining back teeth and proceeded to make a nasty mess of breaking down the hull to get the nut out. I asked myself the same question I always did when I saw her. What happened to her? As a child I couldn't stand her most of the time, but she was beautiful. Red-boned with long silky hair and light brown eyes. Men loved them some Winnie Jacobs, including my daddy, who, in contrast to my mother, was as black as coal, accounting for my just a shade below dark milk chocolate complexion.

"What you looking at me so hard for?" My mother's eyes narrowed.

I shook my head nonchalantly.

"You want some nuts?" She raised the bowl and extended it toward me.

"Uh-uh." I swallowed to fight off the nausea that was starting to overwhelm me. Between the ugly nut scene and the smell, this visit had to come to an end. "It's not going to be much longer before they put you out of here. Are you working on finding a new place to live?"

I didn't want her to wait until they were coming to bulldoze White Gardens and call me to keep her off the streets. Last minute housing arrangements were always expensive.

"My social worker gonna put me in the same place Ebony live," she said, referring to my first cousin. "It'll be ready soon."

I had read that many of the residents of the old Atlanta projects found housing in the suburbs. But some had moved to newer low income housing that wouldn't be called "projects," at least not until the residents tore them up. The suburbs were not for my mother. She liked the familiar. She liked living with the kinds of people she knew, so I wasn't surprised she was waiting for one of the units in Ebony's complex to open up.

"As long as you're not going to be out of a place," I said. My concern was more for myself.

"I'm handling my business. They ain't coming to knock this down for five months. Look," she hesitated, "June Bug needs some more of that stuff you got him before."

I hadn't realized my hand was locked at my hip until I dropped it. "Mama."

"You know he don't have the money, and he's sick. He needs the medicine."

I thought about what I'd had to do the last time to get the "medicine" for my older cousin. Drug addiction—prescription drugs of all things. He needed rehab.

"He gotta have 'em soon. He's almost out."

"Let me give you some money and have somebody go find something for him," I said, reaching into my purse for my wallet. The receipt for this morning's purchases came out with the cash. I lowered my eyes and looked down at my new Salvatore Ferragamo shoes, thought about the check I'd written for them and the balance in my bank account. My budget was already busted. I barely had enough in the bank to cover the four hundred dollar footwear and the unexpected ATM withdrawal that preceded this trip. I threw my head back. I returned my eyes to my mother's, and I could see she already knew what was coming next.

"Nice shoes." She reached for a pack of cigarettes that lay on the end table.

I put my wallet back in my purse. "I got them on sale."

"Sale or no sale, I know 'dem shoes was 'bout a hundred dollars."

I shook my head. "I'll get something for June."

"Good." My mother smiled. "Ain't no point in spending money on drugs. Them hospitals got plenty."

"Yeah, well, they keep them pretty well locked up."

"But you got a key." My mother clucked her teeth and lit the cigarette.

I decided there was no point in telling her they also counted the "drugs a plenty." That would get me cussed out some more. I'd do it this one last time, and then I'd make sure I had enough money to give them to help buy June's drugs.

My mother took a long drag of the cigarette and blew a plume in the opposite direction. She coughed and wheezed. All I could think about was the damage she was doing to her asthmatic lungs.

"I'm going to go." I walked to the door and looked back at my mother. "I'll have something for June by the end of the week.

She nodded. "'Preciate you, Sam-Sam-Marie."

My hand clamped down on the door knob. I turned and

pushed it open. I didn't look back. I couldn't believe my mother had done that—called me by the nickname that only my father had used.

I exited the dank apartment, thanked God for the clean air and the escape. My mother was being mean. Horribly mean. She hadn't sang that nickname in years. New shoes and a new car in the same day. Too much new for her to deal with. She'd always been jealous.

I looked up and saw that the guys who'd been hawking my car earlier had been joined by a fifth person, but this was someone I knew, and he was coming toward me.

"What up, Sammie?" Wang Johnson took a step off the curb and made his way to my car. Wang Wang, as we called him because in the third grade he unzipped his pants and waved himself around at his teacher, had grown up. He was wearing a camouflage Roca Wear hoodie with matching jeans, white Air Force 1's, and some bad ice in his ears. Wang was a small time rapper whose homemade CDs were floating underground all over the south and selling pretty well from what I'd heard. Wang was also my ex-boyfriend, Mekhi's, younger brother and a kid who was about as near and dear to my heart as anyone could get.

I hadn't seen Mekhi in a long time, almost a year, but I had to admit it felt like I was looking at him right now. To look like Mekhi was a good thing because he was as fine as the good Lord made 'em. Tall, brown like a chocolate bar with teeth so white, I swear he had to put a little bleach on them every night.

Wang Wang smiled and the dimples the Johnson boys were blessed with filled his face.

"You being good?" I asked, looking around to make sure Wang Wang wasn't setting me up to get robbed out here. One never knew 'bout busters in the projects.

"Ain't got to be good if you careful." He shoved his hands deep in his pocket. "Ya' moms tight?"

I nodded.

"I know you tightened her up." He poked his lips out and cocked his head in the direction of my mother's door. "Look, while you slumming, you should go holler at ya' boy."

I let my hand fall from my hip and took a deep breath. I wasn't trying to see Mekhi.

"He missing you, Sammie. Talk about you all the time. I think that Negro even wrote a song 'bout cha, or something like that."

I nodded. "I gotta go, Wang; this ain't for me no more, and you know how I feel about Mekhi's business."

Wang's face took on a serious look. "For one, you don't know 'bout Mekhi's business. And two, even if you did and it was dirty, ain't no point in being a hypocrite. Everybody know you supplying June, so what that make you?"

I swallowed hard and felt the hairs raising on the back of my neck. My stupid cousin was running his mouth. I pushed the key fob and unlocked my car. "It makes me family." I snatched my door open. "Speaking of which, tell your mother I said hello." I climbed in.

He strolled closer to the driver's side of my car and tapped the window. I let it down. "No message for my brother?"

I shook my head and started the engine. "Let it go, Wang." I felt the veins in my neck getting tight with my breathing. I forced a smile. "You be cool and stay careful."

He shook his head. I pulled away from the curb and watched as he stood in the street staring at my emissions pipe leave a fine film in the air. He looked sad. Hurt. Had Mekhi talked about me so much that his little brother was out here lobbying for him?

Mekhi. Tall, dark, handsome, and—the worst doggone thing

that ever happened to me. I looked to the right as I passed his building. His late model, copper, Lexus sat in front. It shined like a new penny. Mekhi was writing songs about me. What a joke. What he needed to be doing was writing songs about how he'd dissed me. He needed to be trying to rewrite history.

I pulled back through the rusty front gate of White Gardens. Glad to have that drug infested, crackhead haven behind me. My mama, though I loved her . . . Mekhi—wait, why was he coming to my mind? I hated him. Anyway, they could stay right here in White Gardens until they knocked it down. That was the life they wanted. My world was on the other side of Atlanta, where Dr. Gregory Preston would be walking through my door in less than two hours to help me remember that I was more than my past. And even better, that my future was bright.

Chapter 8

Angelina dropped the phone on its base and said a silent curse under her breath. Another dead end. She'd been making calls for almost two hours and couldn't find a foster home.

The door to the conference room where she was working opened and Katrice peeked her heart shaped face in. Eyeballs like huge marbles swept the room and the tiny little girl entered. Angelina's heart filled with joy and sadness at the same time. She was sad for the little girl's loss, but her sweetness and innocence was a joy because it made her want to forget every ugly thing that was going on in her own world.

"Hi, baby," Angelina said. "Come on in."

Katrice waved and walked directly to her favorite toy in the back of the room—the dollhouse. She picked up a doll and began speaking to her in three-year-old language as she moved her around inside the house.

Angelina picked up the phone and made a call to another home on her list. More rejection. This time the "no" was because Katrice had asthma. That was the excuse most of the foster parents were giving her for not wanting the placement, but Angelina knew better. The child was a hot potato that the *Atlanta Herald* was following around and the truth was, nobody wanted to deal with that.

Angelina wasn't sure how many minutes she'd been sitting there thinking, trying to come up with an idea for what to do with the child, when Katrice bumped her small torso against her thigh. She grabbed Angelina's forearm, climbed onto her lap, took a strand of Angelina hair and began twirling it with her finger. Angelina studied her for a moment. Took a whiff of the baby lotion scent that lingered on the child and smiled even though the tug on her hair was a little too much.

"You pretty." Katrice laid her head on Angelina's chest. When the girl's head touched her skin, she'd also climbed into her heart. Three years old. Danielle, her own daughter, would be almost the same age. Angelina blinked against tears.

"Katrice, come here." The voice startled Angelina, and the tired social worker who was assigned to Katrice's case rushed into the conference room and stood at the end of the long table with her hands on her hips. Debbie something-or-other, Angelina couldn't remember, had been missing this child for far too long to just be finding her now. Katrice didn't raise her head. Angelina could tell the child had been listening to her heart beat in a rhythm that lulled her into that state of peace. Peace had to be eluding Katrice with all the juggling back and forth that had been occurring since her sister's death.

Angelina looked down at her. She hadn't had a baby on her chest since she'd nursed her own. She cleared her throat. A frog of pain had lodged itself there, and she was trying to release it. "She's fine," she whispered, pulling Katrice's bottom farther on her lap to make sure the girl was secure. Then she looked up into Debbie's nervous eyes. "Really. It's okay."

Debbie continued to stand there like she didn't know whether to leave or stay. No doubt she was nervous that she'd let Katrice wander off for almost ten minutes, and then come to find her sitting in the lap of one of the board members. One who had been a county director. One who could have her job as easily as they'd had Katrice's last case manager's job.

Angelina decided conversation would put the woman out of her misery. "Anything on your end?"

Debbie looked relieved. "A family in Valdosta, but they've always had roaches. Even if we paid to have the house sprayed, they'd come back again. They're nice people, but not particularly clean, and it's a very old house."

Angelina rolled her eyes. A dirty, roach infested house was all they had to offer as a long term placement for an asthmatic child. Roaches were a trigger for asthma. "Not an option."

"I wasn't saying it was a good one. It's the only 'yes' I have," Debbie added. "We could monitor the bugs."

Angelina knew better than that. The caseloads were huge. What case manager would have time to stop by and inspect for roaches every week? They weren't trained to do that. The thought gave her the willies. She shuddered just thinking about it. Her sudden movement jolted Katrice's head from her chest. She looked into the child's sleepy eyes. "Not an option," she croaked through tight lips.

Sufficiently chastised, Debbie nodded and left the room.

Angelina made a few more calls, got a few more "no's' before Debbie reappeared in her door with her handbag and Katrice's jacket. Angelina noted it was ten after five. Quitting and dinner time had come at once.

"Come on, Katrice, let's go," Debbie said.

"I wanna see Bobin," Katrice cried, and slipped from Angelina's lap. The two women's eyes connected, mirroring sympathy for the little girl who had lost her only friend. Her only family really, especially since her mother was dead to her for all intents and purposes.

Debbie leaned down and put Katrice's arms in the light-weight jacket. "You know I told you Bobin got hurt, honey. She's not with you anymore."

The words seemed so cold; so harsh. They were words only a grownup should have to hear. Foster children couldn't be told the lies moms and dads would tell their children—that the dead had gone to sleep or they'd become an angel, or even the truth of one's faith, that they were with Jesus. Foster children had to have the clinical, empirical answer that came with no buffer and no sympathy; even for a three-year-old. It was one of the many disadvantages of a child being in the custody of an institution like family services. Human-ness was often not in the policies or practices.

"I want Bobin." Katrice continued to sob.

Angelina could hear her cries all the way down the hall. Her heart broke in her chest. She couldn't believe the grenade that had exploded in the little girl's life. She trembled in the silence; struggled to pull herself together enough to stand and leave the room, the building, and drive home. She felt paralyzed by the events of the day. Pain was all around her, like the very oxygen she had to breathe to survive. She was tired of it.

Angelina pulled into the garage, turned off the ignition, and pressed her head back into the leather of the headrest. What were they going to do with Katrice? Nobody would take her. Angelina closed her eyes and Katrice's face danced through her memory like flashes of light from an old pop bulb camera. She made a fist around the steering wheel. She could still feel the child's baby soft hand on her own, hear her sweet voice when it said, "You pretty." How people could treat their children like disposable paper cups when others would give anything—do anything—put up with anything—to have their own was beyond comprehension to her.

She looked at the time on the digital clock. It was already after seven. Greg said he would be late, and she wondered, *late doing what?* Certainly not any operating that he was supposed to be doing. She let out a sad sigh and reached across the seat for the Chinese take-out she'd picked up after a brief stop by her office and climbed out of the vehicle.

She entered the house, put the food on the kitchen island, and made her way to the stairway that led from the kitchen to the master bedroom. She'd thought it a silly upgrade when the realtor had first raved about it, but now she loved the convenience of two sets of stairs. And this one was so perfect for days like today, when she was spiritually spent from her personal life and work. She began to peel her clothes off before she entered the walk-in closet. She slipped out of her suit and into a pair of shorts, tank top, socks and sneakers. She'd get on her elliptical machine when she finished eating.

She noted her hamper was full and figured Greg's probably was as well. She'd been so busy with her work that home was starting to slip. The one thing she hated was when laundry piled up. Angelina pulled an empty laundry basket from the back of the closet and dumped the contents of her hamper into the basket. Then she went into Greg's closet. She began transferring his clothes into the basket when she spotted a flash of red against a white dress shirt. She pulled it from the pile for closer inspection. Lipstick—high on the collar, and not her shade. She'd discovered the same thing a few weeks ago.

Shirt still in hand, she walked out of the closet and collapsed on the bed. She didn't know what made her angrier—the fact that he was cheating, or the fact that he was so careless about it. Angelina rolled over on her stomach and pressed her face into the comforter. *God, what is happening to my marriage? What happened to the happily ever after this man promised me when I married him?*

She had done everything that she'd known to do. She was a good wife, they had a lovely home, she took care of herself physically, and she was a good cook. She made love to him whenever he wanted, even if her desire was consumed in the drudgery of a day at work. She'd prayed, fasted, and waited for things to turn themselves around since Danielle's death, but they hadn't. And on top of it, he had the nerve to be messing around on her.

Rage filled her belly. She hadn't been this angry since she was a teenager. Not since she had come to a complete understanding of the fact that her father had left not only her mother, but her.

Benjamin Harris had come into her bedroom a couple of days before he left to talk to her. Angelina's six-year-old mind was expecting a bedtime story. The one her father always made up about the African princess who saved the slaves. But the look on his face quickly told her that her father wasn't spinning a tale that night. She hadn't understood much, didn't recall the minute details of it all, but she did remember her mother whispering to her father, "You have to tell her tonight," which meant the decision was not a sudden one.

Her birthday was two weeks away, and she wanted a party at the Dynamo Play Room. Were they going to tell her she couldn't have it there? That's what she'd thought the "tell her" was. Never in her worst nightmare could she have imagined her father would say, "Angel, I'm going to California for a little while."

Angelina hadn't known what California was or even where it was. Her best friend, Zaria, had teased her and filled her sleep with nightmares of earthquakes swallowing her dad like a giant alligator. New Jersey didn't have earthquakes, and it was then that she understood California was far away and not a good place to be.

"I can't find a job, Angel baby." Pain etched her father's face. Angelina knew that if he was sad, she should be sad, so she tried to convince him to change his mind.

"But Mommy has a job."

"Mom needs help paying the bills and buying food and clothes."

"Daddy, my birthday party can be in the yard." She wrapped her arms around her father's neck. "I won't cost any money. I won't be a bill."

Her father removed her arms and laid her down on the mattress. "Angel, this is about more than a birthday party. I need you to be a big girl. There are some things you're too young to understand."

There were some things a child shouldn't have to understand. Angelina shook her head. She tried to shake the memory, but she couldn't. She remembered his eyes. They were the color of caramel and not as bright that night as they had been before. But they held sincerity and remorse over his leaving. Those eyes had haunted her for years. Those eyes that had lied to her and told her to "trust me, believe in me, I love you, Angel." The eyes of the first man who'd broken her heart. Eyes the color of Greg's.

Angelina dragged herself off the bed and went into the bathroom, opened a drawer and pulled out a pair of scissors. She cut the shirt to shreds, taking care to leave the lipstick stained collar untouched. Then she exited the bathroom and laid the shirt on his side of the bed. Greg had some explaining to do, and the explaining was going to begin tonight.

The telephone rang. "If that's him with some excuse for being even later . . ." She hissed as she made her way to her side of the bed. The caller ID let her know immediately that it wasn't him. It was, however, the last person on the earth she wanted to talk to right now. Her mother. Angelina dropped her head back and picked up the phone. "Hi, Mom." She tried her best to keep the tension she felt from filling her tone.

"Hey, baby." Her mother sounded almost cheerful, which was a rare happening for someone who was never, ever filled with cheer. "Hadn't heard from you in a few days."

"I know. We have this situation with DFYS that's been keeping me running."

"You always have a situation with that job that takes up all your time. I don't know how you keep working with those messed up people." Cheer evaporated with each word. "I didn't pay all that money for you to go to Spelman to come out and do that kind of work."

Angelina rolled her eyes upward. Here we go with that again. "Mom, you asked me why you hadn't heard from me, and I'm telling you why is all."

"Well, never mind about that. I'm not interrupting your dinner? I know you eat late."

"No, I just got in. I'm about to eat."

"Well, don't let me keep you. I'm sure Greg is hungry as a bear by now."

"Greg isn't here."

"Oh, he's still working?"

"At seven-thirty on a Friday night?" Angelina rolled her eyes. "He's working, but it's not with a patient."

"What does that mean?"

"Do I really need to spell it out? It means he's cheating." Angelina pulled the phone away and looked at it like it had offended her, then returned the receiver to her ear to absorb the dead silence that came from the other end. "I know there's another woman. He keeps denying it. I'm trying to hang in here, but if things don't better—"

"Slow down. You can't think like that."

"Think like what? Someone who doesn't want to be walked all over? You know this isn't the first time . . ." She let her words trail off. They'd had this conversation before. Angelina sank down on the mattress, scooted across the bed, and pulled her knees into her chest. "Don't you want me to be happy, Mom?"

"Greg is a good provider. You have a lovely life, lovely things." Her mother stated the obvious while ignoring the happiness question.

Angelina rolled her eyes upward. Sorrow enveloped her.

"This is a season. It's not forever," her mother continued. "All men do this type of thing. You don't think your father was faithful to me all those years before he left, do you? Don't be naïve."

Angelina swallowed the words that were on the tip of her tongue. The temptation to remind her mother that hanging in there with her father hadn't done her any good. In the end, she was still alone. He had still left. But she didn't want to hurt her mother. She was already hurting enough for the two of them, plus she knew it wouldn't do any good. Her mother was incapable of being a friend, incapable of thinking about the emotional impact of anything she was going through. Even as a seven-year-old, Angelina had to go through the loss of her father alone.

"Angelina, Angelina." Her mother's voice clamored. "Are you listening to me? Don't be a fool. Girlfriends are a distraction. They never mean anything."

Tears began to stream down Angelina's cheeks. She stared at the shredded shirt, the telling lipstick stain on the collar, and tried with all her might to push the pain in her heart out of her body, out through her pores. She wiped her eyes with a free hand and told her unsympathetic mother how she felt. "She does mean something, Mom. She means something to me."

Her mother's sigh returned to her.

"I want a husband who's faithful."

This time her mother's words did not have the pleading fervor. "Let me give you the reality of your situation. You're thirty-seven years old. Have you heard how hard it is for a black woman your age to find a husband? The odds are better that you'll win the lottery."

Angelina knew that to be true, but did it mean she had to accept . . . Her mother cut into her thoughts.

"Why do you think I struggled and scraped to send you to Spelman? You think it was about your education? No, I wanted my daughter to meet and marry a Morehouse man. A man who would be successful, and you did that. I wanted to make sure you didn't end up with someone like your father. Someone who couldn't find a job."

Angelina resisted the urge to speak her mind, to say *Daddy left, but it wasn't just because he couldn't find a job.* The letters he'd written to her when she was in college told his side of the story.

"Men cheat," her mother continued her lament. "But at least you don't have to worry about paying your mortgage."

Angelina stretched her legs out. "I don't need a man to pay my mortgage. You sent me to Spelman, remember?" Her words were an attempt to counter the argument her mother was making. "I was earning good money before—" She didn't say it, but she meant before she'd quit to take care of Danielle.

"You want children. You can't do that by yourself." Her mother knew how to turn this argument around. Neither of them said anything. Not for a long time. A child—the potential for a child was the big guns. "You are a black woman. You have to be strong, not emotional. Your husband is a surgeon. That man makes more money in one year than I'll make in ten. Do you know how lucky you are? You've got to keep your eyes on the prize."

Sorrow filled Angelina's throat, and she choked out her

words. "If a cheating husband is the prize, what do the losers get?"

"They get old and alone like me. They have to work until they're seventy, and even then they may not have a good retirement," her mother snapped. "You need to figure out how to pull him out of that woman's bed, if he's in one. Who knows? You're so paranoid. Always have been."

That would be because I was raised by you. Angelina closed her eyes and rubbed her temple with her free hand. "I have to go. I'm starving, and I've got a big day tomorrow, so if there's nothing else . . ."

Good-bye hung in the air until her mother spoke. "Nothing else. Just remember what I said."

They didn't say good-bye to each other. They never did. All their chats ended this way. Ended with her wishing she hadn't taken the call.

Angelina put the phone on the base. *Remember what I said.* How could she forget? They'd been having the same conversation for years. Don't let go of the "ideal black man," but Angelina wondered how she could keep something she wasn't quite sure she'd taken a hold of yet. She was starting to believe nothing good would ever come of her union with Greg. Until this very moment, the only thing she could look back and see that gave her real joy in the last five years was her baby.

She reached into her nightstand and pulled out the picture of Danielle. She looked at her daughter's beautiful, angelic face. She'd been four months old in this picture. If Angelina had known she didn't have much more time with her, she would have taken a thousand pictures like this.

"Look at those eyes," she whispered. They were like her eyes, so dark they were nearly black. A startling feature against the baby's cocoa brown skin. From the time that Danielle could open them, she always seemed to be looking right into Angelina's soul. Wise old eyes.

Her mother had commented, when she'd met her grand-daughter, "That child been here before."

Was that why God had taken her away? Was her daughter a mistake from heaven that had to be corrected? Tears returned, but this time they fell like a rain shower down Angelina's cheeks. She pressed the frame against her chest and rocked back and forth on the bed. She did want another chance to be a mother. She wanted that more than anything on God's green earth, but she wasn't getting pregnant. No matter how she timed her ovulation, and no matter how much love making they did, every month her period came like clockwork, and Greg refused to see a fertility specialist.

Angelina had no idea how long she'd been sitting there when she heard the garage door rising, but the tears she'd been crying had long dried up. She brought the picture frame to her lips, kissed it gently, and put it back in the drawer. She stood to her feet and made her way around the enormous California king-sized bed. The shredded, lipstick stained shirt lay on Greg's side; an ugly reminder of her pain and temper that had been abated by her mother's words. *Keep your eyes on the prize.*

Angelina reached for the shirt, opened her closet, and threw it into a corner. She stepped into the bathroom, wet a face cloth, and washed the stains of her pain from below her eyes. She shook out her hair and applied a fresh coat of lip gloss to bring some color to her face. It was time to go downstairs and greet her husband. She was ovulating and all she could hope was that he hadn't left all the virile sperm somewhere else.

Chapter 9

"Sam-Sam-Marie . . ." that crap was playing in my head like music when I woke up this morning. I don't know why my mama did that to me. It was like her way of reminding me of my past, but all it did was remind me of my daddy. He would sing that to me. Sang it until the day he walked out of my life. I shook my head. Probably her daggone way of being mean. Mean was her specialty.

I raked hangers back and forth across the rack in Neiman Marcus like I was trying to see which one would make the most annoying scraping sound. After a few minutes, a sales clerk was at my side, taking a hold of one of the hangers I'd discarded, like I'd bruised her baby.

"Is there something I can help you find?" Her voice had an air of friendliness, but her body language delivered a completely different message. She was annoyed at by my mishandling of the merchandise, and she had come to put an end to my abuse.

I put a hand on my hip, looked her up and down from head to toe before I gave her the evilest eye I could manage. She backed up. Good thing or I would have had her fired before lunch. I wasn't in the mood.

I turned and looked at a rack behind me and realized I'd found what I was searching for. The same, or almost the same, brown suit Angelina had been wearing the other night. I looked at the silk blouses they had flanked with it and chose an etched floral pastel that was similar to the one Angelina sported with hers. It was boring. My preference would have been something red, but if I wanted to be a doctor's wife, I had to look the part. Greg would be impressed, and that's all that mattered.

I took my items to the cashier's desk and prayed my Neiman's card wasn't maxed out again. The hanger police accepted my items with a smile, cleared her throat, and took care of my transaction. I was back in my ride within minutes. I was on my way to *White Gardens* again. I'd had June Bug's drugs for a few days, but thought I'd let him suffer through without them. Who knew, if he started to convulse, maybe somebody would have to call an ambulance and take his drug addicted behind to rehab. But my fantasies of my cousin's painful journey to recovery were not to be so. My mama called last night, looking for the package I'd promised.

My phone rang, and I was pleasantly surprised to see it was Angelina. After the dramatic way I'd scooted out on her, I wasn't sure what she thought of me.

"Hi, Rae. I was calling to see if you were coming to Bible Study on Wednesday?"

I paused like I was thinking about it. That's what a visitor would do. "I'm not sure," I teased. "I was thinking about passing this week."

"Don't pass. Come on out and give us another chance." Her voice was friendly.

I wondered if this was what all churches did to try to get new members. I waited a beat and offered an ambivalent, "Okay. I guess I'll give you all another chance."

Angelina gave me some details about the scripture she'd been teaching from, which I swore I was writing down, and then we ended the call. *Operation Steal Greg* was in start mode. Now I just had to tie up this business with my mother.

***

I had been calling my mama and knocking on the door for almost five minutes. No answer, so I used my key to open the door. I hoped I wasn't going to be walking in on anything I didn't want to see. I knew no matter how much weight my mother gained, she had a boyfriend coming through from time to time.

From where I stood, I could see the living room area was empty, just like the streets outside. My showing up at eleven A.M. was a guarantee I wasn't going to have to deal with seeing any of the losers I grew up with. Except for the few crackheads bobbing around the place looking for their next hit, most folks didn't get moving until close to noon.

I entered the house and closed the door behind me. I heard a rumble that sounded like the garbage truck was parked in the bedroom and knew my mama was in there snoring. I turned the doorknob to her bedroom, and as I suspected, she was knocked out. Thank goodness she was alone. I walked closer to her bed and noted the empty bottle of dark rum. No wonder she didn't hear the phone ringing. If she had finished a bottle of this junk, she would be drooling on her pillow for another couple of hours. I shook my head. I had no idea how many times I had told her that drinking was going to mess with her diabetes, but she clearly didn't heed my warnings.

I reached into my purse and pulled out the envelope with the drugs for June Bug. I also removed a pen and wrote a quick note telling her I had stopped by. I removed a few twenties from my wallet and put them under the envelope. She'd probably buy more liquor with it, but the truth was, I couldn't look at my mother and not hand her something. Everything about her screamed, "I'm broke—give me money." I shook off the bad feelings from that thought and left her bedroom.

I stepped out of the apartment and turned to relock the

dead bolt behind me. The lock was stuck as always and I had to take the time to jiggle the key to get it back out. "Need a locksmith," I muttered under my breath.

"I'll call one and have her hooked up." The deep, baritone voice came from behind me. My heart began to pound, and my body nearly melted at the sound of it. I closed my eyes for a second and took a deep breath before I turned. Apparently, I hadn't come to *White Gardens* early enough. I was looking into the face of Mekhi Johnson. A face I hadn't wanted to see this morning or any other.

Mekhi was dressed in a slick, Tommy Hilfiger running suit. A Rolex watch gleamed from his wrist, and a light sheen of perspiration dotted his bald head and face. Old habits die hard. This joker was still running. Ran cross country track all through high school. Won a lot of medals and trophies too.

Butterflies filled my stomach. "What's up, Khi?" I asked, trying to keep the tremble out of my voice. I pulled my purse tighter across my shoulder, like it was the lifeline that was going to keep my emotions together.

"You know how I do. Keeping in shape," he replied, staring through me like he had X-ray vision and could see all the way to my underwear. "I see you doing the same." He swirled his head in an exaggerated movement to the left and right as he checked me out.

I blushed. I hated that he made me do that, and I had to admit, he was looking good. As sweet as a Milk Dud at the movie theatre. Nothing new in that department. The brother had always been fine.

"How's ya' moms?" he asked, his face taking on a more serious expression.

"You might know better than me. Y'all neighbors."

Mekhi turned his lips up and nodded his head a few times like he was deciphering scientific data. "If I know better than you, that means one thing, Sam. You ain't coming round here enough, and that shouldn't be."

"*That*, isn't any of your business, but I appreciate your concern for my family matters." I rolled my eyes and walked past him. Mekhi grabbed my hand, stopping me in my tracks. The sudden movement snatched the protest from my lips. Our eyes met and danced for a few seconds. He didn't let go. His skin on mine felt like my hand had been wrapped in a warm glove. The heat of his touch was gentle, but felt firey at the same time.

"Everything about you is my business," he whispered, lowering his lips closer to mine. I could smell his breath. It was a mix of mouthwash and some other fruity smell. His scent was potent, and urbane. Where was the funk? He couldn't have been running long, because he smelled too good.

"You got that twisted, Mekhi." I pulled my hand out of his grasp. "I haven't been your business since you showed me what a coward you were."

Mekhi's Adam's apple bobbed up and down. No doubt he was swallowing his pride. I had inflicted pain, which was what I always wanted to do when I saw him. I was satisfied, and this conversation was over. I walked to my car.

"Sam, you really need to learn how to be a more forward looking sister. I mean, how long you gonna hold that over a brother's head?"

"There are things in life that you never forgive," I snapped.

Mekhi closed the distance between us. Probably didn't want the neighbors, who were no doubt peeking out through their blinds at this point, to hear him. "It's been eight years, girl. We forgive what we want to forgive. Remember, what comes around goes around. You may need somebody to let you off the hook for something messed up you do."

Some of the messed up things I'd done skittered through

my mind. I'd been sorry things hadn't worked out the way I wanted, but I can't say I wanted forgiveness. I also could definitely say I hadn't hurt anyone who'd really trusted me, like Mekhi had done to me. But that was a moot point, one I didn't want to keep rehashing with him. As much as the little digs into the past put chinks in his armour, they also reopened scabs on my own heart.

I clicked the key fob for the car lock. "I'll keep that in mind." I opened my door and climbed in. I took one last look at him. His sexy eyes held sorrow, a sorrow that beckoned me to reconsider. His stance, still strong, still hood, was a little less chest out than it had been. I turned away from him, swallowed the sympathy that had risen from my foolish heart, started the engine, and sped away from the curb.

Chapter 10

I pulled into an empty parking space and turned off my car. I could tell Greater Christian had a full house tonight. Mercedes Benzes, Range Rovers, Escalades, Jaguars, and BMWs littered the parking lot. I reached across the seat for the Bible I'd purchased earlier in the day and removed the plastic casing. I'd been coming to these meetings a few weeks and figured it was time for me to look the Bible Study part. I fanned the pages a few times so the book didn't appear brand new.

Many of the women carried well worn versions that looked like they spent their days having their pages turned while their owners absorbed the captivating words in the messages. And while I could tell most of the women were into the Bible Study stuff, I doubted that some of them, the ones like Carol, even opened the book when they weren't in church. Something about them said, "I'm here for the gossip and refreshments." I folded a few pages to add more authenticity to my effort, grabbed my handbag, and popped out of the car.

Music met me in the vestibule of the church. A glance through the beveled glass on the sanctuary doors revealed the movement of bodies. I guessed the choir was practicing or something because a large group of them were in there bellowing as loudly as they could. It didn't sound half bad, for church music.

I made my way to the classrooms down the hall. Just as I put my hand on the knob for the one where Bible Study was held, the door opened. Carol Wright gasped like I startled her and raised a protective hand to her pearls. She was always reaching for her jewelry whenever she saw me, like I was going to rip it from her neck or something ridiculous like that. She annoyed me so much. I could barely open my lips to greet her. "Carol."

"Rae, good evening. Welcome," she said in a tone that screamed the opposite of her words.

I don't know why this heifer insisted on greeting me with the word welcome every week like I hadn't been doing the faithful newcomer thing. Her weekly welcome got on my nerves.

"I thought I was going to be late." I looked over her shoulder. "It seems I'm right on time."

"Of course." Carol glanced at her diamond watch. "Well, I'll be right back." She squeezed past me to get into the corridor.

I watched her walk down the hall. The cow could have said "excuse me," and I would have moved out of her way. I guess she thought a heathen like me was beneath her, not good enough for her pardon me. Too bad I was so busy with Greg or I'd teach that trick a lesson and sleep with her man.

"Rae." I heard Angelina's voice from deep in the room. "Good to see you. I'm glad you made it." She met me midway. Angelina was smiling that same warm, sincere smile she always had for me.

"I finished my meeting early." I put my Bible and purse on a seat on the second row.

"I meant to call you earlier, I have a huge, huge favor to ask," Angelina said.

I snatched my head back. *A favor from me?* I tried to keep suspicion out of my voice. "What do you need?"

"I don't know if you've met Sister Key, but she called me

today and told me she has to go to Alabama for a few weeks or so to take care of her sister. She's ill and has six kids."

Six kids. Oh yeah, she was ill all right. Who in their right mind had six children? I cringed at the thought. That was Stretch Mark City, Alabama.

"We're having a health fair in a few weeks. Sister Key was in charge of pulling it together, and well, now we're stuck with no coordinator. I thought being a healthcare consultant and all that you could take over for her."

One of the other women interrupted us by tapping Angelina on the shoulder, so she didn't see me standing there with my mouth gaped open like she'd just asked me for a kidney. Plan a health fair? I don't do stuff like that. I wouldn't know the first thing . . .

"So what do you think?" Angelina asked, whirling back around. "I know it's short notice, and I promise I won't leave you hanging. I'd be your right hand on this."

"I don't know, Angelina, I'm so busy right now."

"But yesterday you said business was slow."

"I mean, I'm busy looking for paying business."

"Let me let you in on a little secret. If you take care of God's house, He'll take care of yours."

Was she serious?

Angelina continued, "We really want this health fair to be a good thing for the community, and honestly, someone with your expertise would do a better job than any of us."

I considered what she was saying. She was begging with those big, brown eyes of hers. I could see her now, begging Greg and getting whatever she wanted from him because I wasn't even a man, and I was succumbing to their hypnotism.

"I guess I could help, but I'm new to this area, so I don't know much about the needs here. I'm going to have to have lots of help."

Angelina clapped her hands together, then reached out and grabbed me into a hug. "Thanks so much, Rae." She released me like a rag doll and walked to her place at the podium. "Ladies, ladies, let's get started."

Just then Carol walked in. She flashed me one of those disapproving looks she always gave, reached for her pearls again, and quickly made steps to her side of the room.

I took a deep breath and reached for my Bible.

Angelina said a prayer, and then announced that we'd have a brief meeting before we began the lesson for tonight. "Everyone, I'd like to announce that Rae Burns is going to head up the committee for the health fair. Everyone please give Rae a round of applause."

Several of the women clapped like I'd won an Oscar, but Carol raised her index finger, stood, and coughed to get Angelina's attention. "Sister Preston, while I'm sure we can all appreciate Rae's talents or skills in the area of healthcare, I don't know that we can have her head a committee while she's still not a member of the church."

Angelina looked annoyed at first, and then she was thoughtful. I guess I was supposed to be embarrassed or something, but the truth was, they could take the job and shove it. I didn't want to plan any stupid health fair anyway.

"I suppose you're correct. I'll take over as the committee head and Rae can assist." Angelina winked at me.

I knew what that meant. She was going to be a figure head, and I was going to do the work. Cool beans. At least my girl could think on her feet, and we'd be working together. That played right into my plan.

Carol was shaking her head. "I don't know if that's what the church bylaws had in mind."

I looked around the room at the various women. None of them had made much of an effort to make me feel welcome to this little club. The only reason I was still here or had come in the first place was for *Operation Steal Greg*. But since I had been coming for a few weeks, and this was supposed to be a place where there was love and stuff, I felt like they could at least pretend to want to throw some my way.

"Does the church contract with consultants?" I asked, wondering where that had come from, but I knew. For some reason I wanted to show them that I had value; that even though I hadn't been born in a manger or wasn't married to a doctor or a lawyer, I was still a person who had something to contribute in life. I stood. "I mean, if the church had a leaky toilet they'd call a plumber, right? If you were building an addition, you'd hire a contractor. I could offer my services as a consultant." Several of the women smiled and nodded their heads like they were feeling me. "Free of charge, of course," I added. More smiles.

"Sounds good to me," Angelina said. "Unless we have someone else who wants to do it."

No one said a word, including Carol. I had noticed over the last few weeks that these chicks were professionals at dodging work.

"Good. Then it's decided. Please make sure you sign up on the clipboard to volunteer before you leave tonight. Rae and I will pull together a quick agenda and call the volunteers. Please be prepared for a meeting with very short notice. We don't have the luxury of time."

I sat down and fought the urge to look Carol's way, because I knew she was eating crow. That I wanted to see. It was amazing how vindicated I felt after their initial rejection by that one group of smiles from the crowd. Acceptance had never really been my thing, but this felt cool.

Angelina taught the lesson, and I fumbled around in my Bible while she hopped from section to section. It was pretty interesting stuff about people using their God-given talents to do what God wanted them to do. It was a little out there, but the part about us all having gifts had me wondering. The only one I knew I had was getting the attention of men, and I wasn't sure that was something I would consider God-given. But I had to admit, I'd wondered about the successes of some people. I'd thought about how it couldn't be all hard work, education, and connections, but I guess I'd always pegged most miraculous success as luck, great timing, a winning lottery ticket of sorts. Not God.

I left the meeting and hurried home to get dressed for work. The hospital called, and since I needed a shift or two more on the next paycheck, I figured I had to go make this money. I arrived a few minutes early and went in to talk to the nurse in charge. As expected, she was working on the schedule of assignments for the next two shifts. I had perfect timing.

Laura was an attractive white woman, but her attitude was so stank, one could hardly tell. She was a little pudgy, but had a pretty face. Her piercing blue eyes always made me feel like she knew whether I was telling the truth or a lie. I hated that feeling.

"Samaria, I'm so glad you could come in." She clapped her hands together. Her enthusiasm was a little over-done. "I was about to give report."

Report was where we nurses met and received information and updates on patients. I worked on a medical surgical floor, which meant most of the patients on our floor were post operative and required a good deal of care. I took a few steps closer to the desk, grimaced, and dragged my leg like it was injured. "That's why I'm here, I mean in your office. I hurt my knee playing tennis yesterday, and it's not completely better."

"Oh." Laura pushed her heavy chest back from the desk. Charge nurses hated to hear you came to work injured, because they couldn't work you like a slave.

"I was wondering if I could pass meds?"

Laura raised an eyebrow. She was a stickler for rotating duties. I had passed meds the other night when I worked, which meant on this shift I should have a bulk of the patient care duties. I needed to get in the medication room so I could get more drugs for June Bug. Only the medication nurse had keys to the room. I took another step and moaned. "I guess I shouldn't have said I would come in."

Laura picked up her pen. "No—no, we needed you. So it's no problem." I could see her making the change in the assignments.

Satisfied, I turned and limped out of the room. Now all I had to do was remember to keep limping through the rest of my shift.

Chapter 11

Angelina stepped into The Chicken Coup, her favorite lunch spot, and shook off the chill from the cold, wet day. She welcomed the aroma of garlic and other herbs from the barbeque sauce, Sweet Jazzy Reds, which always filled the air. It was her absolute favorite and was certain to help lift the blues that had engulfed her; at least for the duration of the meal.

The restaurant was small, and she could see her best friend, Felesia Sosa, seated at the table they often grabbed near the large window that looked out on the owner's amazing greenhouse. It was the place where he grew vegetables for the organic dishes he served.

"Hey, Mami." Felesia infused the Latino accent that came and went when she chose or chose not to use it. She stood, and the two women shared a hug. Angelina towered over the short, dark complexioned, Puerto Rican that she had roomed with all four years at Spelman College. Felesia stood next to her as the maid of honor at her wedding to Greg and was the first person to hold Danielle after she and her husband got their fill of clinging to their new baby. Felesia, or Fee as Angelina affectionately called her, was her girl.

"You look nice." Angelina admired the Burberry knit dress that clung to Felesia's curvy figure. Felesia made an obscene salary in her position as the only bilingual senior account specialist for Wylinger MoPar, a manufacturing converter for automobile parts. The two women's choices in careers had been the only major difference between them. Both were only children who'd been abandoned by their fathers and raised by overbearing, bitter mothers. Their fast friendship during the early years at Spelman proved to be an enduring glue that both could count on.

No one knew Angelina like Felesia, so when she asked, "Mami, what's wrong?" Angelina knew there was no point in trying to act like she was okay; like her world wasn't crumbling.

Angelina reached for a sweating water goblet that was sitting on her placemat and took a long sip that nearly emptied the glass.

Felesia chuckled. "Dang, chica. Do I need to ask them to bring something stronger?"

Angelina placed the glass down and laughed at her friend's question. "I almost wish I did drink. Drinkers erase the world when they want to. I'd love to disappear."

"Okay, so you gonna fill me in on what's got Ms. Optimistic so pessimistic?"

She hesitated to answer, hating to complain yet again. She lowered hers eyes. When she raised them and met Felesia's, she knew her laments and groans would be received without judgment. "It's Greg." Angelina crossed her arms tightly against her chest. "He's coming in later and later, claiming he's working or golfing or any other "ing" to stay away from home, and he won't talk to me."

"You don't think he's cheating, do you?" Although there was no one near their table, Felesia still leaned forward like she was guarding a Level 5 secret for the CIA.

"I don't care if he's cheating." Angelina avoided Felesia's eyes.

"*Tonterías!*" Felesia threw her back against the padded

booth. Angelina recognized the word as nonsense. "You care if he's running around with some *puta*. You cared the last time he did this. Why not now?"

Angelina's heart hammered a painful beat. "It was a one night stand, and it was years ago."

Felesia guffawed. "The fact that it was a one night stand didn't seem to make it any easier for you at the time."

"That's because I knew that he was trying to prove something to himself. You know he'd just had that fertility test . . ." Angelina twisted her lips. "It doesn't matter. It doesn't matter what's going on with him now. I just want a baby."

"A baby? With a cheating rat that you'll have to leave? So you can subject your child to the same thing we went through growing up? No father."

"Greg will be a better father."

"Oh, like he's a better husband than our fathers were? Come on, Lena. No way you believe that."

"I have to believe it."

"No." Felesia shook her head. "No one has to believe a lie. We choose to believe lies."

Angelina released the tight grip on her arms and began to play with her silverware. She continued to avoid her friend's eyes when she spoke. "I'm not like you, Fee. You'd rather keep your size six figure than give birth. I love children. Look at the work I do. I want to be a mother—again." She let her words trail off. She suppressed the pain she felt in her heart at the thought of Danielle. Then she let her eyes find Felesia's. In them, she saw the sympathy and compassion she was looking for.

Felesia sighed heavily and laid a hand on the one Angelina had on the table. "I know you do, Mami. And you'll be the best doggone mother on the entire planet, but you have to let God work out these marriage problems first. You can't put mess on top of mess."

Angelina laughed inside. It was amazing to her that Felesia had more faith than she did. Felesia had grown up in a dogmatic church that was more like a cult than a denomination. It took years to get her backslidden friend to attend a non-denominational Christian church, but when Felesia reaccepted Christ as her Lord and Savior, without all the doctrine and ritual, she was souled out all the way.

"What am I supposed to do? He won't talk to me, and it's not like I'm a kid. I don't have that many child bearing years left. These eggs of mine ain't getting any fresher."

"Make an appointment with him. He's a doctor, he understands the concept. Schedule a special dinner, and don't let him wiggle out of talking. Do it at a restaurant, but make sure it's some place quiet and intimate."

"What's going out going to do?"

"It'll let him know you're serious for one, and it'll set the tone. Take him out of his home environment where he can go to the bathroom or run down the stairs. If you're sitting at a table, he'll have to talk to you."

Angelina wasn't convinced it would work. "I'll try." She was running out of options for getting Greg to even consider the idea of seeing a fertility specialist again.

"You guys been trying the regular way, right?" Felesia asked, twisting her lips from embarrassment.

Angelina laughed. "Yes, and I make sure to catch him when I'm ovulating. I have one of those kits."

"Uh, sounds like a fun zapper to me." Felesia waved her hand and took a sip of her water. "God is sovereign. You taught me that. Everything works together for the good, for those that are called according to HIS purpose." Felesia quoted their favorite scripture. "Everything, chica."

Angelina nodded, tried to absorb the words, but instead filed them in her memory's to do box. "So what's up with you?"

"Venezuela for a month, Mami." Her brilliant smile filled the room. "And while I'm down there I'm going to meet me a man who's *muy macho* if you know what I mean." Felesia shimmied her chest.

Angelina laughed and slapped her hand. "Don't you get yourself in trouble with the *muy macho* man." Angelina shimmied back at her. "You know you been celibate for a long time."

"Three long years next month. Me and Jesus gonna have to have a talk about this mess. I need me a husband like yesterday." Felesia plopped her chin on her fist and sighed.

"Yeah, well, you been there, done that in a hurry and look where it got you."

Felesia tsked and frowned. "You don't have to bring up my past to remind me. You just make sure you take your own advice. Don't clock out on Greg yet. Give this stuff some time. You two love each other. It'll all work itself out."

Angelina nodded. They loved each other. She loved him. Did he love her? She wasn't so sure. The only thing she was sure of was the fact that she was going to have a hard time getting through the next thirty days without her best friend.

"So tell me about this Katrice."

Angelina looked out the window. She noticed a ray of light breaking through the clouds in the distance. Katrice, the very mention of her, brought the sunshine.

Chapter 12

"I want you ladies to know, I thought about the health fair all weekend, and last night I had an incredible idea." I beamed at Angelina and the rest of the motley crew that had been pulled together for an emergency meeting to help me with the health fair. "Let's not just do the regular old boring stuff like take blood pressures and glucose levels and weigh people. Let's make it a spa day!"

Angelina was thoughtful, but I could tell Carol and the other two women were completely thrown by my suggestion. Their eyes skittered between each other, and the two nervous ninnies looked down at their notepads.

"Hear me out." I was determined to have my say. "Health fairs are a dime a dozen. You can get a mini health physical at the local CVS or Walgreens if you put fifty cents in a machine. What I'm talking about is a total wellness day."

"Go on." Angelina was not cosigning to a big fat no like the other women, but she was still hesitant.

"This is a ritzy area, and a ritzy church. If you really want to do something, make it fun. Massages, facials, reflexology. Serve hors d'oeuvres instead of hotdogs. Have the teens in the church carry them around on little trays. Class it up." I could tell I needed to keep priming the pump, but it was time to do it by being practical. "Stress is killing African American women. I mean, our incidences of heart disease, kidney disease, and every obesity related disease known to man is affecting us. Even stuff like infertility. Our stress is so bad some of us can't get pregnant, and you know that's never been a problem for us." I laughed.

Angelina sat back. She looked like I'd kicked her under the table. *So that was it.* I'd been wondering for months. Why no children? She couldn't get pregnant. A rush of adrenaline shot through me. Major marital issue. The kind I needed to know about. I cleared my throat to quell my excitement.

"I'd like us to come up with some catchy name that has to do with relieving stress. When women come in, they can be screened for all the routine stuff you normally get at a health fair. I'll even try to get a mobile mammogram machine here, although three weeks' notice is not a lot of time for such a thing. But before ladies leave, they have the opportunity to have a ten minute massage, foot rub, and a facial. We'll have them attend a short seminar about stress and how to relieve it through meditation, relaxation, and aromatherapy. We'll make the seminar mandatory before the massage stuff, so we'll get high participation. Their last impression of the church will be of how good we were to them, and how special they felt. Not just a memory of getting their pulse taken."

Carol sneered and snorted. Don't know how she did both at the same time, but she managed it. She was looking down her nose at me again, the way she always did, like I smelled bad. "I appreciate your incredible creativity, Rae, but cost? We hope to have over two hundred women during the day. That's a lot of massages, facials, and foot rub money."

The other two ninnies murmured in agreement. Angelina seemed to have recovered from her blow, but she still didn't say anything. I had to get her on my side. She was the brains of this operation, and she was the official chairperson. If I were going to have to do a dumb health fair, I wanted to do it "Samaria" style; which meant it had to cost somebody some money.

"Angelina." I shifted in my super-padded chair, which, coupled with my internal exuberance, caused me to bounce forward. "We could bring in students from the school of massage therapy. The fair is eight hours. Pay six of them twenty bucks an hour. Students are always looking for a way to make money. And we'd only need three of them for eight hours, the other three could be for four or five hours, during heavy traffic. We're talking less than nine-hundred dollars."

"We have a very limited budget to work with." Carol's tone was snappy. I could tell the idea of some poor woman walking off the street and getting treated to a massage or facial the way she did whenever she wanted was obscene.

"Wellness and healthcare aren't free. What does Greater Christian Life Church want to do? Something relevant, or just be able to say, 'Hey we had a health fair, and everybody left with a balloon.'"

The room was silent. Carol visibly backed down. It was pretty obvious they were waiting for Angelina, and no doubt, hoping she'd shoot my idea down, but she didn't. Angelina Preston turned up the corners of her mouth and said, "I love it. Rae, you're a genius."

I let out the breath I'd been holding.

"What do you need us to do to make sure this happens?"

I did a celebratory dance in my seat and opened my portfolio. I'd spent the entire evening mapping out my plan and each person's to do list. I handed them each a different colored assignment list complete with timelines for completion. As they reviewed them, I couldn't help thinking how cool it was to actually have an interesting consulting job. I mean, I wasn't getting paid for it, but it could go on my lean resumè. Maybe I would become the designer health fair guru of Atlanta and be interviewed by *Fox5* News or something about my revolutionary way of bringing wellness to African American women. I'd have to get the media to come. This could really be big. Greg would be impressed. *He seemed to like his women smart,* I thought, stealing a glance at Angelina.

She was studying her list. I noticed she twisted that huge rock of a ring around on her finger, and at the same time tilted her head in a curious way that belied the confident woman persona. She looked sweet, almost innocent, and I thought that might be something a man—a man like Greg—would find attractive; vulnerability. I thought about myself. Did I do anything coy or cute like that? I was always trying to be sexy, but maybe I needed to appeal to the little boy in a man and copy that head tilting mannerism of hers.

Carol's irate voice pulled me from musing. "Rae, we all have pretty long lists here. Do you mind sharing what you will be doing?"

This wench was dancing on my last nerve, but I wasn't going to give her the satisfaction of knowing. "I will attempt to secure a mobile mammogram machine, and the massage crew. I'll also work my behind off getting all the goodies and freebies we'll give way, including some food that doesn't consist of hotdogs and popcorn. That's going to be a full-time assignment in and of itself. Would that be enough for me to be doing?"

Shut down once again, Carol nodded.

"This is very good, Rae." Angelina put her list in her bag and stood. "I'm really pleased with your creativity, and you've obviously put a lot of thought and work into the planning already. I knew you were the right person to lead this." She smoothed down the front of her silk crepe pantsuit. "Ladies, aren't you excited?"

Carol's crew had versions of smiles on their faces. They spoke in unison that they thought it was a good idea. Carol cleared her throat before saying, "If we can pull it off and the cost doesn't escalate, it looks promising."

"Good." I clapped victoriously. "See, when I began, you were looking at me like I said Jesus was white." I stretched and stood. We all exited the conference room. I was about to ask Angelina if she wanted to have an early lunch when her cell phone rang. She excused herself, walked a few paces, and began to listen to what sounded like bad news. The other women had left the building. Carol and I stood alone, like two school girls fighting for a best friend. We sized each other up. Carol had that demeanor again, the "you're a bad seed" look, and her hands had gone up to her pearls.

"Are those real?" I asked, with a nod toward her neck.

Shock registered on the biddy's face. She stammered over her words. "Of course they're real. What kind of question is that?"

"I was wondering. I used to work a jewelry counter at Macy, and they look like good paste to me." I could see the steam coming out of her ears. "I mean, if they're fake, it's not a crime. Tyra Banks wears cubic zirconia—"

"I assure you I don't have anything fake in my jewelry box. The nerve of . . . Tell Angelina I'll talk to her later," She sputtered and took off down the hall like a bull seeing red.

Mission accomplished.

Angelina ended her call. Her forehead was wrinkled, and worry lines creased her mouth.

"Is it that work stuff with the dead child?" I asked.

She dropped her phone in a pocket on the side of her purse. She was emotionally disheveled. She looked up and down the hall. "Where's everyone else?"

"They left." I ignored the dis. Guess it wasn't work. "So you have time for coffee or lunch?"

Angelina looked at her watch "Yeah, sure. I could use the distraction."

Great, I thought. I could use the intel.

Chapter 13

Angelina was right. She was distracted today. Not that I really knew her, but in the time I'd spent with her, I'd noticed her great attending skills. The eye contact, in particular always, made me feel like the only person in the world. Angelina used just the right mix of titling her head and nodding to make sure a person knew she was engaged; so the woman who sat across from me was one I'd never seen before. This woman was having a hard time being in the room period.

"That's a pretty suit." I hoped to bring her back from Mars or wherever she was. We'd been having this one sided conversation for the last five minutes. Whatever was on her mind was way over the top.

She looked down at herself like she'd forgotten what she was wearing. "Thanks. Lavender's not really a color I care for, but I have an important dinner with my husband tonight, and it's his favorite."

I nodded. "So you're wearing lavender because he likes it, or because you need him weak in the knees?"

She smiled coyly. "You know your men. I need to convince him of something. He absolutely loves me in any shade of purple, and honestly you've got to work what you have to get a man on the same planet as you sometimes." She reached for her ice tea and took a sip, careful not to let any spill on her suit.

I moved my rear end back and forth on my seat. Purple was

news to me. Good intel. I decided to see if she'd share more. "So anything else on the agenda to get him on that planet with you?"

"We're meeting at one of his favorite Creole restaurants. He's from Louisiana, and he grew up on red beans and rice and blackened salmon." She smiled a weak, pitiful smile that lacked confidence. "I'm hoping that'll help too."

"Hmmm," I moaned thoughtfully. "I guess that's why I haven't gotten myself all entangled yet. Seems like too much of a bother to me."

"All relationships involve sacrifice and compromise," Angelina countered.

Always the teacher, I thought; even when she had her own problems.

She continued. "We have to commit to relationships with our parents and other relatives. Friendships. You have to work through things, especially in marriage. Giving someone a foot rub now and then isn't going to kill anyone."

Foot rub. I picked up my water glass. I supposed she was right, but who was compromising in my world? Not my mother. I didn't have any friends, and of course, I was doing all the giving in this relationship with Greg. But that was only because I was the other woman. Once I became the woman-woman, it wasn't going to be his world with me scrambling for nuts.

"So what do you want, a bigger house or something?" I squinted at her.

She looked to her right, and then left, like she was checking the perimeter before she shared a secret. "No, nothing like that." She sat back and waved a hand. I didn't know why she was playing Secret Squirrel. She wasn't telling me jack, or had she changed her mind?

"What did you think of pastor's message on Sunday?"

Water got caught in my throat, and I coughed a little before speaking. "I, umm, didn't go to church on Sunday. I had to work Saturday night."

Angelina frowned. "I assumed being a consultant was a nine to five type thing." Her tone belied that she wasn't pleased that I hadn't gone to church.

"I'm a registered nurse. When my consulting money is lean, I pick up shifts at the hospital. I worked an eleven to seven overnight, and I was worn out." Angelina nodded, and I redirected the conversation. "So how long have you been married?"

The waitress swooped in, put salads in front of us, and filled our drink glasses.

Angelina scooted closer to the table. "Thirteen years."

"Wow." My eyebrows went up. "That's a long time. You married young."

"I was twenty-four." She picked up her silverware.

I wondered if we had to say another grace or if the blessing over the bread would suffice. Angelina began to eat, so I figured the grace covered the entire meal. I picked up my fork. "Do you like being married?"

Angelina nodded and answered between chews. "Most of the time."

"Not all the time?"

"Marriage is hard work, and like anything that's work, we occasionally want a break."

That made sense. I didn't expect her to say it, but it made sense.

Angelina raised her eyes to mine. "Are you dating someone? Thinking about marriage?"

I shrugged. "I don't know. Maybe."

"Marriage can be good, if you're with the right person. It can be nice to have someone to grow old with. You won't always be young."

I pulled back from the table. "So is that why you got married, so you wouldn't have to be afraid of getting old alone? That seems like a long range goal at twenty-four."

Angelina laughed. "I married my husband because I loved him."

"Loved?" My tone asked a question.

Lines creased Angelina's forehead and she answered, "Love."

"Well, I don't think of marriage as permanent. I think that's the mistake people make. They try to make something permanent that should be temporary."

Angelina shook her head. Her disappointment in that statement was as palatable as my salad. "Rae, I know you're a new Christian, but one of the things you'll learn from attending church is that marriage isn't about what you think. God has a design for marriage, and it's a much deeper commitment than a lot of us like to accept."

So she was going to go chu'ch on me. Unbelievable. She had all these ideas about marriage and commitment She was clueless. I rolled my eyes.

"How old are you, Rae?"

"Why are you assuming it's my youth talking?" I asked, my frown in my voice and on my face.

"No, I'm curious." She shrugged. "I've been curious."

"I'm twenty-seven. Not as young as I look."

Angelina didn't say anything.

"Well, what does it tell you? Why I'm so naïve?"

"No, actually, I was wondering how you got so bitter."

Bitter. I flinched. "I'm not bitter. I'm a realist. Men are dogs, and the ones that aren't dogs, you can't count on." Mekhi's face skittered through my mind.

"All men are not dogs." Angelina smiled like she was sure of this fact. Like I was silly for suggesting such.

Well, she was right. Not all. The last doctor I'd tried to get my hooks into hadn't taken me up on the offer, and I was half naked when he said no. But Angelina wasn't living with him. She was living with Greg. She'd obviously convinced herself that he was faithful, and I had the check in the mail to prove nothing was further from the truth.

Angelina's phone rang. She excused herself, stood, and walked away from the table.

The waitress arrived and put down two steaming plates of food left just as Angelina returned. Angelina reached across the booth for her handbag. "I have to go. I'm sorry to run out on you, but the governor and the DFYS chief are holding a press conference downtown."

I threw my hands up. "It's okay. You have to do your job."

"Please have her wrap my plate up and take it for your dinner." She removed money from her wallet and placed it on the table.

I shook my head. "You don't have to do that."

"Of course I do." She put a hand on my shoulder and squeezed. "I'll call you tomorrow." Then she swept out of the restaurant.

The waitress returned, and I instructed her to make Angelina's meal to go. I pulled out my cell phone and my wallet. I had to see what my available balance was on one of my credit cards. It was time to go shopping. I needed something purple.

Chapter 14

The media had turned up the heat on their reports about the death of Robin Edwards. Angelina kept waiting for the reprieve that normally happened when something juicier came along and the cattle of reporters shifted in a herd to torture a new victim. But the metro Atlanta area was quiet, and the only thing they had to gnaw at was The Division of Youth and Family Services. And gnaw they did. A reporter had even done a feature titled DEATH BE NOT PROUD: TEN YEARS OF FAILURE IN THE DYFS SYSTEM, wherein he chronicled every child death the agency had had in the last ten years. Many of which were not the agency's fault. To the reporter's credit, he didn't try to even sway the story in that direction, but the title spoke volumes and sent a negative message regardless of the content.

Angelina's BlackBerry vibrated for the eighth time since the press conference. It was another newspaper calling. She had come to recognize the prefixes on their telephone numbers.

The governor announced that the agency had completed its preliminarily investigation. He assigned blame to high case loads and systemic internal system issues that could have been avoided had the agency been given money to purchase a computer system that kept data in one repository instead of paper records all over the state. Once management pulled case files together for children who had lived in the foster family's home, it was pretty clear there was a pattern of monitoring neglect on the part of the agency. They were in trouble. The commissioner was angry, and the governor was hot. Heads were about to roll.

"I thought you could use this."

Angelina looked up to see Portia, her receptionist, standing in front of her desk holding a steaming mug of coffee. She smiled and accepted the cup from the young woman. Portia, a twenty-two-year-old red head with green eyes and multiple tattoos, was as different from Angelina as night was from day. But the young woman was efficient and sensitive to Angelina's moods, often going out of her way to soothe the ills of the day, like she was doing now.

"Thanks." Angelina smiled and placed the mug on a coaster.

"And there's more." Portia pulled an envelope from behind her back and stuck it under Angelina's nose. They made eye contact, and Angelina noticed Portia was blushing. The reddening of Portia's porcelain skin meant she was excited or angry, and since she was giddy, her coloring meant excitement. Angelina felt her heart skip a beat. They had a donation, likely a big one, and boy did they need it.

Angelina removed the check and letter from the envelope. It was notification she'd been awarded the grant she'd requested from Murray Sporting Goods and a check for ten thousand dollars to fund a summer mentoring program for pre-teen boys. She wanted to cry, but instead, she put Portia to work. "Call the community relations manager, what's his name, Van something from the Atlanta Sparks."

Portia nodded and made rapid steps to the door.

"I'm going to send an email to the director about that campground in Conyers and see if they still have space," Angelina continued. "Would you pull the file for me?"

Portia nodded.

"And after you reach Van, get me contact numbers for V-103's publicity department."

Portia threw her hand up and saluted Angelina. "Will do, boss." She turned to exit.

"Oh, and Portia," Angelina called before the young woman disappeared. "Thanks for the coffee and looking out for the good news."

Portia winked and disappeared through the door.

Within minutes, Angelina was on the phone negotiating the details of a summer program with the Sparks community relations manager. The basketball team had been willing to match money they received from a sponsor, so they had twenty thousand dollars. It would be an awesome time for the kids. The plan was to sign up one hundred pre-teen foster boys and teach them everything from how to tie a tie to how to start a small business. In addition to a few of the team's players, she was hoping to get the attention of a local celebrity entertainer—hip hop star or radio personality—to really make the week special. This was what Something Extra was all about. This made DYFS's failure less of a burden on her soul.

Angelina locked up her small office. Once Portia was gone, that was it for staff at Something Extra. Volunteers came and went, but usually finished their day by three P.M. to avoid getting stuck on the interstate. She looked at her watch. It was after five. She was a little pressed for time, but if she didn't hit any pockets of traffic, she'd be at the restaurant by six, as promised, for her dinner with Greg.

She climbed into her automobile and pulled into the thick of cars heading out of downtown Norcross. Choosing a restaurant in Atlanta had been a good choice because she was actually moving against most traffic.

She was on cloud nine. After the grueling press conference,

where angry words and accusations flew around like planes over the airport, things were looking up. She prayed her luck wasn't about to run out at dinner. She'd been anxious all day about their meeting, but the truth was the conversation could go well with Greg. He, like she, had a chance to mull some things over and really think about their future. An earlier text message from Felesia had reminded her to remain positive about it all. She'd been doing that, or at least trying, until the phone rang.

Chapter 15

I knew my relationship with Greg had kicked up a notch. I could tell by the way he looked at me when he walked out of the door. It was that "I don't want to leave" look. The one a man gets on his face when he's satisfied completely. And satisfy him I did. It began with the phone call where he'd answered and I'd whispered, "I'm wearing purple panties." Within an hour, Greg was stretched out on the lavender silk sheets I'd picked up on the way home. I'd sat next to him in my new lavender satin "Merry Widow" getup I'd gotten at Fredrick's of Hollywood on my last stop. I kept a credit card for the store for emergencies like this one. Just like I hoped, they had this God awful-uncomfortable set hanging in the back on a display. And that wasn't it, I was in luck—purple was in fashion. I purchased everything from thongs to elbow length gloves. He was never going to see so much purple in his life. Angelina had no idea how I welcomed that little tidbit of information.

"Where did you get that sexy get-up?" he'd asked, loosening his tie.

I helped him remove his jacket. Then I pushed him down on the couch, hard. I straddled him. "Don't you worry about that."

I fed him from a fork like a king, rubbed his feet like I *now* knew he liked, gave him some mind blowing sex, and sent him on his way. I was exhausted. Stealing a man was hard work.

I stripped. Ready for a long, hot soak, I climbed into my Jacuzzi tub. Just as I reached for the knob to turn on the jets for the water massager, the telephone rang. I cursed. One glance at the caller ID, and I could see it was my mother. Reluctantly, I answered. "Hi, Mama."

"Hey, baby, you busy?"

She wanted something, but it wasn't urgent. When it was urgent, she didn't care if I were busy. "I'm taking a bath."

"A bath. Why you wanna take a bath when you got a shower?"

She was stalling with that question. Whatever she wanted was going to really piss me off. "I'm worn out, and a bath is relaxing. What's up?"

"You the tiredest young girl I ever seen. Whatcha doing to get so tired?"

All I want is this soak. "I work. A lot on several different jobs and projects. Tell me what's up?"

There was a long pause before my mother spoke. "I know you gonna be upset, but ya' cousin need some more of those pills."

I sat straight up, water sloshing. "What do you mean more? I gave you ten pills. I can't take anymore. I'll get caught!"

"He gets his check the end of the month, and he can buy some more."

"The end of the month is more than a week away. What happened to what I gave you? He couldn't have taken that many so fast."

"He dropped some down the drain." Her voice was nervous with the lie.

Dropped some down the drain. Now I know she thought I was a fool. Those were the lies I told when I stole the dang pills: dropped them on the floor, patient refused them but I had already contaminated them, patient spit them out, etc. etc.

to account for needing to get more. So I knew a rouse. I created one every time I went to work.

"Mama, is June selling them?"

"No. Why would you think that?"

"Because I don't believe a drug addict would drop a pill down the drain. A coke head wipes the table clean. Nobody addicted wastes drugs."

"Well, he did. You know he got that bad arm. So unless you got money to buy some, I need more," she barked and then got humble. "'Til the first."

Those pills were at least fifty dollars a piece on the street. No way could I buy enough to keep him going for ten days. I didn't have any cash, and my credit cards were maxed out. The lavender had taken me over the top. This was insane. "I can't do it. I'll get caught and fired. I could lose my license."

"It's just one more time. Then we'll . . . I mean, he'll buy some."

"Mama, June has got to get help. He can't afford a hundred dollar a day drug habit." I let out a breath. "I can give you some money, and he can pick up some Demerol or Percocet."

"No!" she screamed. The shriek startled me so that I almost dropped the phone in the tub. "I can't live with him when he ain't got his stuff. He start yelling and acting crazy."

"But—"

"No 'but,' Samaria. I told you we gonna have money at the end of month. I need you to give me some more pills. Just this last time." My mother's breathing became ragged. I could hear her taking a breath from her inhaler. "Ya' cousin, June, is all I have left of my dead sister. I promised her I would take care of him, and I'm trying."

"Mama, you not going to have June if he's overdosing on that stuff, and uh, he's almost thirty years old. He's not a kid."

"I been talking to him about rehab. We working on it. I'm working on it. I need you to just help me 'til I gets him there."

I nodded, although I did not believe her. "Okay. I'll try."

"Can you get the green ones? They stronger. He breaks them in half."

"I'll get what I can, but I'm telling you, this is the last time."

I hung up with my mother and reached for the loofah to wash my body. Then I turned on the jets and tried to let the heat and rhythmic flow of the water relax my muscles. This was getting crazy. I had never done this before in my career, and to think I was doing it and it wasn't even for me. I had turned into a drug supplier, and I didn't know how to get out of it. And June was getting worse about feeding his habit. He'd gone from the white to the pink and pink to peach, and now he was begging for the green ones. OX was bad stuff, which meant this couldn't end good. I had to stop supplying him. I couldn't afford it from my wallet or on my job, so he'd either start stealing or killing to get more and end up in jail. That would break my mother's heart.

I closed my eyes to the problem and tried instead to focus on Greg. I said his name over and over again out loud to hypnotize myself and bring my world back into the order that my mother's call had shattered.

Greg. I loved the crazed look in his eyes when he'd seen me in the lingerie which was heightened when he entered the bedroom and saw the lavender rose petals leading to the bed. I had worked the heck out of that little piece of information Angelina shared. Worked it until only the motion of the water could remove the ache. Greg was a stallion. The only man I'd known who'd ever been able to keep up with me in bed had been Mekhi.

My heart rate sped up just thinking about Mekhi. He

looked so good last week. Greg was fine, but he was an older man. I had no idea how much we'd have in common when we did eventually get together. I envisioned him wanting to listen to old school music from the eighties, or heaven forbid, he was into neo-classic jazz or some fusion music or crap like that. I liked hip-hop and rap. That music was in my blood, which brought my memory full circle back to Mekhi.

Music always made me think of Mekhi. He loved it. Taught me to love it. Taught me to understand the beats and the rhythms. How to feel the music in my heart instead of just hear it with my ears. He and I would spend hours chillin' on the roof of his building with a boom box listening to Jay Willie and Busta Lee's early underground stuff while Mekhi wrote silly little poems and love songs. We mapped out our future; planned our escape from White Gardens.

It was also when Mekhi introduced me to the business.

"Girl, we gonna make this money and get up out of here." Mekhi's white teeth shone in the moonlight. "I'ma buy you a phat house off Cascade or in Buckhead. Wherever you wanna live. I got you."

I was lying on my back. Mekhi was perched on one elbow next to me, his clear eyes staring at the moon and the stars. What he was talking about seemed like it was as far away from our world as the Milky Way, but fantasies were all we had as teenagers. Our reality was so bad. While Mekhi had dreams of living the lifestyle of the rich and famous, all I wanted to do was get away from my mother's boyfriends; their filthy looks and even filthier hands.

I raised an arm and reached around the back of his neck and pulled him to me. All my hopes and dreams for leaving these rat and roach invested projects were tied to this man; his plans, his lips, and his body.

"You promise you're going to take care of me, Mekhi?"

I asked, looking deep into his eyes, always making sure he never flinched or blinked when he assured me he would. We sealed our dreams with kisses and teenage love making that had gone from being clumsy to being as sweet as the fantasies that preceded it.

My experiences and my mama had taught me that I couldn't trust a man. Yeah, I'd known Mekhi since I was eight years old. Yeah, Mekhi had been a friend before he'd become my boo. Yeah, Mekhi had me wearing FUBU and Phat Farm and blingin' with YSL and Gucci bags. Yeah, Mekhi was the reason I didn't ride the crappy school bus. We rolled everywhere in his Honda Accord on twenty-inch spinning rims with his base stereo announcing our arrival. Mekhi was my savior. My mama kept warning me. "Girl, don't get yourself all in love with that boy. As sure as the sun rises, he gonna let you down. Something about being male makes them all stupid."

Mekhi's tape played louder in my head than my mother's. When he thought I was ready, he had brought me into his business. Boosting. Mekhi taught me how to steal any clothing item that wasn't nailed down, and we were moving on to jewelry. "You can do this, Sammie. Ain't nobody gonna get caught." His voice was strong. His words sure. I trusted Mekhi Johnson one hundred percent. Trusted what he said and what he did.

Slam! Bars closed in my face. The sound was so real it startled me. I bolted up in the water which was now chilly. My heart raced with such velocity I thought blood would come out of my ears.

"*Argh,*" I moaned. I stood and reached for a towel.

Mekhi Johnson was history. Bad history. I stepped on rose petals as I moved across the bathroom floor. They paved the road to my future. The rose petals, sheets, and lingerie I'd discarded on the floor. Forget Mekhi. I had to focus on Gregory Preston.

I thought of Angelina. How disappointed she had to be when her husband called and cancelled dinner. I thought about how proud she'd been of me when I shared my ideas for the health fair. She liked me, which was interesting because women never did. Especially women like her. I wanted to blame it on stupidity, but I knew Angelina was no dummy. She was just kind and genuine. Pure, even. I hated that her good heartedness and naivety were going to cost her so dearly because I was going to bust up her marriage and take her husband if it were the last thing I did.

Chapter 16

Angelina wanted to knock that lying smile off his face. An emergency consultation. Oh it had been a consultation, but it had nothing to do with anything medical.

"Can we talk now?" She still wanted to accomplish her agenda. Still wanted a win despite the diminished aura of the atmosphere. It was killing her to speak to him calmly, civilly.

Greg was peeling his clothes off. She could smell the cologne from his woman all the way across the room. Or was her mind playing tricks on her? The scent was the same as hers, but it seemed so fresh. She hadn't sprayed herself since she'd gotten in the car when she was on the way to the restaurant for the dinner she'd so carefully planned. "Can we?" she repeated the question that had come back unanswered.

"I'm tired, Lena." He went into the bathroom.

Angelina flew off the bed and went into his closet. She pulled his shirt from the hamper and buried her nose in it. Perfume. Her perfume, but it was so strong. What was going on? She was losing her mind. She dropped the shirt in the hamper and thought about the one she'd cut to shreds the other day. Maybe it was her. Maybe she was imaging all this drama; imaging that Greg was cheating. Maybe he was working and doing all the things he said. She was going to acquiesce and let it all go when she saw it. Stuck to the back of his shirt. A rose petal near the hem that fell off when she reached for it. A lavender one.

She waited until she heard the water go off in the shower and walked into the bathroom with her evidence. Greg was toweling off. She extended her hand. "What's this?"

Greg looked at the rose, his face a mask of confusion. "Where'd you get that?"

"It fell off your shirt."

"So are you doing laundry this late at night or snooping through my clothes again?"

"Does it matter how I found it? Tell me where it came from?"

Greg turned his back, wrapped the towel around his waist and reached for his electric toothbrush. She grabbed his hand before he could turn it on and shoved the petal closer to his face. "Tell me where this came from?" She applied pressure to his fingers until their bones met. Until his cold stare forced her to release him.

"Don't get started with that nasty temper of yours." Greg shook his hand, no doubt to work out the discomfort from her grip. Then he applied toothpaste to the brush. He did it so casually that she would have been impressed with his ability to stay placid under pressure if she hadn't been so disgusted. "It's nothing."

Angelina looked from his face to his reflection in the mirror. "It's a freakin' rose petal, and I want to know how it got in your clothes."

"Freakin'?" He leaned close to her. A sarcastic grin came over his face. "Come on, Lena. If you're going to curse, be a real woman about it. At least use the word." He turned on the toothbrush and proceeded to do his three minute brushing routine. She stood there determined that tonight he was going to answer her. He was going to tell her where he'd been, or he was going to find out how nasty her temper really was.

"I'm not letting this go, Greg." She opened and closed her hand around the petal.

He turned off the toothbrush. "It's nothing. It's a flower petal."

"You stood me up for your tramp!" she yelled. "I drove all the way—"

"What are you talking about? There is no tramp, and I called you," he interjected, walking out of the bathroom.

"I was almost there." She followed him. "How could you do that to me? I told you I had a special evening, and you cancel—"

"Lena, I had to work." He turned back to her. "You know this happens."

"Where were you working, in a flower garden?"

Greg sucked in his cheeks and let out a long, frustrated breath. "You really want to know where that came from?"

"Yes." She guffawed. She knew he was stalling, trying to think of a lie. "I want to know."

"You and those outrageous delusions of yours have spoiled my surprise. I stopped by the florist on the way home this evening and ordered roses for you. I intended to buy some, but the only ones she had left were wilted, so I ordered them to be delivered at your office tomorrow. I felt bad about cancelling tonight. It couldn't be avoided. I wanted to make it up to you."

Angelina was not convinced. Her gut told her Greg was lying, so she pushed. "It was not on the outside of your clothes, it was inside. How did a rose petal get in your pants?"

"What?"

"You heard me. How did the petal get *inside* your pants?"

Greg threw up his hands. "I don't know. I was in the place looking around. I guess I bumped up against something." He walked into his closet and pulled pajama bottoms from the bureau. He removed his towel and stepped into them.

Angelina's glance darted between her husband and the evidence in her hand. She didn't believe him, and now it was time to let him know that. "Where's the receipt?"

Greg shook his head. "What?"

"The receipt for the flowers?"

Greg dropped his chin to his chest and sighed, then met her eyes with a shake of his head. "You're the snoop. Go look in my wallet. Look in pockets. I'm not going to hand it over like a child. If you want it, you find it." He pulled a T-shirt over his head and walked out of the bedroom.

Angelina closed her eyes, but a tear escaped and ran down her face. *Liar, liar, liar.* She collapsed on the bed. Did she go through his pockets, check his wallet, and embarrass herself with the hope that he was telling the truth? She opened her fist and looked at the crushed petal in her palm. She wished she could make it disappear. *Lavender.* How ironic that the very thing she thought would serve to bless her today had done the opposite and cursed her.

Chapter 17

Angelina stared at the lavender roses sitting on her desk. They'd been delivered before she returned from court this afternoon. The search through Greg's wallet and pockets had been futile. There had been no receipt. Not that she expected to find one. She trusted her instincts. They told her he was lying.

"They pretty." Katrice pointed her tiny finger in the direction of the enormous vase that took up most of the space. Angelina smiled at the little girl and returned her gaze to the blossoms. He did have good taste. Too bad his attempt to fool her left such a bitter taste in her mouth.

"Let's see." Angelina stood and removed one of the flowers from the arrangement. She broke the stem off close to the bud and pushed the flower into the child's wild, kinky hair above her ear. Angelina reached into her handbag and removed a compact. She showed Katrice her image, and the little girl laughed with delight.

"Pretty," Katrice said.

While Angelina appreciated the woman who'd finally had the nerve to step up and temporarily house Katrice, she was white, and the child's hair was a wooly mess of cultural misunderstanding. Katrice needed an African American foster mother, and she needed one bad.

Angelina stared into Katrice's beautiful brown eyes. What was the world coming to when someone as sweet and affectionate as this baby could be displaced? She'd had a not so nice visit with her mother. Angelina had observed it with her own eyes through the one way glass outside the visitation room. Afterward, she decided rather than send the child back to the daycare center with a hundred other kids, she'd give her one-on-one attention that no one else in the world had time to share. It was uncustomary, but so were her feelings toward the child. She did what she deemed best and didn't worry about protocol.

Katrice reached up and touched Angelina's hair. "Your hair pretty."

"Thank you," Angelina said, and then she had a brilliant idea.

She picked up her phone and made the call that was necessary. Then she closed Katrice's file and locked it in her desk draw. "Let's go, baby. Let's go make us both prettier."

An hour and half later they stepped into the McDonald's across from the Shine and Swing Hair Salon where Angelina had a standing weekly appointment. Katrice was a vision in cornrows and beads. The little girl was so excited. She'd had a wash and got to sit under the dryer. Terri, Angelina's hairstylist, was in between clients, so she gave the little girl special attention. Katrice even got a coat of clear nail polish from the manicurist. It was the most fun Angelina had had in a long time, and there was a light in the little girl's eyes that she'd never seen.

McDonald's was an adventure. Angelina had to admit she'd never really paid attention to the play areas for children. Katrice behaved like she'd never been inside one. Angelina had no doubt that the little girl hadn't. After all, her foster mother's level of trifling had only been exceeded by the child's natural mother's.

"I think it's time for us to leave," Angelina announced when Katrice came out of the ball pit for the third time and took a sip of her fruit punch. Angelina glanced at her watch. She hated for the fun to end, but it was getting late. It was almost seven, and she'd told the foster mother she'd have her home by seven-thirty. "I have to take you back to Ms. Henry's house."

"I don't wanna go Ms. Henry. I stay with you."

Angelina sat back in the chair. A wave of emotions assailed her because in truth, she was beginning to feel like she didn't want to let Katrice go. She had facilitated foster parent certification classes for years. One of the standing lessons in the course taught that foster parents could not get attached to children. They had to be prepared at any time for the children to go home. Now she realized how preposterous that statement was. How does one not fall in love with a child like Katrice? She was sweet, well-mannered, and that smile . . . it was melting Angelina's heart more and more every time she saw the child.

"Don't you want to show Ms. Henry your pretty hair? I bet she'll be glad she doesn't have to tussle with it tonight."

Katrice's face was marred with a frown, and her eyes filled with tears. "I wanna stay with you."

Angelina let out a breath and reached under the table for the child's shoes. "Come on, baby, I have to take you home, but I promise we'll do this again. We'll make your hair pretty and we'll come to McDonald's, okay?"

"Not home." Katrice shook her head. She raised her leg and let Angelina put her feet in her sneakers. All the joy that the little girl had been exhibiting seemed to slide down on the floor and disappear into the concrete.

***

They arrived at the Henry home a minute before Katrice's promised delivery time, and Angelina removed the child from her car seat.

"Remember what I said," Angelina whispered in a soft, affirming voice. "We'll do it again real soon. And I'll get my hair and nails done too, so we'll be like best friends." Angelina was careful not to use the word sisters.

"But I want you to be my mommy," Katrice responded, big eyes shining with tears.

Angelina felt the wind rush out of her lungs. *Mommy.* She wanted to be somebody's mommy so terribly bad, and all Katrice wanted was to be somebody's child. They were two of a kind. Both alone and looking for someone to love. "I'll be back. I promise." She knew she shouldn't have said that. It was unfair to make promises to foster children. Her professional training taught her that was a no-no. But her heart—her heart was a part of her soul. The one Katrice had climbed into with every tender smile and word the little girl said.

Ms. Henry retrieved her at the door and thanked Angelina for getting Katrice such a pretty new hair-do. Angelina instructed Ms. Henry on how to care for it, handed her some hair products complete with a silk head scarf, and walked back to her SUV. She was determined not to turn around and see Katrice's anguished face. She climbed in, started the vehicle, and finally unable to stop herself, she looked back at the house one more time. Nose pressed against the glass, Katrice was still standing there.

"I want you to be my mommy," she'd cried. Angelina wanted to cry with her because she wondered why she couldn't be somebody's mommy.

Chapter 18

"Angelina, you're not going to believe this." I turned my laptop monitor around so she could read an email.

I watched her scan it, and then her face broke into a smile. "You're amazing."

I beamed. Getting Curvaceous Fitness Center to come and do body fat measurements had been an idea that came to me early yesterday morning when I was brainstorming. "Cool that they said yes. We are going to have so many booths and stations and giveaways. It's going to be a really successful event."

"I hope the local media shows up and takes some pictures." Angelina beamed. "It would be good publicity for the church."

I bit my tongue. I wanted media coverage too, but I couldn't pursue it. I was working undercover. Samaria Jacobs couldn't be caught being Rae Burns. My fabulous health fair could make it on the nightly news broadcast, and Greg might see me. So while I was sure this was my big chance to get on *Fox 5 Atlanta* or one of the other stations and sell my consulting business, the media was out. Greg's checks were a definite thing. My mama taught me about having a bird in the hand.

"Have you tried to get some PR?" Angelina asked.

"I've contacted all the major media outlets." My shrug was indifferent. "So we'll see." I didn't want Angelina to make calls to local television and radio stations herself. Although I doubted I needed to really be concerned about that. She didn't seem to have time. She was busy every day with the child death case family services had botched up. The media wouldn't let it go. We'd been working together pretty closely every day, and the text messages and phone calls about the case never stopped. I was starting to feel sorry for her. The worry lines were aging her. A sista needed a massage and facial herself.

Angelina picked up a note in my pile of things to do. "I see you still don't have the banner for the opening."

"I've been trying to find someone to pay for the thing. Haven't gotten a taker."

"Don't worry about it. I'll ask my husband's practice to donate it." She reached into her bag. "But before I forget, let me get him on the phone."

Angelina removed her cell phone and pressed what I assume was a speed dial number. I'd never seen her talk to Greg up close. I couldn't wait to see how they interacted, even if it were a one sided observation.

"Hi, babe, how are you?"

Angelina did some nodding and mumbled some yeahs and um-hums before saying, "I'm at the church." More yeahs and um-hums. "Look, before I forget, I wanted to ask for a favor. You know we're having the health fair, and we don't have anyone to pay for the banner for the door. I was wondering . . ." After a couple of seconds a smile filled her face. "Thanks, hon." She made an okay sign with her free hand. "Look, I'd like to talk to you this evening. We still never had our conversation." She nodded and listened for a minute or more. Then she said, "Okay," and ended the call.

No "I love you" was exchanged.

I couldn't read her. She looked pretty neutral about it. Either he had blown her off again and she didn't want me to see it, or he had agreed, and she was nervous about it. I was dying to know what she wanted to talk to him about.

"Your husband is pretty generous. What kind of business does he run?"

"He's a physician. A surgeon. He has a practice downtown." Her voice had dropped an octave.

"Oh, I didn't know he was in healthcare. What's his specialty? I work with a few hospitals. Maybe I've met him."

"Neurosurgery."

"A brain surgeon." I threw my hand to my chest. "Impressive."

Angelina looked me right in the eyes and nodded. I could tell she wasn't impressed.

"Will we see him at the health fair?"

She laughed, but the throaty sound was not filled with joy. "Not as long as the grass is still green at the Dunwoody Golf & Tennis Club."

"What about church? I know I haven't been that much; does he attend?"

"No, I wish he did. He went to church in college, but after we got married, he started working long hours during his residency, and then he stopped. It's been a long time since he's attended regularly." Angelina had a sad, forlorn look on her face. "But he's a good man," she added. "He has a good heart."

Good hearted. Hmmm. Not sure I would use those words to describe Greg, especially with respect to her. "What would you do if you found out he wasn't the person you think he is?"

"I'd be disappointed, but I wouldn't be surprised. Why? Are you going through something like that yourself?"

I thought about Mekhi. I had been through something like that, but I really asked the question to find out where her head was. "No, I mean, maybe. Tell me why you wouldn't be surprised?"

"Because when people are backslidden or unsaved, you

never know what they're going to do. They don't have the
Holy Spirit guiding them the way a person does who's in relationship with Christ."

"So you'd forgive him for anything?"

She looked at me like I was silly. "I'm not saying that.
But I know we're unevenly yoked, which means not on the
same level spiritually. So we're going to have issues because
of that."

"See, that's why the Bible is a trip to me. What's with the
yoke talk?"

Angelina laughed. "The Bible was written more than two
thousand years ago, and it was translated by scholars and
scribes. They talked like that."

"Well, I need a plain English Bible. One that tells it like it
is." I laughed, and she laughed with me. "But seriously, if you
and your husband are uneven, shouldn't you go try to be with
someone you're yoked right with?"

"It's not that simple. First of all the Bible tells us that God
is a covenant God. Vows to God are not supposed to be broken. Secondly, the Bible also tells us that God hates divorce,
so He expects us to try hard to make our marriages work, not
quit on each other."

Even when lavender panties are involved, I thought. "Those
don't seem like reasons to stay in a marriage if you're not
yoked." I kept throwing my new word out. "Seems to me to
have the peace you keep saying Jesus brings, you need the
right man."

My cell phone rang, and I picked it up quickly when I heard
Greg's special tone.

"You get that." Angelina stood. "I'm going to the ladies
room."

I opened the phone, but waited until I was sure she was out
of ear shot. "Hey, big daddy."

"I was about to hang up," Greg grumbled. "Look, I can't make it tonight."

I rolled my eyes. "Why not? I was looking forward to giving you a real special treat."

"I'm sure you were. Something's come up with my wife. I have to have dinner with her tonight or she's going to blow a gasket."

"Can we get together early?"

"I'm not out of surgery until around three, and by the time I clean up and head home, it'll be too late. I can't swing it."

"But Gr . . . baby." I changed my tune when Angelina walked back into the room. "I have to work for the next three nights. We won't see each other."

He groaned. Angelina sat down and began shuffling through papers.

"Three nights in a row? You've never done that before."

"I had to take the work they had. You never know when it's going to be a lull in the schedule." The truth was, three nights were going to give me the latitude I needed to steal drugs.

"Well, I guess we'll have to try and do an early morning. I have to go home tonight."

"Fine. I'm in a meeting, so let me finish up, and I'll talk to you later." I closed the phone.

"Soooo," Angelina sang through a wide smile. "There is a man?"

I nodded and put my phone in my purse. "Yes, I've been dating him for a little while."

"Is it serious?"

"I don't know. Depends on what you mean by serious."

"Is he important to you? Do you love him?"

"No, I'm not coo coo for cocoa puffs if that's what you mean. He's important to me, but love—I love his wallet." I chuckled to myself. "I love that a lot."

"A wallet can't keep you warm at night."

"With money you can buy a *Ralph Lauren* goose down comforter that can."

"But the pleasure of the comforter only lasts until the new smell wears off. Then it won't matter what's on the bed, only who's in it."

I had to give it to her. That was a good comeback. Still easier said than done when you had it all. "I think I'll have to see that for myself." I handed her a flyer for the event. "Brother James is going to have the youth put these on car windows at the mall and three of the supermarkets this weekend to advertise some more."

Angelina looked at it and nodded. I could see she had retreated back into her thoughts about Greg.

"So." I decided to go for it. I had to get her talking or all this mentoring stuff wasn't going to benefit me. "Do you want to share this big topic you want to talk to your husband about?" Angelina looked at me like I had two heads. "Sometimes it's good to get an objective person's thoughts, and since I hardly know you and definitely don't know him, I could be a good sounding board."

"It's nothing I need an opinion about. We have to discuss something and make a decision."

"Oh." I crossed my arms and feigned indignance. "I thought this thing with us was a two way street."

Angelina let out an easy breath. "It is, but there's no pressure on either side to talk."

I decided to go for the juggler. I mean, why not? I was a juggler cutting type of gal. "Angelina, do you mind if I ask you something personal?"

"I don't mind if you don't mind if I don't want to answer." She winked at me.

"You've been married for more than ten years, right?"

"Yes. Thirteen. I think I told you that before. Why?"

"I was wondering why you don't have kids?"

Angelina shrank like a balloon that was losing its air, but it wasn't air, it was blood. I had cut the juggler vein, and she was bleeding. Visibly. The look on her face told me that this was an extremely painful topic for her. I had to find out the deal. I needed to know if it were something I could use, but I did feel guilty.

Angelina reached into her pocket for her vibrating phone. She took one look and stood from the table. An escape. How convenient for her. I listened to her side of the conversation. Something about a budget cut. When she was done, she began to pack her things. "Sorry to leave you hanging, but I have to go."

"But we're not finished."

"Rae, you are more than competent. I trust you to make good decisions on anything else that has to be decided."

She was rattled, and it wasn't just the phone call that had her smashing things into her Coach bag like she was putting waste in a trash bag. With the way she was behaving, I really wanted to know.

"Angelina, did I upset you?"

"No." She answered too quickly. She was unconvincing. "I have to get to the office. We're trying to allocate some money for a program that may help with foster home evaluations and oversight."

"You were upset before the phone rang. You were upset when I asked you why you never had children."

Angelina put her handbag on her shoulder and picked up her attaché. She looked like she was using them to hold herself up. I had bought up children, and the molecules in the air had adjusted, made it harder for her to breathe, but I wanted to know, so I pushed. "I'm sorry if I upset you. I was curious; you seem to really love kids. I mean, you've got the non-profit and you're on the DFYS board. Lord bless you for that. Seems you would make a good mother. I was wondering why you never had any of your own."

Tears wet her eyes. Sadness seemed to leak from her pores. She opened her mouth, closed it and swallowed hard before speaking. "I did have a child. I had a baby girl, but she died two years ago."

Both hands flew to my lips. "Oh gosh. I'm sorry. What happened to her? I mean, if you don't mind. Oh no, I'm sorry . . . I shouldn't have asked that." I was stumbling over the words in earnest. I mean, a dead baby. That was messed up.

"SIDs." The word came out of her mouth, but I could tell it made a painful journey from her soul.

"Oh," I whispered, not sure what else to say.

"I have a hard time with that mysterious cause of death, but that was it. One moment she was here, and the next she wasn't."

I stood and wrapped my arms around her. I had no idea where that instinct had come from. It was she who stepped out of my embrace. Tears had stained her face. I reached into my bag for a tissue and handed it to her. "I'm sorry I made you think about it. I'm really so sorry. It was silly of me."

"No. It's okay. I get asked all the time, and really, I think about Danielle everyday anyway."

"Danielle is a pretty name." I decided to pass on saying anything deeper. I couldn't imagine what would be appropriate.

"She was a beautiful baby." Angelina seemed like she was a million miles away when she said that.

"I'm sure with such great genes. I mean, she had to be, right?"

"But now she's in heaven, so—I mean." Angelina stopped. "I'll have to keep trying to live the best life I can so I can see her again."

"You mean like in the after-life?" I asked, unable to mask that I didn't believe that crap.

"We'll have to talk about it one day, Rae. I'd love to really talk about Christianity with you. I can tell you have a lot of misgivings, but I believe there's something that drew you to Greater Christian Life. I'll call you later, and we'll set up a real girl-to-girl study session."

I nodded. She patted my hand and walked out of the room.

Wow, I thought the woman had bad eggs. It never occurred to me that they had a child that died. I really felt guilty. I had to. I'd actually hugged her. I never hugged anybody that didn't have testosterone, not even my mother. Hugging came real natural to Angelina. I noticed that from the way she grabbed all the other sisters in church, and the way she wrapped her arms around me with such ease. Hugging was church protocol. If I hung around her much longer, I'd be hugging everybody too.

I closed my files and put them in my briefcase. I needed to focus less on this woman mentoring stuff and more on why I was here in the first place because there was one more thing I had noticed when the church sister of the year had pulled away from me. Angelina Preston was wearing a new perfume.

Chapter 19

"I wasted medication," I announced. Perspiration covered my upper lip and my hands shook as I closed the lid to the small sink like bowl. "Can I get someone to sign for me later?"

Nadine, one of the new per diem nurses on the floor, asked, "Why would you put it in before you let me see it?"

She was referring to the pills I'd dumped down the sink where we disposed of the ones that were no good. "Oh I'm sorry," I said, sarcastically, "we all trust each other on this floor to sign because we're busy."

"But I'm standing right here," Nadine said. "I could have witnessed and signed for you."

"But you saw me."

"I saw you near the sink, but I don't like to sign unless I see the drugs myself."

I picked up the chart for my next patient. "Then don't, Nadine. I can ask someone else." I walked away. It didn't matter. I could get any one of the nurses I worked with to sign for me that the meds were not useable. I didn't need Nosy Nadine.

I entered my next patient's room and removed her medication from the cart. She was a cancer patient who was recovering from surgery. The surgeon had ordered a Fentanyl patch. It was applied to the skin and medication slowly released over a three day period. I raised the patch and stared at it in the light. This was what June needed. One of these things that would last for days. Although I had heard crazy stories of ways people stole them, I didn't dare even think about taking one of these babies. Stealing one of these involved withholding pain meds from the patients; no way was I going to do that. That was cruel.

I applied the patch to my patient's arm, completed my charting, and just as I turned to walk out of the room I nearly collided with Nadine. She was such an annoying little person. She had dirty blond hair, bad skin, and no fashion sense whatsoever. Her uniforms looked like they came straight off of Dollar General's sale rack. I shuttered at the thought. "Need something?" I asked, walking back to my cart.

She hesitated for a moment. "I was wondering if you could cover me for my break."

We exited the room, and I turned to look at her like she was as crazy as she sounded. Miss Technical about wasting medication had just committed a major customer service no-no. "You came into a patient's room while I was administering medication to ask me to cover your break?"

"I have an important phone call to make, and it needs to happen in five minutes," she replied. "I promise you won't miss me."

Well, she did have that right. I certainly wouldn't. I shrugged. "Go do what you gotta do."

I finished the last of the medication rounds and my charting, and then gave report. I was glad when the shift was over. I climbed into my car, leaned against the headrest, and closed my eyes. Stealing was stressful. More stressful than it had been so many years ago when I was taking jeans and leather jackets from Macy's and Dillard's with Mekhi. He'd teased me.

"You good, girl, but you gotta stop looking nervous. I'm going to make a professional thief out of you yet," he'd said the day I'd unhooked my first leather coat from a chained rack in Wilson's. He'd been proud of me. I'd been proud. Funny how it never occurred to me until just this moment how much Mekhi's words had come to pass. I was good at stealing. I was stealing all the time—men, pills. All these years later I was still taking things that didn't belong to me.

I reached into my scrub pants pocket and removed three small pills, one green, one peach and one white. Oxycontin, the opid of champions, or of fools depending on who was taking it. I opened the center console of my car and removed a small white envelope. I dropped the three pills in with the two others that I'd managed to get last night. I needed two or three more and that was going to be it. If I kept wasting pills they'd be all over me like barbeque sauce on ribs. June was going to have to get some help, or settle for something cheaper I could pick up on the street without breaking the bank.

Rap . . . rap . . . rap . . . the loud knock on my window almost caused me to pee my pants. I looked at my driver's side window and there was that dang Nadine. I folded the envelope and quickly tucked it in the top pocket of my scrub shirt. Then I let down the window. *What did this heifer want now?*

Nadine leaned in toward the window, closer than I would have liked. "Thanks," she said.

I cocked my head. "For what?"

"I really appreciate what you did earlier. I wanted to thank you." I knew I looked perplexed because I was. "For covering my break. My boyfriend is in prison in Nevada, and he gets to call me at exactly eight P.M. their time, which is ten here. I really wanted to talk to him."

I nodded. Surprise of all surprises. Nadine didn't strike me as the type to have a man in prison. Actually she didn't strike me as the type to have a man period. I, for sure, would have pegged her for the type who couldn't buy a date. Not with that ugly eighties haircut and those jacked up glasses. "What's your man in for?" I didn't really care, but I figured I was sup-posed to be curious.

"Selling Ox," she said, solemnly.

I had to do everything I could to keep my face straight. I mean my eyes seriously wanted to eject from their sockets like a jack-in-box that had been sprung. "That's messed up." I turned the key in the ignition.

"Really messed up. He was a pharmacist. He had a bad hiking accident a few years ago, fell off a trail down the side of a mountain and hurt his back. The doctor prescribed Ox and he got addicted. I didn't even know he was out there that bad."

She seemed really sad. I almost felt sorry for her. Almost, but I was too busy thinking about the fact that ole boy got caught and was in prison, to be empathetic.

"He messed up, but I love him you know."

"Yeah." I shook my head. The hairs on the back of my neck rose, and my heart was racing like crazy. "Look, I gotta go."

She stepped back and raised her hand to give me a signal that the coast was clear for me to back up. I waved to her and noticed that Nadine was looking at me strangely. I almost thought I saw some kind of weird sympathy in her eyes, and for some reason, I felt I had been warned.

Chapter 20

Angelina had been trying to wait Greg out. She'd talked to Felesia on the phone for twenty minutes, looked at the proposal from the Sparks for the teen camp, and now she'd stared at Rae's perfect schedule for the health fair until she couldn't look at it anymore. Still, he was engrossed in a novel.

She put the files in her attaché, made bustling movement out of the bed, and went into the bathroom. With no particular reason to be there, other than to kill time, she checked her appearance in the mirror. She was wearing an above the knee length lavender and white negligee. An Internet order that had come in the mail today. It was as sexy as the picture online, and fit her toned figure perfectly, if she did say so herself. Well, she had to say so herself, because her husband hadn't noticed it.

Angelina picked up her scented, shimmering body lotion and applied a little more to her neck and chest area. She was already glowing; adding more was going to turn her into a nightlight. There was nothing else to do in here. After tossing her hair a little to give it a slightly wild look, she reentered the bedroom, dimmed the overhead lights, and approached the bed. Her husband didn't look up.

She called his name. He pulled his eyes away from the book and raised his eyebrows like she was intruding. He scanned her form with little interest and returned to his reading.

Angelina swallowed her anger and her pride, pulled back

the comforter and climbed into bed. Trying to seduce him had not worked, so she decided to get to the point. "I'm ovulating."

Greg grunted. "That's sexy." He kept reading.

"You look like you're getting sleepy." She hated begging him. "I was hoping you'd put the book down."

Greg groaned. "Then you should have asked me to put the book down." He kept reading.

Angelina bit back frustration, then closed and reopened her eyes. "Greg, would you put the book down?" She asked as sweetly as she could, but his attitude was making it difficult. His attitude was going to make it difficult to make love period.

"Not tonight," he replied, turning a page. "Not with all the ovulating you're doing."

Angelina shook her head. "Was that really necessary? Do you have to be so nasty?"

"I'm not some science project in here that you can tell to stand at attention at will."

She did everything she could not to take his book and throw it across the room. "Why can't you give me what I want? That's the least you can do." Her words reverberated off the walls. She'd yelled them louder than she'd meant, but she had his attention. The book was closed.

"What's that supposed to mean? The least I could do."

"You *are* my husband. You're the only one in this marriage with what I need. You could at least help me . . . fill this void." She paused. She didn't want to cry. Didn't want him to see her cry again. "I need another baby. I want one now."

Greg surprised her when he reached for her. He stroked her arm. "And we've been trying."

"But you know you . . . we had that problem before, with . . ."

Greg let out a loud breath and tossed his book off of his

lap and onto the floor. He stepped out of the bed and went to his closet. When he emerged he was dressed in jeans and a T-shirt.

"No, Greg," she begged. "Where are you going?"

"For a drive."

"A drive, this time of night?"

"I need some air."

"Please don't do this. Stay with me. Let's talk about this."

He shook his head. "I need some air."

"Don't go. Let's make love and see what happens."

"Not tonight."

"Please, if we can't come together on this—"

He stood at the foot of the bed for a moment. His six foot two frame, glistening hair, and wolf-like hazel eyes were a startling image in the dimmed light. He would have looked perfect if it weren't for the angry set of his jaw and the steely look in those translucent eyes.

Neither of them said anything for at least thirty seconds, but those seconds felt like minutes, hours, as she waited and hoped he would change his mind about leaving. When he spoke his voice was husky. "I don't think you realize that Danielle wasn't just your child."

Angelina shook her head. The tears she'd been holding back were winning. The first one fell and then others followed like water from the dam of her soul.

"She was my daughter too. And to make it worse, she was with me. Have you ever thought about how that made me feel? I'm a doctor. I save lives for a living. I save the lives of strangers." His words sliced her. She felt the pain that thickened his words. "I was sitting eighteen feet away, and she stopped breathing."

A beat passed before Angelina spoke. Before she found the courage to challenge the hurt. "Just because she stopped breathing, doesn't mean we have to."

That wasn't what Greg wanted to hear. She knew it because he made rapid steps to the door.

"We are still here." She called after him. "We're still alive, and we'd still be good parents."

She was talking to no one. He was out of the door, down the hall and stairs. Sixty seconds later Angelina could hear the garage door open and Greg's car pull out.

She lay down on her bed. Pain, fury, and confusion all swirled around in her soul with their competing interests. Pain for her loss. Fury over her loss. Confusion over her loss. Where was her God? They both needed Him so badly.

Angelina stared at the ceiling. She wanted to hear from God. Wanted to feel Him. She wanted Him to make this right for her. *Don't I deserve it? Don't you owe me? I've lost so much. At least give me another child.* She banged the mattress with her fist and threw a pillow across the room.

"I'm angry," she cried. "I'm so angry I can hardly breathe." She thought about what Felesia had told her earlier. To trust God no matter how dim things look. Felesia had begged her to read her Bible, to find comfort in God's Word. Angelina looked at the book on her night table. She noted the worn tabs she'd indexed that took her to the scriptures that often saved her during times like these. Times when she felt so low she wanted to die. She also thought about praying to soothe her soul, but she did neither. Instead, she rolled over on her side and cried herself to sleep.

Chapter 21

I stepped into my condo, dropped my purse, and kicked my shoes off in the coat closet where I kept them. I flicked the light switch and nearly jumped out of my skin when I saw Greg sitting in one of the club chairs near the bay window. "You almost gave me a heart attack." I raised my hand to my chest. "What are you doing here?"

"Where have you been?" He stood and came toward me.

"Working. I told you I had per diem—"

Greg closed the space between us and covered my mouth with a hungry kiss. He raised his hand and reached for my body like he hadn't touched a woman in ten years. I could feel the envelope shifting out of my pocket, but before I could pull away, pills began to spill on the hardwood floor.

I dropped into a squatting position and quickly tried to pick them up, but Greg leaned over to help. "What's this?" he asked, picking one up of the green ones. I took it out of his hand. "It's a pill."

"That's pretty obvious, but what is it? What are they doing in an envelope in your pocket?"

I moved around him and headed for my bedroom.

"Don't tell me you're stealing from the med room." He followed me.

Okay, so I won't.

"Are you addicted to this stuff?"

I turned sharply. "No, of course not." I couldn't believe I

had been caught by Greg. If it hadn't been for that darn Nadine, I would have put the envelope back in the car console. These pills wouldn't be here. "I have a sick aunt."

"A sick aunt without a prescription?"

"A sick aunt without a med plan."

"You can't steal pills. They'll catch you, and your career will be over. Forget your career. You'll go to prison."

Did he think he was telling me something I didn't know? "What are you doing here?" I asked.

"I came to see you."

"That's pretty obvious since I live alone, and there's no one else to be seeing, but I thought we had an agreement that you wouldn't show up without calling."

"Don't be annoyed." He closed the space again. "If you needed money to fill your aunt's prescription, why didn't you ask me?"

"I didn't want to involve you." I was careful with my words. *Stroke his ego.* "You're already so generous."

"You know I'm here for you. How much is the prescription? Add it to the invoice you send to my office."

I feigned relief. "Thanks, baby. I've been really going broke helping with all her medical bills." I decided to see if I could get more.

"Well, stealing is not the way to help her. What would she do if you got caught? They have ways of knowing . . ."

"I know. It was just this one time. I won't do it again."

He looked concerned. I supposed it was a good sign that he gave a rat's behind about me, but I really didn't want him in my business like this. Especially knowing the bad. What kind of doctor's wife would a thieving medication nurse make?

"Why don't you take a shower? I don't have much time," he said.

I looked at him. This midnight drive by was a booty call.

He'd fallen out with Angelina or couldn't get her to give up the goods, so he got in his car and told me to go wash it off and give him some. I was starting to wonder if I were fooling myself about this man. His marriage was busted, but he never talked about his wife. It was time for him to give up some information.

"Greg, it's midnight. I don't usually press this issue, but what is going on at home that's got you out here in the middle of the night?"

He rolled his eyes upward. "I was thinking about you. I miss you. It's been a few days."

"Umm, hum, and I suppose the cow jumped over that full moon out there."

"Samaria." He put his hands on either side of my arms. "Please don't add to my aggravation with these questions."

I moved out of his grasp, put my hands at my hips, and continued to wait for his answer.

"My wife and I have been having a tough time," he offered. "We're at an impasse about something she wants that I don't want."

"Would that be children?" I asked.

His eyebrows went up. "Why would you assume that?"

"Because you don't have any. You're forty-four, and she's whatever age she is. You've been married forever, and you don't have kids."

"I'm aware of all of that, and if I wanted to be talking about it I'd be at home, right?"

"So it is about kids?"

He shot me a nasty look. I didn't want to piss him off. The younger model's job was not to piss the man off by reminding him of the older model. "I'd like to know if I'm the substitute for someone you can't have or someone you don't want." I stepped closer to him, slid one leg between his and placed a hand on his chest. "Tell me. I think that's a fair question."

He hesitated for a moment, looked in my eyes, and stroked my hair. "You are not the substitute for anyone. You're your own person. Unequivocally. Trust me; my interests in you are singular."

I resisted the temptation to roll my eyes and went into the bathroom. *What in the heck kind of answer was that?* I turned on the shower and stripped out of my clothes. I laid June's envelope on the sink and copped a squat on the toilet while the water got hot. I needed it to match the angry tears I was fighting.

Greg was treating me like a whore tonight. I mean, who walks in the door and tells you to wash your butt and lie down but a pimp? No "How are you? How was your night?" He let himself in because he paid the mortgage, and now he was lying on my bed because paying the mortgage paid for me. My mother had taught me to sell myself to a man. That was the only mother-daughter lesson: Don't give it away for free. But somehow I couldn't help feeling like the price I was paying to get this money was more than it was worth. Getting this money was actually costing me.

Chapter 22

I had to show up in church or be excommunicated from the women's Bible Study. I knew that I dare not disappoint my new mentor who for sure was going to ask me, "What did you think of Pastor's sermon?" like she always did.

I choose the eleven o'clock service. Seven A.M. was out of the question on a Sunday, and I was glad I'd arrived on time, because it was a packed house. Angelina was front and center. She'd seen me when I made the rounds for the collection of tithes and offerings, smiled like a proud mother, and pointed to the empty space next to her like she wanted me to move from my back row pew to join her. I waved and scrunched up my nose. I wanted to sit in the back. Heaven forbid she try to push me to the altar. Plus depending on what the message was about, I might need the cover of the rear in case I fell asleep.

The preacher was standing up there talking about some lost sheep, lost coins, and a lost son, and he would have lost me, except the stories were kind of interesting, or at least his presentation was. In particular I was struck by the one about the lost sheep. He, or rather the Bible, said that if a shepherd had one hundred sheep, he would leave the ninety-nine to go look for one who was lost, and that's what God does with us. He wants all of us to be saved, not just the Christians that are already in the church. Same thing with the coins, that if one out of ten was missing, the Lord would frantically search for the one because it had value too. Then there was the prodigal son. I got that. Two kids, you don't give up on one, but a hundred sheep? I'd grown up in a world where you cut your losses and kept on moving. Nothing had value, nothing was worth fighting for.

I could remember the countless times we got evicted. It happened at least once a year until we moved into White Gardens when I was eight. I would come home from school and find the sheriff had come and gone. Our things were strewn up and down the street like trash. Mama had packed some clothes in garbage bags, grabbed the food she wanted, but left the rest for the neighborhood vultures—human and animal—to pick through.

I hated that we always had to start over. We'd go to the Salvation Army like vultures ourselves, picking through rich people's leftovers for new sheets and new curtains and new pots. I mean, none of it was new. It was gently used and new to us. It didn't make sense to me that we kept leaving behind the stuff I'd gotten attached to, so one time I got up the nerve to ask. "Mama, why you always gotta leave our stuff on the corner?"

I don't know if it was my huffy little tone or my mother's own frustration that caused her to react to me so strongly, but she reached back as far as she could and slapped me across the face so hard that for a moment, I thought the taste buds had come off my sharp little tongue.

"Don't question what I do." She looked like a monster more than a mother. "We don't need that mess. Cost more to move than to get some more."

She was still that way today. Even though she'd been in White Gardens for almost twenty years, the apartment was sparsely furnished. She didn't care to paint or really hang pictures. It was like she was waiting for the sheriff to come and tell her to get out. She still wasn't collecting anything worth moving.

"How many of you are living on God's good grace?" The preacher, or pastor, as Angelina called him, yelled into the microphone and rattled me to attention. "How many of you are living your life any old kind of way because you think God doesn't care what you do?"

He had stepped down from the pulpit and was making a slow sojourn up the aisle. I wasn't often paranoid, but I would swear that man was looking directly in my eyes when he asked that question. The back of the church wasn't quite far enough. Who knew the man would take his show on the road when he started trying to go after the prodigal coins like me?

"Beloved. The truth is God is gracious. He loves the saved and the sinner, the righteous and the unrighteous, the lost and the found. Every thought of His heart, every action of His power, goes toward reaching out to the needy, the guilty, and the lost souls. The sheep that need to be bought back into the fold."

I shrank, averted my eyes so he couldn't catch them—tried to melt into the pew. After a few more words he called for people to come to the altar for prayer and salvation and the ordeal of a church service was over.

"I'm so glad to see you today." Angelina gave me the church sister hug.

"I know it's been a few weeks, but I usually take up residence here with the amen choir on the back pew." I laughed and waved my hand toward the seat I'd vacated.

"Awesome message, wasn't it?"

I nodded. It was pretty powerful if you believed that kind of stuff.

"Have you met Pastor?" Angelina asked.

My eyes bugged. "Oh, no. I don't—he seems so busy—I really should be going."

"It'll only take a second." Angelina grabbed my arm and pulled me to the front of the church to join the line of people who were waiting to shake the *Honorable* Bishop Winston Bennett's hand.

"Angelina—really, there's always next time." I had no interest in shaking that man's hand. He had an aura about him. Made me think he was Jesus incognito.

My mother had taught me that pastors weren't nothing but pimps with Bibles, but she was wrong. The flip flopping in my stomach told me this man was the real deal, and I was afraid when he touched my hand he would see all the dirt I had been doing.

Angelina and I waited our turns, which came quickly. She stepped up, thanked the Bishop for something to do with DYFS, and then said, "Pastor, I want you to meet Rae Burns. Remember I mentioned the industrious young woman who was helping us to pull together the health fair?"

He nodded and hesitated before his teeth split his lips in a wide grin. "Yes, Ms. Burns. I'm told you've been a tremendous asset. Welcome to Greater Christian."

He stuck out his hand. I closed my eyes and slid mine in his, waited for the lightning bolt that would strike me, the new and improved version of Mary Magdalene. I did know some Bible.

"I appreciate you being of service to Sister Preston and all that you're doing to make the health fair a big success for us." I opened my eyes. He continued. "I know you've been attending women's Bible Study, but please make sure you join us again on Sunday morning. Come on up to the front row next time." He chuckled, winked, and released my hand. There was no tremor of the earth, no lightning bolt from the sky. Bishop Bennett moved on and grabbed the next parishioner's hand and began a conversation with them about a son in college.

I let go of my breath. He wasn't clairvoyant. I had not been discovered as a fraud.

Chapter 23

I didn't do this often, but I needed help making sure my mother was going to have a place to live like she'd told me. In particular I wanted to find out if she were getting into my cousin, Ebony's, complex, so I decided it was time to do some checking on my own. I called Ebony.

"Hey stranger," Ebony said. Ebony was the daughter of my mother's oldest brother, Jimmy Ray. Jimmy Ray was dead. He'd been shot for cheating in a poker game when Ebony was ten years old. A good looking man and natural born talker, he'd had a well paying job driving a tour bus around the city of Atlanta. It was packed daily with people; mostly business travelers, who wanted to sightsee and shop without the bother of renting a car or taking public transportation. Shortly after Jimmy Ray was killed, Ebony and her mother moved into White Gardens because it was the only place Emma, Ebony's mother, could afford working as a hotel maid.

I could hear the little tribe my cousin called children screaming in the background. "I thought you had gone off and married some rich sheik in Saudi Arabia," Ebony teased.

I smirked. "Not yet, but I'm working on it."

"No doubt." Ebony's smile came through the phone. "So to what do I owe the honor?"

"I need a favor. I'd like to stop by the complex and see what's up with my mom's application. Is the management office open today?"

"It ain't been that long since you was renting. You know all the leasing offices are open on Sundays. We got to have some place to complain after Saturday night." Ebony chuckled. "I didn't know your mother was moving over here."

I pursed my lips. My mother not telling Ebony her plans was suspect. "Eb, give me directions."

I pulled off I-20 onto Panola Road and made the few quick turns it took to get to Farrington Gardens. It amazed me that the word garden was used in so many low income housing complexes where there wasn't a shred of green landscaping, and the only thing growing was crime, drug use, and teenage pregnancy.

Farrington Gardens was a rehabbed townhome complex. The owner received a huge amount of federal funding to do the renovations provided he reserved a certain percentage of units for low income residents. It was kind of a win-win for the owner because the tenants had HUD vouchers, and they paid what HUD didn't. The problem was most of the current non-low income residents would move out leaving the place to be occupied by all low income residents; hence, it became a better looking project. This wasn't the intent of the relocation program, but it was better than White Gardens, for now.

Ebony had called me midway through my trip to ask me not to knock because she had gotten the kids down for a nap. When I pulled in front of her unit, she opened the door and sprang out with her husband, Tyrone, on her butt. He grabbed her hand, pulled her back, and gave her a peck on the lips followed by a look that said, "Don't be too long." No wonder they had four kids in six years.

Ebony skipped to my car. The smile dropped from Tyrone's face, and he waved to me. I could see reluctance. Tyrone didn't like me. He was broke, so I didn't care.

"What's up, cuz?" Ebony slid onto the butter leather seat and closed the door. Wide eyes admired the interior. She scrunched up her face. "When you get this?"

"A few months ago." I backed out of the parking space. "Which way am I going?"

Ebony gave me directions to the management office. I made my way to the back of the huge complex, and we climbed out. There was a line of people in the waiting room, most complaining about needing this or that repaired, slow trash pickup, or noise from their neighbors during a rowdy party the night before.

Ebony reached into a tiny purse and pulled out a pack of gum; offered me a stick which I declined. She popped one in her mouth. "So when did ya' moms put in her application? I think they got a long waiting list over here."

I let out a sigh. "I don't know. She said her housing social worker did it."

Ebony shook her head. "That don't sound right. We had to do the applications ourselves. They told us how much money we could spend, and we had to find our own place. I been trying to talk to Auntie 'bout what she was gonna do, but she keep telling me she working it out."

"That's what I was worried about." I was glad I'd enlisted Ebony's help because no way was the leasing agent going to be willing to tell me anything about my mom's application. I knew my cousin. She had a chatty personality, and I had no doubt that she was in good with the staff.

"Hey." Ebony tapped my shoulder. I had been looking in the opposite direction. When I turned to her, she was looking me up and down like the fashion police. "Where you coming from all done up? If I didn't know any better, I'd think you went to church."

I raised my chin and cocked my head. "I did. I go to church, Miss Smarty Pants."

Ebony laughed. "Uh-uh. What you going to church for? You got to be scheming on some poor pastor or deacon."

I dropped my chin and cut my eyes. "I know you think you've got the church of the Lord on lockdown, cousin, but there is room in the house for those of us that have been lost. I'm one of the ninety-nine sheep the shepherd is looking for." I rolled my neck.

This time Ebony's laugh was an out and out cackle. "Girl, that would be the one sheep. The ninety-nine are found, and if the shepherd is looking for you, he gonna need to take a map and some hunting equipment. Heck, he might need an exploration team or something."

I squinted and started to say something when the leasing agent let us know we were next.

Ebony was real cool with her. Just like I knew she would be. Ebony explained who I was and asked about my mother's application. Their friendly banter got her past all the confidential privacy stuff, and the agent looked in her computer file for all the pending applications. Just as I suspected there was nothing for Winnie Jacobs. Ebony inquired about how long the waiting list was. The woman told her it would probably take two years to clear off, and no way could they move names around. That was a locked file that the manager kept. We left.

"You have time for an early dinner?" I asked when we climbed back in the car.

She shook her head. "I don't like to go to restaurants without my family, so I'ma have to say no."

"We can go to Applebee's and order take-out for your crew. You won't have to cook dinner, and everyone will get hooked up." I knew she'd like that offer.

Ebony stuck her hands in the pockets of her jacket and knitted her brow. "My kids are too young for Applebee's, but there's a new place on Covington Highway we been dying to try."

"Doesn't matter to me." I pulled off and headed in that direction.

The restaurant was a cute little place. I wasn't a big soul food eater. Grease and fat and butter did not make a banging body. But the smell coming from the kitchen was enough to lure me out of my fried chicken moratorium. I'd have to hit the gym later.

We gave our orders to the waitress; she collected the menus and left us alone. That's when Ebony knit her fingers in front of her on the table and asked, "So what you want, Sam?"

I sat back like she had smacked me. "Dang, why it gotta be like that?"

Ebony smirked and rolled her neck as she spoke. "Heifer, please, you know it's like that. Don't nobody hear from you unless something's up."

I pretended to be insulted, but I knew it was kind of true. The real thing was I avoided Ebony a lot of times because she was always preaching at me. Like she would for sure do before this dinner was over.

"I need my mom settled on a place to live. I've got a ton of projects going on for my business, and I don't have time to run all over Atlanta looking at apartments and putting in applications with her. I was wondering if I gave you a couple of dollars if you'd do it for me."

"You want to pay me to help my aunt?"

"I want to pay you for your time," I said.

"You ain't got to pay me to help Aunt Winnie. All you had to do was ask."

That was it. A commitment from Ebony, and it was a done deal. I reached into my purse and pulled out two hundred dollar bills and slid them across the table. "Gas isn't free. I appreciate you, girl."

She raised her eyebrows. "That's a lot of gas, and I hate to think about how you got that and the car."

"I work, Ebony. Every day."

"Yeah, well, Panola Medical is right up the street, and I see them nurses pull up every day. Ain't none of them getting out of no new Beamers."

I swallowed a protest and slid the money closer. "Take it. I know it could come in handy. Maybe you and Tyrone could take the kids to Six Flags or something on Auntie Sam."

With that, she reached for the money and tucked it away in her purse. If nothing else, Ebony was a great mother. She wasn't going to pass on doing something for her kids.

The waitress delivered the drinks and salads we'd ordered. I was starved and started to dive in when Ebony said, "Ms. Lost Sheep, can we say grace?"

I bowed my head, and she led the blessing.

"So how's Tyrone?"

"You know my boo is good." She did a little dance in her seat like thinking about him had her body singing. "He's still working at the church with the audio-visual equipment and stuff. They paying him for that now, so it's a part-time job. Plus he's painting and doing all the other work he can get."

I nodded. Tyrone was fine. He was sweet actually, and he and Ebony were about as in love as in love could get; had been since eighth grade. But a part-time job at the church and painting when he could with four kids? I wanted to throw up my salad.

"He's working on something else. A little something with Mekhi."

I resisted rolling my eyes, but my jawed clenched. I knew what was coming now.

"Gosh, Sam." She put her fork down. "Why you tripping on Mekhi so hard? You act like he did something to you."

"You *act* like you know he didn't."

"I know Mekhi is a good brother. He's got a good heart. And ain't nobody perfect, including you and whoever you laying with, so you need to think about that." Ebony turned up her nose. "You gonna be real disappointed if *Mr. Knight in Shining Armor* don't come through and Mekhi done moved on and got him somebody else instead of sitting around trippin' about you."

"You don't know the deal about what went down between Mekhi and me, so please don't sit across the table and judge me." I slammed my fork down, which got the attention of the people next to us. I avoided their stares by reaching into my purse for my ringing cell phone.

The waitress arrived with our meals. She stood looking between the two of us as we sat there with our arms crossed over our chests.

"We gonna need you to wrap this up to go," Ebony said, looking me in the eye. "And I need to see the menu again. I'd like to place a takeout order."

Ebony and I had reached that point again. The point where we would no longer enjoy each other's company. My business with her was completed, so I eased out of the booth and returned the call I'd just missed from Greg.

Chapter 24

Angelina Preston was a woman of her word. She'd called just like she said and invited me to a picnic lunch at the church where she and I would get down and dirty about the Bible. This was going to be interesting. Although I knew I'd never be one of those Holy Roller type devoted Christians who believed in the evangelical, whimsical, all-knowing God, I had to admit there were some things I was curious about.

"Okay, my first question is about the whole creation thing," I said, and we were on a roll.

Angelina knew a lot about the Bible, and it was pretty clear she believed everything in it. The most interesting fact among them was the idea of this Trinity—Father, Son and Holy Spirit. The Holy Spirit, in particular, was the voice in our head and our hearts that tried to speak to us. The voice I thought of as a conscious or instinct. Angelina had me thinking about how many times that voice on the inside had niggled at me or downright warned me about things that I paid no attention to, and then ended up sorry for later. Like walking into Bergdorf's that day almost eight years ago. *Slam!* I let out a deep breath. Would I ever stop hearing those bars come together in my memory?

"The last thing I wanted to talk about was grace." Angelina pulled me from my memory.

"Grace," I repeated. "Your pastor must have said that twenty times yesterday."

"Yes, because those parables all illustrate the grace of God. God's grace is one of the gifts of salvation. When we lose our way, we can always come back home. God wants us to come home. Sometimes He looks for us like in the case of the sheep and the coins, and sometimes He waits for us."

"Like the Prodigal Son." I was surprised that I remembered so much.

"Right." I could tell Angelina was pleased. She looked at her notes. "There's another story I want to share with you. Turn in your Bible to the book of John, chapter four."

"John. He was one of the gospels."

"Yes. His book is one of the four gospels." She corrected me with a smile.

"If I don't get anything else today, I've got those four names down."

"You're getting a lot, Rae. You've asked me some of the most thought provoking questions anyone has ever asked me. I can't tell you how much I appreciate you challenging me this way. This has been just as good for me as I hope it has been for you."

Angelina really looked like she meant what she was saying. I couldn't imagine. I nodded and kept turning. "Okay, so I have John . . . chapter four."

Angelina reached for a glass of juice. "You read this time. Keep going until I say stop."

"*The Pharisees heard that Jesus was gaining and baptizing more disciples than John, although in fact it was not Jesus who baptized, but his disciples. When the Lord learned of this, he left Judea and went back once more to Galilee. Now he had to go through Sam . . .*"

What was this? I stopped and looked at her. Did she know who I was? Was this some kind of game she was playing with me? She was just sitting there, as Angelina-ish as always with that guidance counselor slash friend expression on her face.

"Keep going. The pronunciation is Samaria." She sounded out my name.

I forced my eyes back to the pages, looked at my name, and then at Angelina again. I had to be sure I wasn't being played. "My mouth is dry," I whispered, and I reached for my bottled water. I took a long drink, cleared my throat, and regained my composure. *"Now he had to go through Samaria,"* I continued and read the passage all the way down until I finished the twenty-sixth verse.

I was paralyzed with some emotion I couldn't qualify or quantify. It was a weird sense of displacement, like I knew who I was three minutes ago, and now I wasn't so sure. I shook my head. Tried to clear the cobwebs. "What's this about?" My voice croaked.

"The story has a lot of issues, and like most of the stories we have talked about today, it can mean different things at different times to different people," Angelina began, "but the one message that never changes in this story is that God loves us regardless of what we've done. We have grace through God's love. We're all His children."

I shook my head again. The Samaritan woman was a whore, but God loved her. "I don't get it."

"Rae, the Samaritan woman at the well was no angel. She was from the wrong side of town, and she was mixed up with some of the wrong crowd. She had a reputation. She'd had a bunch of men in her past and still didn't have it right with the one she was sleeping with. He was a married man. So from this story we learn that God doesn't accept a sinful or carnal lifestyle. We talked about that earlier, you remember?"

I nodded.

"If we want to be in right relationship with God, we can't live to please ourselves and our wants. But the story also shows that a well of grace is always there to renew us, to refresh our souls. It's like I told you earlier. Jesus came not for the healthy, but the sick. The church is about helping the sick, and none of us, church people, Samaritan women, lost sheep, none of us are perfect. It's only God's grace that makes us acceptable."

I stared at the pages. I couldn't stop looking at my name. I couldn't stop thinking about the parallels between my life and this woman's. I couldn't believe the irony that of all these stories in this humungous book that she would chose to share this one. I had the same feeling I'd had the other night when Nadine had told me about her boyfriend. I had the feeling that I was being warned, but maybe it wasn't a warning. Maybe it was the Holy Spirit trying to talk to me.

No. I pushed that thought away. I wasn't falling for that. What would God have to do with me? He'd never paid attention to my life before. I closed my Bible. "That was an interesting story."

"It's not just a story. It's the reality of our faith. Think about it. Reread the scripture tonight and read the parable of the lost sheep again. Pray. The Lord will give you clarity about the meaning for you. Always trust that voice inside. It's God inside of you, and He's never wrong."

I helped Angelina clean up the picnic lunch. I thanked her for teaching me the things she thought someone considering Christianity should know, and then I hugged her. Not because it was a church sister thing to do, but because I wanted to. It felt strange. All my life I'd only ever gotten hugs or gropes from men. I'd never had a girlfriend who hugged me. My mother had never in my entire life hugged me. It was weird, but it also felt—I don't know—nice. Like it was something I needed.

Mentor-a-Sister. Angelina's heart was so pure. No wonder she could believe all this stuff about grace and mercy and forgiveness. She'd probably never done a corrupt thing in her life. I was a liar, a fraud, and a thief, and I didn't care how many undesirables Jesus had flanked around Him when He was crucified on the cross. He didn't have anyone hanging next to Him like the likes of me. I had slept with Angelina's husband last night and hugged her today. Grace, mercy, forgiveness, and all the water in the deepest well on the earth weren't going to wash away my sins. Nobody was going to convince me that Jesus was leaving His flock to look for a sheep like me.

Chapter 25

The call from my cousin, June, came just after three o'clock. My mother had been taken to the hospital. For what, that knuckle head didn't know.

"She was acting strange. I got scared and called for a bus," he said, using the word folks in the hood called an ambulance. "Holla back when you find out somefin'." The line went dead.

June was useless. Mama told me he hurt his arm in some kind of accident on the job. That's how he'd started taking oxycontin. That's when his drug use got out of control. While I was sympathetic to the fact that he had been injured, I kept wondering why that Negro couldn't just be a crackhead like all the other drug addicts in White Gardens.

I took a seat and lay my head back against the wall. My cell beeped a reminder, and I pulled the phone from my pocket. *Bible Study.* I was supposed to bring a refreshment item to the meeting. I dialed Angelina's number and hoped to heaven she didn't answer. I didn't feel like talking. Just when I thought the voicemail would come on, I heard her voice. "I can't make the meeting tonight. My mother had to come into the emergency room."

"Oh." I could tell she was stunned. "Is she okay? Is it serious?"

"I don't know. I haven't been told anything." I paused. "I'm sorry. I know I'm supposed to bring a snack."

"Rae, it's all right. It's cookies, and we're talking about your mom. How are you?"

"Scared," I admitted, letting out a breath. "For someone with a background in healthcare, I'm a complete punk when my mom is sick. She's a bad asthmatic, she has high blood pressure, and some other chronic health issues, so I've been here before."

"We're all like that when it's our own family."

"And I hate this hospital. They take so long to give you updates. They're always short staffed." I ran my free hand through my hair and pulled it into a knot at my neck.

"What hospital is it?" Angelina asked.

"Atlanta South Regional." I rolled my eyes wishing I was anywhere but here.

"Okay, I'm going to get somebody to teach the class for me, and I'll be right there."

"What? No. Angelina, that's not necessary."

"Of course it is. You shouldn't be alone. I'm coming." And the line went dead. Angelina Preston on this side of town. I stared at my phone. Were there any limits to this woman's Christian charity?

I found myself pacing the floor and constantly checking my watch. I had arrived more than an hour ago, and no one had told me anything about my mother. I'd even tried to pull the professional courtesy thing. Talk to the staff, nurse to nurse, but the emergency room was swamped with patients. Nobody had time to massage another nurse's ego.

"Somebody had better tell me something soon," I whispered.

"They will, and it'll be good news."

The velvety timbre of the masculine voice came from behind me. I closed my eyes and Mekhi touched my shoulder. A tingle radiated from my neck to my knees. "I came as soon as I heard."

He turned my weakened body toward him and massaged my upper arms in his strong, but gentle grip. "She gonna be straight."

Something yummy filled my nostrils and set my heart to racing. My eye lids popped open. I wondered if this man could ever not look good. Ever not smell good. I stepped out of his grip and took in his complete appearance.

Mekhi was wearing a suit; a black, single-breasted, three button, peak collar designer number that hung on his six foot frame like he'd had it custom made. He had Eel wingtips on his feet. He was looking fine at a level that left me speechless.

"You didn't need to come here." I was eye level with his enormous chest, and that was all I could think to say. I was trying to keep from trippin' on how he looked.

"You an only child, and I heard June was too messed up to ride in the bus with her."

"You still didn't have to come."

"Nobody should wait in this place by they-self." His voice grew huskier. "I'm trying to be a friend. Can't you think of me as a friend?"

I rolled my eyes and stepped back again, trying to distance myself from his scent.

"Dang, Sam. We used to be good friends." Annoyance peppered his tone, but his eyes were begging for forgiveness.

We used to be lovers, I thought, looking at the sexy set of his jaw. He always did look good when he was getting heated. I sat down in a nearby chair and stared at my hands. I couldn't look at him anymore. The worse thing about looking into Mekhi's eyes was that I wanted to stand back up and fall into his arms. I wanted his strength. I wanted him to hold me. I wanted to lean against that chest, but I couldn't go there, couldn't go back. Not with him. I had to resist this power he had over me because it was so crazy. Especially when I was feeling vulnerable, like now.

Mekhi took the few steps necessary and stooped in front of me. "Sammie I'm just trying to be here for you."

This Negro. I wanted to scream. He was on my mind more and more these days. I kept seeing him, in person and in my memory. Why, after all these years, was he resurfacing like this? I had to release the tension that was gathering in my gut. I did it the only way I knew how. I got nasty. "I don't do friends. And even if I did, I definitely wouldn't consider you to be someone I could trust like that," I said. "We passed friendship a long time ago."

Mekhi let out a deep breath, stood, and dropped into the seat next to me. "Look, I didn't come here to talk about us. I told you I was through doing that. I didn't want you waiting by yourself." He looked at me sideways. He smirked, and when his lips twisted a long dimple appeared in his cheek. I loved those dimples.

We sat there for a few minutes, neither of us saying anything. My mind had finally drifted back to my mother, where it should have been all along. The wait was really getting on my nerves. I didn't trust this place. Didn't trust these overworked, underpaid employees. Mekhi seemed to sense my anxiety because he reached for my hand, which I promptly snatched back.

"Uh-uh." I shook my head. I didn't look in his eyes. I was afraid I might melt. I might grab his warm, strong hand and lay my head on his shoulder. I was scared, and I was tired of being strong all the time. I wanted somebody else to be strong for me, like Mekhi used to be in the old days, before he left me hanging.

"Rae." I heard Angelina's voice before I saw her, and I sprang from my seat.

She gave me a tight squeeze. "Do you know anything?"

"Not yet. I'm thinking they'll have to tell me something soon."

Mekhi stood.

"I'm sorry to interrupt." Angelina's eyes moved between us. I noticed she stole a glance at Mekhi—a head to toe sweep. She had to be impressed. He looked like a million bucks. "I don't know why I assumed you were waiting alone."

"No, it's okay. He was leaving." I pinned him with a look that said "go."

Mekhi raised his eyebrows. "It's like that?"

I didn't hesitate. "You know it."

"I don't want to intrude," Angelina said. Like Mekhi, she was looking like a mint standing in this crappy hospital in a Chanel suit with matching bag and shoes. I thought I could dress. She was light years ahead of me and definitely out of place in this dump.

Her attire wasn't wasted on Mekhi either, he looked her up and down, and then returned a disapproving gaze to me. "No, it's cool. I think she'd rather be alone than be with me anyway."

An uncomfortable beat passed between us all, and then Angelina stuck her hand out at Mekhi. "I'm Angelina Preston. Rae and I go to church together."

Mekhi shook Angelina's hand and cleared his throat. "Rae." His expression said what he couldn't.

"Mekhi is a childhood friend, Angelina. Nobody called me Rae as a child," I stuttered over my words. "I don't go by nicknames anymore, Mekhi," I said it with the same firmness I implied in the look I gave him. He was a con artist. He got my game.

Mekhi's head moved in a disapproving shake, and then those optic white teeth of his filled his face. He looked at Angelina and said, "It was a pleasure." He gave me a nod. "Call and update me on your moms. I'm out."

Angelina and I watched him stroll out of the waiting room.

I let out the breath I'd been holding and turned to her. I could tell she was curious about Mekhi, but before she could ask a nurse entered the room. "The family of Winnie Jacobs."

"I'm her daughter." I moved like an Olympic sprinter to get closer. Angelina was on my heels.

"We've stabilized her," the nurse reported. "We'll let you see her once we get her to ICU. She had a couple of seizures—"

I interrupted. "Seizures."

The nurse put a hand up to let me know to let her continue. "Her blood pressure was elevated, and we've got her on a ventilator. She had a severe asthma attack."

A ventilator. It'd never been this bad. I closed my eyes tight to block out the image. I'd cared for many patients on ventilators, but the thought of my mother not breathing on her own was more than I could bear. Angelina squeezed my hand, and I opened my eyes. The nurse continued. "We've sent her blood work to the lab, and we're doing some other tests. We're trying to pinpoint the cause of the seizures." I nodded. "We'll let you know as soon as we have more information."

I nodded again. I didn't know what else to do. Tears were brimming in my eyes. A seizure . . . that was something new. That didn't have anything to do with her blood pressure or her asthma. The nurse left the room.

Angelina put her arm around me. "Let's sit down."

I followed her lead to my abandoned chair. I reached into my handbag, trying to find a tissue when Angelina handed me some. "I grabbed a bunch on the way out the door," she said. "I know how it works when you're in a place like this. We women can't turn off the water works."

Angelina was looking around the dingy gray room, looking at all the other people waiting. It was a motley crew. One ghetto fabulous chick with gold teeth, finger nails too long to wipe a butt good, and hair as high as a 1960's beehive was on her cell phone chewing somebody out about missing money. Three young men that looked like gang bangers clad in white T-shirts and jeans with red bandanas tied around their heads were waiting to hear about their friend who'd been stabbed. I'd heard that report earlier. Then there were the two transvestites in the corner that were dressed like rejects from a Patti Labelle and Lady Marmalade revue. It took all kinds to capture the essence of poverty. I would have bet good money that Angelina would have been scared in this environment, but she wasn't. She was cooler than I was, and it made me wonder about Dr. Preston's wife's background. For real.

"So tell me about your mom," Angelina said. "Are you close?"

I chuckled. "Close. I wouldn't call it that. I'm an only child, so I'm the only one she has, but we've never really been close in the mother-daughter sense. My mom isn't one of those people you get real close to."

"Humph," Angelina grunted. "I know what you mean. We have something in common. I'm an only child too, and my mother drives me up a wall."

I laughed. "Really."

"She has these ideas about how my life is supposed to be, and she won't let certain things go. I get tired of it. Sometimes you want someone in your corner, even if you're making a mistake. I can't get that from my mother."

I was in shock. "You couldn't have surprised me more if you told me you're mother was in jail, girl." I laughed. "I guess I pictured your mom and you attending some Sisters of the High Tea Secret Society meetings every week."

"Not even close." Angelina laughed. "My mother is in New Jersey, Asbury Park, where I grew up, and I'm glad she isn't close enough to attend anything with me. It's hard enough talking on the phone. I think that's why my friendships are so important. I've always protected my female friendships. They make up for what I lacked with my mom.

"So that's why you do Mentor-A-Sister?"

"Probably; my deep seated need for an older or younger sister. Being an only child is lonely."

"But you have a husband." I almost bit my lip. I actually felt guilty about bringing Greg up.

Angelina's smile didn't reach her eyes when she responded. "That's a different kind of relationship. Plus, men are men; you know—self-absorbed. Not like your girls. Your girls are there for you through thick and thin."

I didn't know. I had no idea. Had never had a "girl." Had never wanted one.

We were quiet for a moment, and I felt compelled to share. "My mother is different from yours. I don't know what she feels about me. She worked a lot when I was growing up, had way too many boyfriends that always had her attention, and now she only calls me when she needs something, which is a lot. I always felt like I was a burden. Like she resented me after my father left."

"Well, that's something else we have in common." Angelina smiled. This time it held appreciation. "My daddy left too. And my mother? I have never heard her talk about a man. If I found out she had one, they'd have me stretched out in one of those beds in there." We both laughed. "I think she hates men, but she also seems to think they're the answer to every problem a woman has. It's a strange thing going on in her head."

I lay my head back against the wall. "My mother is three hundred pounds. She's ignorant and she's crass." Tears burned my eyes. "If you went in there right now and she was able to speak to you, she'd say something crazy, and I'd be embarrassed."

Angelina reached into her purse for more tissue and handed them to me just as the first of two hot tears escaped the prison I'd tried to hide them in.

"It doesn't matter." Angelina exhaled. "She's your mother. She's not someone to be ashamed of."

More tears spilled down my face. "You haven't talked to her."

"We can't choose our family. The only thing we choose is what we do. And as for shame, we all have something we're ashamed of."

"Oh, yeah? I can't imagine that's true of you." I looked at her sideways. Tried to imagine what she could be ashamed of. We were killing time, so I asked. Teased her with my tone. "What's your secret shame?"

Angelina paused for a moment. I could tell she was trying to decide if she were going to tell me. "I'm ashamed of how I treated my father before he died." She turned to me and her eyes were misty. "My dad left us when I was six. He worked construction and there wasn't any work in New Jersey at the time. Or as my father said, the Portuguese had taken over the jobs brothers did back then on the construction sites." She laughed. "Anyway, he got a job, but it was in California, so he went out there to work. I remember he used to call me every week, but then the calls got fewer and fewer, and then they stopped all together." She paused. "When I was in college, I heard from him. He was still in California. He wrote me some letters, begged me to come see him. He said he was sick, and he wanted to see me before he died. I wanted to punish him for leaving; for leaving me and Mom. For leaving me with Mom." She laughed through tears. "So I didn't respond. I don't think I really believed that he was dying." She shook her head, and I squeezed her hand. It felt like the right thing to do. It's what I would do if I were comforting a patient at work.

Angelina continued. "After I graduated, I became curious. I tried to contact him, but he didn't answer. So I flew to Los Angeles to try to find him."

"What happened?"

"I found my daddy buried in a pauper's grave. He'd been writing me from a church mission that housed homeless men. He had hepatitis C. He'd been an I.V. drug user, but he got saved when he got sick, and he was trying to reach out . . ."

I squeezed her hand again. It seemed to give her the strength to keep talking.

"I let my daddy die alone because I wanted to punish him." She threw her head back. "The only person who ended up punished was me. That was a year of his life that I could have had with him, but I was stubborn and angry." She sniffed and a slow, joyless smile crept over her face. "Try to find something to love about your mom. She's not perfect. None of us are, but she's here. She didn't abandon you."

I nodded. Thought about how I could share my daddy story, but chose not to. My daddy, the singer who sang my name every day until he walked out the door when I was five. He didn't have a job waiting in California. He hadn't made empty promises, and he hadn't said good-bye. He had just left. That wasn't anything to share.

"And I don't know anything about that Mekhi, but I can tell that he loves you. It's in his eyes, and you feel something for him too. It's obvious."

I let her hand go and stood. "Oh no, sister-friend, we're not going there. Mekhi and I have too much bad history."

"What did he do? Hurt you, disappoint you?"

"You could describe it that way."

"He's not the man you were talking about the other day. The one you're dating because he has money."

I shook my head.

Angelina crossed her legs. Seemed to settle in for more of this soliloquy. "People do things wrong, but forgiveness goes a long way. Remember what I taught you about Jesus. He forgives us, and we must forgive each other."

I turned my back to Angelina's pleas and took a few steps to my left toward the dirty window that looked out over the trash compactor. Mekhi's face filled my memory. I rolled my eyes and sighed. Mekhi let me sit in jail. All the begging and showing up at hospitals wasn't going to change that, and that wasn't going to change how I felt about his betrayal. "I hear what you're saying, but sometimes that's easier said than done."

She nodded. "I agree, but we still need to forgive. It's more for us than it is for the other person. When you don't forgive, you hold on to anger and hate. It fills you up, and you can't fit any love and peace inside of you."

"But what if they do it again?" I asked.

Angelina was on a roll. "I'm not saying you have to keep a relationship with them." She stopped and measured her words. "I'm not saying you have to have a relationship with Mekhi. But at least forgive him and see where it goes."

I looked back out the window at all the trash. It was a mess like my relationship with Mekhi, my best friend, my lover had become. I'd been angry with him for so long, I didn't know how not to be.

"Consider this, Rae. Especially since we're standing here in a hospital. If you only had one week left to live, who would you want to spend it with? Who would make you laugh and feel happy? Mekhi, or Mr. Ralph Lauren comforter?"

I nodded. "I'll think about it," I said, trying to convince Angelina – and myself. "I'll work it out in my head." *I'm just not sure how.*

Chapter 26

I stood over my mother's hospital bed, looking at all the tubes attached to her body. The vent tube in her mouth gave me the chills, but the beeps and other sounds from the machines gave me comfort. Even though she wasn't conscious, I knew the numbers on the digital screens were good, and she was only on the ventilator as a precaution. They were sure they'd be able to take it out tomorrow.

I watched her sleep. Drugs. They'd found an excessive amount of oxycontin in her system. I remembered what she'd said that night on the phone. She'd used the word we."

"*We just need some until the end of the month.*" How had I missed that?

"Mama, I'm going to get you some help," I whispered. I kissed two of my fingers and pressed them against her forehead.

I didn't know about June, but my mother wasn't going to kill herself taking drugs. Not if I could do anything about it. I stepped out of the room. Angelina had been waiting by the door.

"It's time to leave." I could hear weariness in my own voice. "She's sedated, so she's not waking up tonight."

Angelina nodded. "She's going to be okay. I'll be praying for her, and I'm going to ask the prayer ministry to pray for her."

I nodded my head. If a prayer could help, I wanted it to

be done. I hadn't told Angelina about the OX. Even though she'd shared that her father was a drug addict, I wasn't ready to give that information up. It was too new even for me.

We exited the hospital through the emergency room doors. Our vehicles were parked close together, so we were about to go our separate ways, but I was curious about something and I had to ask her. "Why did you tell me that story, about your dad? It was so personal."

"Because you needed to hear it." I waited for her to explain herself the way I knew she would. "As Christians, our painful experiences are not only about us. We have to be willing to share what we've been through to help others. I wanted you to know that shame was not a burden you bear alone. So I'm Dr. Preston's wife. I have my own business and a big time position with *Youth and Child Services*. I've got on a suit I paid way too much money for." She laughed. "And I drive an eighty thousand dollar car. My daddy was a heroin addict that I had to dig up out of a state grave to give a decent burial." The smile that had touched her lips was gone. "Everybody's got stuff, Rae. None of us are exempt from pain and drama. But we have to talk to each other, so we don't feel alone in our trials. That's what we do for each other, as sisters in Christ."

"Sisters." I sighed. "I don't think I make very good sister material. I've done horrible things, Angelina. I can't believe someone like you is even here with me." I swallowed to keep my emotions inside.

"We're all a work in progress. We sister-friends gotta hang in there with each other." She smiled and rubbed her arm. "Oh, and speaking of which. I almost forgot." She reached into her handbag and pulled out a picture. It was of her and me at the church. "Sister Green took this a few weeks ago. Remember when she came in all excited about her new camera? I was going to give it to you tonight."

I accepted the picture. Looked at our twin smiles. Sister-friends she'd called us. We really did look like sisters. It actually hurt my heart because as the younger model, I looked like her. I wonder if she saw the resemblance. I looked in this woman's eyes. *What was I doing? How could I keep doing it?*

Her phone rang. She pulled it out of her bag. "This is my husband. I'll see you tomorrow." She gave my arm a squeeze. "Call me as soon as you have an update on your mom, or if you need anything."

I nodded and watched her rush to her car. It was nine. No doubt the good doctor, or no-good doctor was home trying to find out where his woman was. Angelina pulled out of the parking space and waved as she sped off. I went to my car and climbed inside. There was an envelope stuck under the windshield wiper. I climbed back out and retrieved it. It was a greeting card. A homemade one with a beautiful, calligraphic writing. It read:

> *Sammie,*
>
> *I said I wasn't gonna beg no more, but I don't have that much pride. I'll beg forever if I have to.*
>
> *Love, Mekhi.*

I got back into my car, dropped the card on the opposite seat, started the engine and pulled out.

I thought of the words Mekhi had said that day outside of my mother's apartment. *"We forgive what we want to forgive. Remember, what comes around goes around. You may need somebody to let you off the hook for something messed up you did."*

And then Angelina's plea tonight. Who would I want to spend the last week of my life with? That was deep. It was easy for her to talk about forgiving Mekhi because she didn't know the skinny on what went down. Would she forgive Greg if she knew about me? There were limits to what we could forgive, even when we loved people.

Chapter 27

I pulled into my garage and made a hurried trip to my condo. It was almost ten, and I was tired. Really worn out. Emotional, more than physically because I had a new problem. Bigger than the ones I woke up with this morning. A drug addicted mother—that mess was over the top in the realm of problems that needed solutions.

I collapsed on my bed and rooted around in my purse for the picture Angelina had given me. Sisters in Christ. She loved using the word *sister*. If she'd only known, I was as far from a sister as any chick could ever get. I was every woman's worst nightmare. I was the other woman, and the only reason she even knew me was because I was devious enough to step to her with my *Operation Steal Greg* plan. I emptied my lungs of a long breath and propped the picture against a lamp on my nightstand.

My cell phone rang. It was the fifth call I'd gotten from Greg. I figured I'd better answer before he showed up again and used his key.

"Where have you been? I've been calling you."

"I had a family emergency. I didn't have my phone with me."

"My wife was out this evening. I wanted to see you."

Hmmm. Was there something I was supposed to say? I mean, it was obviously time lost. I guess this was his version of a lecture for being a bad mistress. I rolled my eyes. I was starting to hate him.

He kept talking. "I'm on my way home from the gym. I was thinking I'd stopped by for a few minutes."

I swallowed hard and cleared my throat. "Not tonight, Greg."

"Excuse me?" His voice strained.

"I said—not tonight. I'm tired, and I'm stressed from this family business."

"Maybe I can help you work through the stress." I could imagine him smiling on the other end. *Jerk. Was he kidding?*

"It's not likely you can help me work through anything in a few minutes."

He was silent for a beat. I could see his face, the angry set of his chin when he was displeased. I'd only seen that once before. The time I tried to make him jealous by throwing out another man's name in conversation. He set me straight in a way that only a man who was paying the bills could. I hadn't done that again. "Besides," I said, thinking I needed to clean up the mess I was making with my attitude. "I have my period. Got it yesterday."

"Your period. Do all you women get them at the same time?"

His question made me think of Angelina, which embarrassed me. I squirmed in my seat. "You must be mixing me up with your wife. Too many periods in your life."

"You get in touch when your PMS or whatever you've got is over. I didn't call for this." His end of the line went dead.

"Of course not," I whispered. "You called to use me." Tears brimmed my eyes. Greg had never, ever stopped by or called just to say hello. It was always "I'm thinking of sex" or "Can I come get some?" He hadn't even asked me what was wrong, what my emergency was. I was nobody to him.

If you only had one week left to live. Who would you want to spend it with?

Not him.

I tossed my cell phone and settled back in the pillows on my bed and picked up the pile of bills I'd gotten from the mailbox. Student loan bills, Macy's, Nordstrom, Visa, Lord & Taylor, MasterCard. All of them due and overdue. I threw them across the room and rolled over on my side. The picture of Angelina and me came into view and anger boiled inside of me. It wasn't directed at her. I was pissed with myself. What the heck was I doing getting nasty with Greg? If I didn't get these bills paid, I was going to be messed up big time. I needed him. I needed to stay on track with *Operation Steal Greg.*

"Stay focused. You've come too far to get mushy now." I opened my nightstand drawer and put the picture face down inside. I reached across the bed for my cell phone. I could still call Greg back. All I had to do was tell that Negro I was wearing a purple thong, and he would be here faster than roaches on food left out on the stove in the projects. He'd forgive the menstruation lie.

When I went to dial, I saw I had a missed text message. I opened it first and it read:

Rae, remember, I'm praying for you and your mom. Love, Angelina.

D'rn her. I tossed the phone again. This heifer was really messing with my head. She was under my skin deeper than Greg. She'd come and sat in that dirty hospital waiting room for hours. Angelina had called me sister. Hugged me. Not even I could mess around with her husband tonight. I reached into the nightstand drawer and returned the picture to its place against the lamp. I wasn't fooling myself that she and I would be the best of friends, but even I knew about giving a situation its due. Angelina was trying to be a sister-friend. I'd never had one of those, but I had one now, even if it was an inconvenient one.

Chapter 28

The Greater Christian Life Heavenly Spa and Wellness Day had turned into a huge success. We'd planned for two hundred attendees, but it was barely noon, and it seemed like we'd served a hundred people already. And it was a pretty event. We'd decorated with chocolate brown and red balloons—Angelina and my favorite colors. The family life center was filled with them, and the centerpiece at the registration table was a commanding masterpiece of latex and ribbon.

The kids wore black pants and white shirts— balanced hors d'oeuvres trays piled high with donations I'd begged up from restaurants, culinary schools, and even Sam's Clubs and Costco stores all over the city. The highlight of the event was the section roped off in the back of the room, the *chocolates and cherries* treat section where I'd hung brown and red privacy drapes. The spa area. The women of the community were positively giddy over the fact that they were going to receive a free massage, facial, and foot rub. I was amazed at how many low income people were coming in for blood pressure and glucose checks.

I guess I'd assumed this side of town was for Atlanta's money folks, but these women were the ones who cleaned these people's houses and worked in the local restaurants and took care of their children. They were piled like sardines in two bedroom apartments where they lived with six and seven people, mostly children and abandoned grandchildren. How naïve I was to believe that poverty was confined to the gates of White Gardens and other places like it.

"Rae, you are a genius. Girl, we need you on the Youth and Child Services Board." Angelina threw her arms around me in a hug worthy of a win on Grammy night. "I'm so proud of the work you've done. Isn't it fabulous, Carol?" Angelina winked at me.

Carol's hands went to her pearls, and I rolled my eyes. "It's a fine job. The people seem to think it's special."

"It is and—" Angelina's words were cut off by a little girl that ran and slammed into the back of her legs. She turned to find the intruder and the joy that had been apparent in her face kicked up one hundred percent. "I didn't know you were here."

A short, red headed woman who looked to be about forty-five walked up with a small Barbie backpack and handed it to Angelina. "I'm sorry. When she saw you she just took off."

"It's okay, Ms. Henry." Angelina leaned down and squeezed the child. "Hi, Katrice."

"Hi, Angelina." The little girl made a mess of Angelina's name, but she was cute to death. Hair braided with a million rubber bands. Darling little Baby Phat outfit and matching kicks on her feet. "I got new clothes."

"I know," Angelina cooed. "And you look pretty in them."

Angelina stood, and Katrice grabbed her hand.

"Ms. Henry, these are my church sisters, Carol Wright and Rae Burns. Rae is the coordinator for today's event."

Ms. Henry was admiring the panache of her surroundings. "So this is a health fair?"

"A total wellness day," I corrected her politely. "You should stay and have a massage while you're here."

Angelina pointed. "You'll have to stop at a few of the booths and have blood pressure checked or weight or even your body fat percentage if you want to know it. After you've gotten four marks on the registration card, the spa services are a gift from the church."

"Marvelous idea." Ms. Henry looked at her watch. "I think I'll take you up on that. I don't remember the last time I could afford a massage."

"Bye, Ma Henry," Katrice said. The child was obviously thrilled to be turned over to Angelina.

"You be a good girl for Ms. Angelina, and I'll see you tomorrow," Ms. Henry said looking down at Katrice. She redirected her attention to Angelina. "Thank you so much for allowing her to stay with you overnight. Twenty year anniversaries only come around once."

Angelina and Katrice's eyes caught each other's. "No problem," Angelina said. "I'm looking forward to Katrice and me having a nice sleepover."

"Mind your manners, Katrice." Ms. Henry scooted away. She was clearly psyched about getting a massage. I was hoping she'd visit the body fat table. The first step to getting help was knowing the scope of the problem, and from the rear view, Ms. Henry needed to be in the know.

"So," I said, turning my attention to Katrice, "who's this little beauty queen?"

Angelina held the girl's hand out like she was presenting her at a royal ball. "This is Katrice. Katrice is a very special friend of mine."

"Oh," I said, feigning surprise. Angelina had been talking about Katrice non-stop for weeks. "What a pretty name for such a pretty little girl."

Katrice chuckled at my compliment, but then she whispered, "Thank you."

Angelina positively beamed when she looked at the little girl, and the little girl was looking at her like she was completely in love. If Angelina couldn't see this homeless, parent-less, child was the baby she was looking to fill that void in her life, I wasn't about to tell her. She was going to have to figure that one out all by herself.

"Katrice and I are going to help Sister Green at the mammogram sign in table. They're a little backed up with the paperwork."

"And I'm going to leave," Carol announced.

"Carol?" Angelina's tone rang with disappointment. "You can't leave. Rae needs to leave early. Her mother is in the hospital."

"I have a hair appointment. I couldn't reschedule." Carol patted her bob like touching the perfectly coiffed hair would convince us it was in need of a roller set. "Besides, Rae has this all running like a well oiled machine."

"It's okay. My cousin is with my mother." I threw my shoulders back. "Besides, I prefer willing workers."

Carol sneered at me before she walked away.

"Well, she'll kick herself in the morning when she finds out my surprise," Angelina said. "Come on, Katrice."

Surprise? What was she talking about? "Angelina, is there something I need to know?"

"It's a surprise." Her eyes twinkled with mischief. "A good one. Trust you won't be disappointed."

She walked away. I imagined she would have some special plaque made for my extraordinary efforts. There were lots of them hanging in the Hall of Fame at the church outside in the main hallway. She probably had some cool presentation all planned where I would be named Sister of the Year or some corny crap like that. I let it go and figured I'd accept my kudos, especially since my delivery from the infamous Justin's, a.k.a. P. Diddy's restaurant, had arrived. Now that was wellness food. I was starving, and I wanted to taste every one of those yummy appetizers before anyone else could get their hands on them.

I should have given Angelina's surprise more thought. If I had, I would have guessed it, but I'd been too busy working to consider the fact that Angelina had hooked up a visit from the media. Not some local nobody media. She had gotten us a spot on Atlanta's biggest station: Channel 2. Biffy Baskin, the "roaming reporter on the metro scene" was in residence with a hulking cameraman who looked like he doubled as a bodyguard. With a smiling Angelina to her right, Biff and her flunky walked toward me. There was no way I could escape.

"Rae, I know you tried to get news coverage for this event, but I called in a favor. One of my sorors is programming manager, and she was able to get us a camera. Isn't this great?" Angelina's excitement was bubbling out of her pores.

I thought I was going to throw up artichokes, cheese, and tiny wheat biscottis. The one time I didn't want attention drawn to myself, and my face was going to be splashed all over the six o'clock news.

"Rae, are you okay?" Angelina's eyebrows wrinkled. "You look a little green."

Nausea nudged my ribs. "I . . . I'm camera shy."

Angelina laughed. "Yeah, right."

"No no, really, Angelina," I said, grabbing her arm. "You do the interview. I'm not even a member of the church."

"You did all the work. I'm not going to take credit for it. Plus you need the business this could generate. You wouldn't have to work all those shifts at the hospital."

"But—"

"Am I going to get one of you ladies on the camera or what?" Biffy asked, raising an impatient brow.

Angelina stepped back and stretched a hand toward me.
"This is your girl." The cameraman lifted the heavy equipment up on his shoulder and pointed.

"It'll take three minutes, doll," Biffy, a former Miss Georgia
beauty pageant finalist, pulled a compact out of her pocket
and checked her face. "Jake, you ready?"

"Rolling," he replied.

Biffy returned the compact to her pocket and started her
script. "Today, I was roaming around town and guess what I
happened upon? The most unique church health fair I think
any of us in the metro area has ever seen."

I wanted to disappear—fall into the floor. I was caught. On
tape like on that stupid show *Cheaters*. I couldn't hide from
the television. Everyone was going to know I was a fake. Everyone at work, White Gardens, and most importantly, Greg,
and then Angelina. I was done.

I entered my apartment, slid my bag off my shoulder, and
kicked off my pumps. What a day. I needed a soak in the Jacuzzi, but I was too tired to even run the water.

I flopped down on the bed. I'd stopped by the hospital
to visit my mom. She was back to her old cranky self and
was clearly suffering from the effects of not having her drugs.
Thank goodness she was being discharged in a couple of days.
Between the commuting to the hospital and her nasty mood
when I got there, I was exhausted, and my problems were
growing by the day. Now I was going to be all over the news.

It seemed where Biffy went all the little media hawks followed. Several local weekly papers showed up. While I hid
in the bathroom like a punk, they took pictures of Angelina
and some of the other women and went on their way to, no
doubt, write up a front page story about Greater Christian

Life Church and their awesome women's wellness day. With the exception of one cameraman, I was able to stay clear of the newspaper journalists.

I couldn't believe I'd gotten myself so played. Angelina had scheduled her TIVO to record the news at six and eleven to make sure she got to see the story about our event. I could see her now, lying in bed with Greg and saying, "There's Rae, the woman I've been telling you about," and Greg losing his dinner at the sight of me.

Operation Steal Greg was a wrap. I'd outdone myself this time. All I had to do was be a mistress, the girlfriend, the heat on the side. Greg was paying up. He was doing what men like him did; he was writing checks. But no, I had to be ambitious. I had to try to break up a marriage. My mother had warned me. *"Married men don't leave they wives, but they know they gots to pay to keep you happy. Don't be no fool. Get paid."*

I rolled over on my sick stomach. Hot tears began to fall from my eyes. When Greg cut me off I wouldn't be able to keep up with the bills: the condo, the car, my student loans, credit cards. I screamed out loud and began to beat on the bed like it was the source of my misery. I buried my face in the comforter. For the first time since I'd bought it, I didn't care if my designer linen got wet. I wanted to cut off my oxygen supply and smother myself to death so all this drama I'd created would go away.

Chapter 29

Angelina and Katrice entered the house through the garage. Katrice's presence stunned Greg. He looked like he had seen a ghost. Angelina realized he must have, since Katrice probably looked like Danielle would she have lived to reach this age. Greg coughed a few times and pulled himself together. "We have a guest."

"This is Katrice, my special friend that I've been telling you about." Angelina put her purse on the island.

"Wow." Greg swallowed. "If she were older, you'd have a twin." Then he directed his attention to Katrice. Greg was good with kids. He adored little girls, so he smiled, took her hand, and kissed it like a southern gentleman. "Hello, Katrice."

Katrice gushed and said hello back.

"She's staying over tonight. I know you're playing poker later, so I thought she and I would have girl time."

Angelina knew he didn't approve. Her work wasn't supposed to come home, but he nodded and said, "Fine by me," in a voice that was less than fine by him.

A beat of silence passed as Greg looked between Angelina and Katrice. Angelina realized she'd been in the house long enough for him to have inquired about the fair.

"Ask me how it was?" Greg raised an eyebrow, and she cocked her head. "The health fair."

"Oh, yeah. How was it?"

Angelina gave him a quick recap of the day. She included the news that Biffy Baskin came and did a feature.

"Biffy who?" Greg never watched the news, because he said it was too sensationalized. He only read the paper.

"The roaming metro reporter." Angelina put a hand on her hip. "You know the blonde with the big hair."

Recognition shone on his face. "Oh yeah, and the big –" he stared, and then smiled when he looked at Katrice. "The big hair."

Angelina pursed her lips. "Yeah, the big hair." She walked to the refrigerator. Katrice was right behind her. "I TIVOed it, so we can watch it later." She removed a juice box, pushed the straw in, and handed the drink to Katrice.

"I don't think so. TIVO's full. I've been meaning to clean it off for a while."

Angelina's hand went to her hip. "So I'm not going to get it."

"No, but if your fair was newsworthy, it'll run again at eleven or in the morning. I'll dump some stuff and get it ready for you." He stood. "So Katrice, did you enjoy the fair?"

Katrice nodded. "Yes."

"Good." He stuck his hands in his pocket, rocked back on his heels and looked at Angelina, then Katrice. He was clearly uncomfortable. "I'm going to shower." He's found an escape. "What's for dinner?"

"I thought I'd order pizza. We've all had a full day. It's fast, and it's Katrice's favorite."

"That's fine. Been awhile since we had Angelo's," he replied. "Get a Philly cheese steak for me too."

Katrice and Angelina watched him leave the kitchen and jog up the stairs.

"He nice," Katrice said.

Angelina smiled, thinking the nice came and went with

the changes in weather. She reached for the wall phone and dialed the number for Angelo's.

Katrice and Angelina spent the evening like sisters. They played dress up, watched a Disney movie, and drank homemade strawberry smoothies in the Jacuzzi. By the time she put Katrice in the guest bedroom, the little girl was completely pooped, and so was Angelina.

She heard Greg's car enter the garage, and she took the stairs down to greet him. The silly cigar he always smoked when he played cards was hanging out of his mouth. He was smiling, which meant he'd won, and Angelina hoped his luck would transfer to her.

"How much?" she asked, taking the kiss he offered.

His eyes twinkled. "Two hundred twenty bucks, and I had horrible cards. I bluffed all night."

A light chuckle escaped her lips. "Are you hungry?"

"No, Malcolm ordered pizza from Angelo's of all places, so I've had my fill of bread and cheese. Where's the kid?"

"Sleeping. We had fun. I enjoyed having her." She smiled thinking about their evening. Playing makeup had been their favorite part, but Angelina realized she'd need to get some inexpensive cosmetics and keep them on hand for repeat makeup sessions. No point wasting the good stuff.

Greg nodded, and then the understanding gave way to concern "You're not getting attached to her, are you?"

"You say that like it would be a horrible thing."

"Well, she's a foster child in the middle of a pretty nasty lawsuit. I'd think you'd need to keep professional distance."

"Is that what you were thinking?" she asked, knowing full well it wasn't.

Greg shook his head. "Okay, I was thinking about Danielle and hoping you weren't transferring some instinct to be a mother on her."

Angelina breathed deep through her nostrils and a knot of tension settled in her belly. "I like her. She's a little girl, who, at this point, is all alone in the world. She's living with white people, which as an agency, I appreciate, but as a black woman, I don't. I don't think there's anything—"

Greg threw up his hands, cutting her off. "I'm not trying to fight about this. I'm just asking." He reached into the refrigerator, pulled out a bottled water, and opened it. "I'm concerned about you."

"Really?" She shook her head. "So why doesn't that love transfer into action?"

Greg put the water bottle down on the counter hard. A spray of it flew up and hit the light fixture above the island. "It's been a good day, Angelina—don't start this tonight."

"A good day." She guffawed. "I have a hole in my heart the size of the Grand Canyon. It's never a good day, and if you were so concerned about me, you could see it."

Greg didn't respond. He took a sip of water, but it wasn't keeping him cool. She could see him boiling under the surface.

"You refuse to go see Dr. Luke."

"You're right. Nagging me about it isn't going to change it."

"You're being so unfair. It's not like I'm the one with the problem." She regretted the words as soon as they came out of her mouth.

Greg leaned forward like he hadn't heard her. Then he grinned, but it wasn't a smile. "Oh yeah, that's good. Rub that salt right in the wound."

"I meant—"

"I know what you meant."

"Greg," Angelina pleaded. "The process worked before. Why can't we do it again?"

"Because you have no idea how humiliating that entire *process* was for me." Angelina could tell she'd hit the hot spot. He was enraged. "Going into that room with those magazines and that cup. You don't know what that was like."

"No, of course not. I was too busy dealing with the headaches and pain from injections to think about what your process was like." Angelina decided it was time for them to have it out. It was time to say what they'd both been thinking. Time to address the pink elephant that had been walking around their house and trampling over their emotions for two years.

"I didn't like it," Greg barked. "I hated it, and I don't want to do it again."

"So what, you don't think Danielle was worth what we both went through?"

Greg moved to the other side of the island and banged a fist on the counter. "Don't do that. Don't make it like I wouldn't do it all again for her."

Angelina slid a few feet closer to him. Begged with her eyes. "Then why not for another child?"

"Because maybe that's what was wrong with her!" He yelled, and the words that had been hiding in his heart reverberated off the walls. "Did it ever occur to you that the little in vitro fertilization weakened her in some way?"

Angelina was stunned. She took a few feet backward, toward the table, and fell into an empty chair. Neither one of them said anything for long moments. "Is that what you think?"

Greg washed his face. "I don't know what to think. All I know is we did this unnatural thing, and then our baby died."

"Greg, you're a physician. You know better—"

"I don't know any such thing. Do you know how much of

what we do is guesswork? Some of it is really untested." He shook his head and turned his back to her. A painful sigh filled the quiet.

Angelina stood, went to him, and wrapped an arm around him from the rear and rested her face against his back. After a minute he pulled her body to the front of his and used a hand to smooth her hair. "I love you, Lena. And I almost lost you after Danielle died. The only thing worse than losing her would have been losing both of you. I don't want to take the risk of that happening again."

"We can't live our lives in fear. We have to trust God that everything will be okay."

He released her. "You're kidding?" He tossed his empty water bottle in the nearby trash. "I don't know how you continue to do this whole God and church thing. If God cared about us, about you, then that would be our child upstairs and not someone else's."

Angelina opened her mouth to say something, but he cut her off again.

"If God cared about anything, would that kid's sister have broken her neck on the stairs of a foster parent's house? Come on, honey. You can't ever, ever talk to me about God. I don't believe in Him!"

The tears that Angelina had been trying to suppress fell at the same time Greg's fist hit the counter. "You used to believe," she whispered. "When you were in college and you were struggling to pass a test or even move up in your career, you prayed. You asked me to pray with you."

Pain etched his face, and he nodded. "That was before I buried my daughter." He left the kitchen, went into the library, and closed the door behind him.

Angelina's heart had been pounding, but now it was shattered into a thousand little pieces. She sat there, head in her hands, tears streaming through her fingers until she cried herself empty. She reached for a nearby napkin and wiped her face.

That was it. The pink elephant had left the house, but its exit had torn the frame off the door. There was no reaching Greg. He wasn't going to see Dr. Luke, and most assuredly his low sperm cell count hadn't reversed itself. If she didn't get pregnant on her own, they wouldn't have a baby. The chance of that happening naturally would be a miracle. Something she wasn't sure she believed would occur. At least not for her.

Chapter 30

When I arrived at work the next night, my charge nurse announced that all staff on our shift was required to complete random drugs tests. I wondered what was random about an entire shift being selected.

Last week, administration released the employee newsletter where they explained revenues were down due to declining admissions and escalating facility and pharmaceutical costs. As a result, a drastic spending cut was in place until further notice. I remember concluding that what they needed to cut was waste. These drug tests fell in the category of spending, so I began to wonder if this randomness had something to do with me. Were they looking for a drug addict who was stealing OX and using? The idea that they were on to me had me looking over my shoulder all night.

To add to my angst, I was on pins and needles about the Angelina and Greg thing. I hadn't heard from Angelina all day, nor had I heard from Greg. Not that that was uncommon on a Sunday, but surely they'd watched the TIVO of the newscast by now. Didn't somebody want to cuss me out?

I had watched the broadcast on the Internet. My face was screaming fraud on national television. Thank goodness I had a private telephone number and very few people had it, otherwise my phone would be ringing off the hook. Folks in the hood always watched the news and read the obits. Who got arrested, who got shot, and who got dead. That was big talk in

White Gardens. The news made for juicy gossip, which I was certain to be the subject of today. My mother had called and left a message. She'd seen the broadcast and wanted to know why I was fronting with the name Rae Burns. She also wanted to know when I was going to get her out of the hospital. I knew she was itching to get more pills.

I'd done some Googling on the Internet for rehab centers. There were some free ones, but their websites indicated they had waiting lists. The ones that weren't free were extremely pricey. Mama and I had yet to have the talk about her drug use. The right time just hadn't come up, and as stubborn as she was, she wasn't likely to say she'd go, so it was hard to know what I should do. What I could do.

If I kept supplying her, she could end up in the hospital again, or worse yet, overdose; not to mention the little fact that I'd be jobless or homeless feeding her habit. If I didn't supply her, she'd get the drugs on her own. I had visions of her turning into a toothless, fifty-year-old hooker. Doing unthinkable things and taking endless abuse to earn enough money for her stuff.

"Jesus, what do I do?" I rolled my eyes to the ceiling. Now I knew I was in trouble. I had called on God. Did God help drug addicts? Did He help fifty-year-old ex-strippers who were hooked on drugs? Angelina believed so. She had me so confused with all that talk about grace and mercy and salvation. I didn't know what I believed anymore. It was so much easier believing it all rested on my own shoulders. That way I didn't have to worry about the disappointment of God not coming though for a sista. Besides, how did a person plan if they were waiting for a miracle? I was a planner. I didn't like when life took me by surprise.

"Samaria, I would have sworn I saw you on the six o'clock news yesterday." Nosy Nadine had crept up beside me. "Something about a health fair at a church in Roswell."

"I have a twin sister," I replied, and went into the medication room where, surprisingly, I was scheduled to work again. I had already made up my mind. I wasn't taking anything tonight. I needed to work a shift where no drugs were wasted so pharmacy would not get suspicious every single time I came in.

I pulled my meds and rolled the cart out of the room. Nadine was waiting for me. Didn't this woman ever take care of her patients?

"An identical twin. That must have been interesting growing up."

I didn't respond, just kept moving my cart. She followed me.

"Most twins have matching names. You know like Jean and Jane or Hailey and Bailey."

I grunted. "If you must know, her name is Ramaria. She goes by Rae."

She seemed satisfied with that, but she still continued to walk alongside me.

"Nadine, if you don't mind. My little visitor came today, and I'm really feeling a little crabby. I'd prefer to work alone." Her face didn't register my meaning. I let out a breath and said, "My period, my cycle . . . I'm on the rag."

"Oh." Nadine turned red and tried to censor a nervous laugh. "Sorry. Where I come from we call it our friend."

"You white girls would," I snapped, and she went back down the hall.

There was something about her. I couldn't put my finger on it. She hadn't worked here long. In fact, she'd come from out of nowhere and started getting assigned to shifts on our floor. She didn't talk to all the other white women, but seemed to have lots of conversation for me. I wondered if her man was a brother. Sometimes when they were down with black men, they tried to align themselves with sisters. I'd have to ask her about that.

Angelina would say I needed to trust the voice of the Holy Spirit. Know that He was trying to tell me something. I needed to quell my suspicions; that was for sure. But I preferred to follow my street instincts more so than the voice of an omnipotent God. My instincts were saying check her out, and that's exactly what I was going to do.

Chapter 31

I got my mom settled in her recliner and put her medication bottles and a tall glass of water on the table next to her. She'd refused to come to my condo, even for a day or two, but I had made a deal with one of her neighbors, an out of work certified home health aide, to check on her a few times a day.

"I don't even need this stuff," my mother complained. She picked the plastic prescription bottle that held the teeny tiny pills that would limit future seizure activity.

"It's a precaution. Just do right, Mama, and take it for now." I busied myself straightening a pile of untouched magazines I'd purchased for her while she was in the hospital. "I put food in the fridge. It's all cooked. You just have to stick it in the microwave. Don't let June eat it all up."

My mother's head jerked up and our eyes locked. "This is my house. You bought the food. Don't tell me who I can give it to."

I swallowed my frustration. This woman was going to drive me crazy. "June is a grown man, and he hasn't been sick. So let him fend for himself like he's been doing all week while you've been in the hospital."

My mother grunted. Her annoyed smirk irritated me. How much more did I have to do up in this place to get a little respect? How much more time and money did I, her daughter, have to spend to get treated half as well as she treated that stupid cousin of mine? And it wasn't like she didn't owe me. She owed me for the messed up way she'd done my father, cheating on him with his best friend. He left her because of it, and when he left her, he left me. She also owed me for the messed up way she let her boyfriends get their jollies staring and pawing at me.

Find something about her to love. Angelina's words came back to my memory, but all I could see was the contorted face of a woman who I was starting to think didn't even like me.

The door flew open, and June's hulking figure filled the entrance. His high induced, glossy eyes fell on me, and I knew instantly that he was up to no good. The Negro looked guilty. Of what? Probably the Ox I was sure was in his pocket for my mother. She'd used her cell phone in the car. Mumbled that she was on the way, and now I know who she was talking to. She hadn't been home thirty minutes, and he was here with more drugs.

"What up, Sam?" June asked, closing the door. He slid across the room and fell onto the old pleather couch that bore the imprint of his body. He didn't wait for my answer. "How you doing, Auntie?"

My mother barked out complaints about the hospital, the food, the television service that had too few channels, and the stupid doctors and nurses that prodded and poked at her all day. June nodded and shared his hospital war stories with her, but I could tell the exchange was small talk. They were using the banter to fill space and time. They were waiting for me to leave.

"Mama," I said, cutting into June's stupid conversation. "We need to talk about how you gonna get off this drug. It almost killed you, and I—"

"They gave me some papers to look at." She picked up the remote control and punched the power button. Noise filled the room. "They told me about some drugs I can get to help. Something with an s."

"Drugs to get off drugs is not the way to do it. It's another addiction," I said, raising my voice over the volume of the reality television show she'd flipped to. "And it's only part of treatment. They're not going to keep giving it to you without counseling."

My mother rolled her eyes and pushed the mute button. I could tell by the way she was looking at me that she wished I had a mute sensor too. "The peoples at the hospital told me what I had to do. But it ain't like I'm hooked on the stuff. I was just taking a few pills for my back." Her eyes cut to June and back to me, nervously.

I looked at June, and he looked away from me. I dropped my head back and bit my lip. My mother unmuted the television and shifted in her seat toward the screen.

June laughed at some ridiculous wig pulling off cat fight on the screen. Both of them cackled about the show, ignoring the fact that I was squatting between them trying to talk to her about getting well.

June reached into his jacket pocket for a pack of Kools, and lit one like my mother wasn't sitting there recovering from the worst asthma attack of her life. "Let me get one of them," she said. June bounced off the chair and walked over to hand her a cigarette and the lighter.

"Mama . . ." I started to protest, but swallowed my words. The people at the hospital had told her no smoking. She knew she wasn't supposed to be doing this crap. I stood and walked to the door. "I'll see you later," I said. It was a struggle for me to look back at her. She nodded a good-bye. I heard June's body hit the pleather again. I didn't bother to say anything to him. No way was I acknowledging his stupid behind; not when all I wanted to do was strangle him.

I stepped out the door. Thought about the scene I was leaving: June and my mother, smoking, no doubt about to pass off an oxycontin pill that June did God knows what to get for her, and possibly drinking later. Those two were co-dependent abusers, and I was going to have a hard time saving my mother from herself.

Chapter 32

I raised my hand to knock on the door and held it there suspended like my nerve. I couldn't bring myself to do it. *What was I doing here anyway?* Just when I was about to turn and leave, it swung open with a loud creak. Wang Wang snatched his head back. "Well I'll be. It's Rae Burns in the flesh. What up, girl?"

"Cute." I rolled my eyes and pulled my bag tighter against my side, strengthening my resolve. "Ya' brother here?"

Wang scratched his chin hairs. "Nah, he running. Been gone awhile though. He'll be back in a minute."

I released the grip on my bag, reached into it and pulled out a business card. "Will you give this to him for me? Tell him I need to talk to him."

Wang waved off the card. "Tell 'em ya'self, Sammie. Dang, I told you he'll be back in a few. Cop a squat on the sofa and wait."

I didn't move.

Wang grabbed my arm. With reluctance, I allowed myself to be pulled into the apartment. "Chill. Ain't nothing in here gonna bite you. Mekhi be glad to see you anyway." He pushed the door closed.

I relaxed some, sized up my surroundings, and nodded.

Wang looked at his wrist watch. "I gotta go out and do my sales thing. Tell Mekhi he need to pull a message off the machine. Sound important."

I continued to be mute, acknowledging his instructions with another nod. Wang moved to the door, snapped his fingers like he forgot something and went back toward the bedrooms. He emerged a few minutes later. "I'm out. Holla, and don't be a stranger." He opened, closed, and locked the door in what seemed like one motion.

I looked around at the place again. I was amazed at the difference from the dank, tore down apartment my mother leased. Mekhi's place was hooked up like a shot out of *Metropolitan Homes* magazine. Plush carpet, a metallic treatment on the walls, African art, and some bad to the bone brown leather furniture. His stereo system was hot too. Boosting must be good business. Shame it hadn't gotten him out of the projects. All his dreams of the life of the rich and famous, and he was still living with the broke and nameless. At least until they tore this dump down.

I'd been browsing through their extensive music collection when I heard a key in the door. I sucked in my breath and didn't let it out until he entered the apartment. Mekhi didn't notice me at first, but once he did he just stared for a moment like he was waiting to see if I were a mirage that would disappear when he blinked. Then he dropped his keys on the table by the door. He reached for the tail of his shirt, pulled it over his head revealing a bare torso with six, eight, ten pack of stomach muscles. I swallowed. Hard. I was staring, and he was looking at me like I was something to eat.

"I'm gonna take a shower."

All I could do was nod.

"Make yourself comfortable. I'll be quick." He disappeared down the hall.

"That's twisted about your moms," Mekhi said. "Somebody

oughta kick June in his head for getting her turned on to that mess."

I was sitting on a stool at a waist high bar by the window, looking out at his Lexus and my Beamer gleaming in the mid-day sun. I noticed a few heads coming out of buildings on the prowl for drugs. A couple of older women and young mothers were sitting on their stoops watching children play on the red clay that probably wouldn't produce grass even for Martha Stewart. I turned back to face Mekhi.

"Might not have been June. Mama is good at helping her-self to stuff. Pills probably in the bathroom or something. All that weight on her, and she had been complaining about her back."

Mekhi nodded. Carrying a half empty bottle of Powerade, he moved from the refrigerator to the living room. Concern had etched deep folds into his face. I was relieved to have someone to tell all this stuff to.

"I don't know what to do. This has gotten way out of con-trol. She's has all these health issues, and she's already back on the Ox. There's no state medical for people who don't have kids, so her real prescriptions and home health aide are costing me a small fortune." I rubbed the creases on my fore-head. "Paying to take care of her would be okay if she weren't using, but she is, so it's good money down the drain, and I can't keep stealing from my job."

"Yeah, I was wondering where you was getting the drugs you was hooking June up with."

I raised an eyebrow.

"Er'ybody know 'bout that. But ya' moms, that's on the low. Don't nobody know 'bout Ms. Jacobs being strung out."

"And I don't want nobody to know." I pinned him with a firm look.

"Shoot, I ain't gonna tell nobody. You know that. That's

why you here." Our eyes locked for a moment, and Mekhi moved to where I was sitting. He put his Powerade bottle down on the bar next to me.

I dropped my eyes from his. I was here because I was desperate. I was here because I had no one else to call. I was here because other than that one time, Mekhi always came through for me. I suppressed the sound of the bars slamming in my memory, which was easy to do with the way Mekhi was making me feel. Silence continued to pass between us, and I raised my eyes and let them fall on his biceps and triceps and thigh muscles. It was getting hot up in this apartment, and it didn't have anything to do with the temperature of the room. Mekhi was standing way too close.

"I'll take care of it for you." He reached past me. CK One filled my nostrils, and I held my breath to stop its seductive assault. "I need a few days to get the right price, and then I might have to go up north and be my own courier." Mekhi drew his hand back and slid a toothpick he'd picked up into his mouth. "She got enough pills to hold her over?"

I let my breath go. I thought he was going to touch me. I shook my head. "She called me yesterday and asked for pills, but I can take care of it for a few days. How are you going to—what are you going to do?"

Mekhi was thoughtful for a moment. He moved away from me to a large computer desk on the opposite wall and dropped his weight into the leather executive chair in front of it with a loud squish. I was glad he'd distanced himself. His cologne was messing with my senses.

"I'll get her onto something low dose. Try to wean her while you work that rehab angle."

"What if she takes more than one?" I asked.

He shook his head. "She ain't gonna have but one at time. Called spoon feeding that monkey. She'll be dealing with me direct."

I nodded understanding. "That's a lot of oversight, and she isn't going to be cooperative. What's it gonna cost me?"

He shrugged. "Ain't gonna cost you nothing."

I cast him a 'don't play with me, Negro' look.

"What you think I'm gonna ask you for, some booty or something?" His dark eyes swept my body, and his lips slowly spread into a small smile. "Come on, Sam. You know me better than that. I likes my women to be willing, much more fun that way."

I wondered about that for a moment. Wondered about Mekhi's woman or women. I found myself feeling jealous. I mean whoever she was, she was one lucky trick to have a man this fine.

"What you doing for yourself to roll out that kind of money for a friend, Mekhi?" I swirled my hand around the apartment. "I mean, unless all this stuff is hot, you got about ten thousand sitting in this living room."

Mekhi leapt from his chair and once again closed the distance between us. "Everything in this apartment is paid for with the truth. My days of making dishonest money came to an end."

My mind went back to the suit he was wearing in the hospital. I assessed him now in his Sean John muscle shirt and designer jeans. "Oh yeah, so when did you stop boosting? Yesterday afternoon?"

Mekhi placed a hand palm down on the surface of the bar to my right and bought his face within inches of mine. His eyes flashed with fire. "No. More like six years ago when I realized how much stealing had cost me."

I swallowed hard again. His minty breath and cologne had me trippin. My own breath was coming harder. "So." I fought stuttering over my words. "If your money is so tight, why you still in the projects?"

He laughed and let the smile hang on his face for a few seconds. "Come on, Sammie. Don't you remember, I promised I wasn't leaving White Gardens without you?"

My heart slammed into my chest like a bag of bricks. My cell phone rang, and I wanted to thank God for the reprieve because if we hadn't had that interruption, I was going to kiss him so deeply that he was going to know I was worth waiting for. I leaned to the side for my bag, and he returned to an upright position to give me room. It was Angelina, and I was almost afraid to answer it. Especially if I were going to get cussed out. I clicked talk and said a cautious hello.

"We still on for lunch?" Angelina's voice had a lilt that was chipper. With a breath, I inhaled a bit of calm. *She didn't know.*

"I'm sorry," I said. I watched Mekhi move across the room. He opened a laptop and pushed the power button. "I forgot. I'm on the other side of town, handling some business for my mother."

"Well, I was on my way out of the office, and I wanted to make sure you could still make it before I got in the car," Angelina said. "By the way how is your mom?"

"Much better," I lied, turning slightly on the stool as if I could hide from Mekhi's intent stare.

Angelina definitely didn't know about the Rae Burns thing. She sounded like she didn't have a care in the world. "I know you're tired from the weekend. I'm still worn out myself," Angelina chuckled.

"I think it's more my mom than the weekend," I said, wondering how I had escaped the technology of TIVO. "Angelina, let me call you back."

"Sure, sure. We'll get together later this week, or at least see each other at Bible Study."

I confirmed that was cool, ended the call, and put the phone on vibrate.

"Is that somebody looking for Samaria Jacobs or Rae Burns?" Mekhi asked, closing his laptop and giving me his full attention. I looked away. "Sammie, what you into?"

"A smaller mess than it looks like, and I'm getting out of it." I surprised myself that I'd said that because at that moment I meant it. "And speaking of messes." I cleared my throat. "There's something else—I need another favor."

"Whew, you needy today." He smiled and chuckled like it was music to his ears.

I rolled my eyes up. "Anyway. I was hoping you could help me with this woman at work." I filled him in on what I knew about Nadine.

"Sound like a nosy white girl to me." He scruffed up his chin. "But I can have this dude I know snoop around for you."

"What's that going to cost me?" I asked, thinking I already knew what he would say this time.

Mekhi didn't hesitate. Through a cocky smile he said, "You keep trying to pay for what I'm willing to give for free, and it's gonna cost you. I might ask for a kiss."

I had been in this apartment with him too long. I gripped my purse; my palms were sweating around the straps, and my nerves were shot. "That sounds like more than I'm willing to pay."

Mekhi leaned closer. His irises danced mischievously. "You know, Sam, you might find out that a brother done got better at some things than he was when he was nineteen."

A large lump went down my throat. I cleared it and shook my head. "Stop messing with me," I hissed. "Either tell me what I have to pay in cash, or let it go."

Mekhi laughed a throaty roar from deep in his belly. He took a few steps back. "No sweat, girl. I appreciate the fact that you here." He took a few more steps backward and collapsed on the bulky leather sofa. "We making progress."

"Don't be so sure." I wasn't ready to crack my veneer. "I'll have to see how you deliver on all these promises you made today."

Mekhi's smile was all dimples and confidence. "One thing you gonna find out about me is I'm a man of my word." He winked.

I slid off the bar stool. "We'll see about that, won't we? Not like you haven't left me flat before."

"C'mon, girl, you ain't gotta remind me of what I did," Mekhi said. "Not like I can forget."

"Well, you've got a chance to redeem yourself." I cocked my head. "I'm going to go."

Mekhi nodded, gave me a hard once over with his sexy eyes, then smiled. "You sure 'bout that kiss?" I know I could see all thirty- two of his teeth.

"I appreciate your concern." I walked to the door. "And your help."

Mekhi flew off the sofa. He beat me to the door in record time. Both our hands were on the knob. His brick hard body brushed against me as he turned it. My resolve was melting like an ice cream cone in the hot sun. "I'm glad you came to me. Glad to know you trust me some."

I didn't move. I was afraid to. Mekhi used his free hand to sweep my hair from over my ear and whispered, "I still love you, Sammie."

I looked at him over my shoulder. My eyes fell on his lips. He licked them, and I turned my head. "You don't even know me anymore."

Mekhi hesitated for a moment, like he was considering my words. Then he chuckled. "Girl, what you talking 'bout? You ain't changed." His laugh came harder. "'Cept your name. Rae Burns."

I countered his playfulness by throwing an elbow in his gut, then I stepped through the door. It didn't close behind me, so I knew he was watching me as I made my way down the hall. I could still feel the heat of Mekhi's gaze clinging to my body as I approached my car. I looked up and found that he was indeed at his window. I climbed in the vehicle, turned on the engine, and threw my head back on the head rest. I'd come that close to letting Mekhi touch me. And it wasn't just because he was fine, and he was offering to bail me out of my mess. Mekhi had said he loved me. He'd been the only man in my life to ever tell me that. I needed to hear those words because my world was unraveling, or at least it felt like it might at any moment. Was he being honest? The voice inside my heart said he was, but I couldn't escape the memory in my head.

Slam! The bars opened and closed all day. I was glad they were closing behind me this time. I had a visitor. I had no idea who. My mom, one of my cousins, or Mekhi. I was praying it was him. He was the only person I wanted to see, but when I entered the main visiting room I saw my cousin, June, sitting at one of the small tables.

"Where's Khi?" I asked, sliding onto the bench across from him.

June scanned me from head to toe. "Girl, you look a mess."

"June, Khi. What's going on? Why hasn't he been here? Is he locked up?"

June hesitated for a moment and said, "Ain't nobody seen Mekhi. I talked to Wang today, and he told me his brother was in Florida."

I slammed my palms on the table. Caught the eye of a grumpy guard and recomposed myself. "Wang said he scared or something. His mother got him hiding out until this thing is over."

"Until it's over. I got a public lawyer, June. I need Mekhi to get up here and get me a decent lawyer."

June sat back and crossed his arms over his chest. "Look, I'm the messenger. Ya' moms asked me to let you know what was going on. Mekhi is gone. You need to try to work this out yourself."

I shook my head. I had worked it out for myself, or rather

I'd gotten lucky. The county was piloting a new pre-trial intervention program for first offenders under age twenty-one. I was perfect for it. All I had to do was keep my nose clean for five years, and I wouldn't have to go to jail. I wouldn't even have a record. I'd done that for all these years, but I continued to hold the contempt I felt for Mekhi in my heart.

"I still love you, Sammie." I could still feel his warm breath on my neck. I fought hard to not hear those words, to not feel his heat, to not want them both. I didn't want my lifeline to be Mekhi, but just like he'd been the raft I needed to survive the last time, he'd somehow become it again. I started the engine and prayed this time, he wouldn't let me drown.

Chapter 33

Angelina pushed herself. Her muscles strained under the pressure of the incline on her Stairmaster. Sweat trickled down her face and back. She looked at the calorie counter and for all she'd done, she'd only burned about two hundred fifty. She became disgusted with the entire workout. It was so much like everything else in her life. Like her marriage. She was putting in a ton of work, exerting a bunch of energy and getting nowhere. She pushed the button and let the machine come to a stop. There was no point in continuing to put off the inevitable. There was a decision to make. Did she continue to pray and wait for Greg to come around, or did she leave him?

She stepped off the machine, used a towel to wipe her perspiration, and exited the home gym. She needed to talk to Felesia. She picked up the phone, hoping she could get Felesia before she started work. Caracas was only forty minutes behind Eastern Standard Time, and Felesia might still be in her hotel room. She knew her friend wasn't a breakfast eater.

The phone rang a few times and went to voicemail. Angelina didn't want to leave a message about the real reason she was calling because that would be too depressing for anyone to receive on the other end. She pretended she was calling to follow-up on the message Felesia had left her the other day about the change in her flight home. "Hey, Fee. I wanted to let you know that I received your message. Just call me when you get home. I miss you, girl. Can't wait to see you." Angelina smiled and ended the call.

The phone rang as soon as she placed it on the base. She was hoping it was Felesia calling her back, but she had a feeling it was the one other person who would call her at this hour. God help her, the one person on the earth she was not in the mood to speak to; her mother. She entered the kitchen, picked up the extension, and said hello.

The chatter began about some stuff Angelina did not care about. "I ran into one of your classmates at church. You're going to get an invitation to your high school reunion," her mother said. "Won't that be nice?"

She moved past the fact that her mother hadn't greeted her. Hadn't asked her how she was doing.

"You get to come and show everybody how successful you are."

Angelina shrugged off the depression that was invading her soul. Just moments before the phone rang, she had been deciding if she were going to submit to what would be the biggest failure of her adult life—a failed marriage—so she wasn't feeling like a success. She tuned her mother out and continued to think about where she was in her life.

People had harder decisions to make. People were choosing between life and death things like chemo and radiation. The president was deciding if we went to war or continued to negotiate with our foreign enemies. Being an adult was tough, and decisions were hard. Greg and she simply weren't on the same page. She was not going to sacrifice having children because he was prideful or he was scared. That was the problem with him being backslidden. When the tough choices had to be made, that really needed to be thought about from a spiritual perspective, Greg checked out on her. Maybe it was time for her to check out on him.

"Angelina, did you hear what I said about your reunion?" Her mother raised her voice.

"Yes, you said I was getting an invitation."

"I said that when you first answered the phone. I told you they're holding it at *The Breakers* in Spring Lake. It's going to be fancy."

Angelina washed her hands and started the coffeemaker. Still listening to her mother's chatter, she went back through the front of the house, turned off the alarm, and stepped outside for the morning papers. When she stepped back in, Greg was descending the stairs. She met him at the bottom, and he kissed her on the lips. "Tell your mother good morning," he whispered and removed the *Wall Street Journal* from her hand.

"Is that Greg?" her mother asked.

"What other man would it be at this hour, Mom?" Angelina shook her head.

"Let me let you talk to your husband. You know I told you not to be on the phone when you're husband is around."

Angelina nodded. "Yes, you did, Mom, but you called me, remember?"

"I remember. I'm not senile. Call me later. I have to tell you about my neighbor. She got a collagen injection in her lips and she looks like a cartoon character."

Angelina laughed, promised her mother she'd call later, and pushed the OFF button.

When she entered the kitchen she found Greg pouring coffee into a mug. He took a seat in front of his breakfast bowl, and Angelina dutifully poured cereal and milk in. "Do you want an egg?"

He looked up from his paper. "No, this is fine."

"You'd be better off with some protein in the morning."

"I'd be better off if I could lose this five pounds around my gut," he responded. "You spend an hour on that Stairmaster every day. I've gotta keep the younger men away from my wife."

Angelina poured a cup of coffee and took a seat across from him. She supposed he was trying to flatter her. She wanted to tell him that the only reason she'd be looking at a younger man, or any man, was because he could or would get her pregnant, but she snapped open the *Roswell Weekly* and began to peruse the pages while she waited for her coffee to cool. She was flipping through it so quickly that she almost missed the story; a write up about the health fair and a picture of her and Rae. She smiled and stretched the paper across the table to Greg. "Honey, look."

Greg took a few seconds to pull himself from the financials, grunted a bit, and accepted the paper. "What is—" he started.

"It's our health fair." She proudly raised the coffee mug to her lips.

Greg stared at the paper. For a moment he looked confused, and then he looked bothered. "Who—who is the woman next to you?" The words came out like someone had tazered his tongue.

"It's Rae, Rae Burns. The woman at the church. I've mentioned her to you a few times. She was helping me with the health fair."

Greg stood to his feet. "Rae?"

"Yes." Angelina knew she'd mentioned Rae's name a number of times over the last few weeks. "She's my new mentee."

Greg looked funny. She couldn't put her finger on it, but she would swear he was suddenly ill. "I have to go."

Angelina stood. "What's wrong?"

"What do you mean?" Greg asked nervously.

"You look funny, and you haven't touched your cereal."

"I'll grab something later."

"Why would you grab something later when you have something in front of you?"

"Because I have a long surgery this morning. I shouldn't have milk. It's been getting to me lately." He looked back at the paper. "I might be getting lactose sensitive."

"That's new." Angelina was mystified. The man ate bran flakes every morning.

He folded the *Weekly* under his arm. "I'll read this article later."

She nodded. He was acting strange. Real strange, and then something occurred to her. "Do you know Rae?" Angelina asked, crossing her arms.

Greg stuck his neck out. "What?"

"Rae, the woman in the picture. She's a nurse. Maybe you've worked with her."

Greg snatched back his head. "No. No. I don't think so. I was noticing in the picture how much she looks like you."

"Really?" Angelina pulled the paper from under his arm, unfolded it, and took another look at the picture. Rae and she were standing close. She was smiling, but Rae wasn't. She'd remembered how nervous she'd been when the photographer snapped the picture, said she was camera shy, which didn't fit in with the woman's personality at all. "Hmmm," Angelina mused. Now that she was looking, she could see some resemblance. Bone structure—the shape of their eyes. They did look alike. "You're right. We do favor a bit." She handed the paper back to him. "Are you sure you don't want me to cook you something?"

"I've got to go." Greg folded the paper and leaned in close to her. Instead of giving the customary peck on the lips, he kissed her deeply, took her breath away really, and then gave her a hug. She followed him out of the kitchen and to the front door like a whoop puppy. One kiss, and she was already reconsidering her early lament about leaving him.

Suddenly he turned around. That weird look still on his face. "What are you doing today? After work?"

Angelina was caught off guard. He surprised her with that question. She couldn't remember the last time he'd asked her that. "Uh, nothing until Bible Study."

"Let's have dinner. I want to make up for last week."

She shook her head. "It's my Bible Study night."

"Please. I—we should talk."

Greg looked so serious she thought no way could she pass it up, but she hated that he was being so discourteous when he knew it was Wednesday. "I'm teaching."

"Lena. Tonight. We need to talk tonight." He was so firm that she wondered what had come over him.

"Have you thought about what I—"

He cut her off and raised a hand. "I'm thinking about a lot of things. I'd like us to have a nice dinner, okay?" He kissed her again. Not as lingering as the last time, but not a peck. "I love you. Please call me when you're on the way home, and I'll meet you for dinner."

Angelina nodded. He walked out the door. She turned the lock and let her body fall against it. *I love you? Dinner in the middle of the week?* He *had* been thinking about her. Thinking about them. One moment he'd shut her out with the *Wall Street Journal,* and the next he was kissing her like they were still in college. She made the slow climb up the stairs to get dressed for her meeting and prayed the passion he'd felt toward her wouldn't wane with the passing of the day.

Chapter 34

I entered my apartment and was shocked to see all the lights on. I was a little nervous at first, but then I realized Greg had let himself in again. He was getting bold about using his key. Maybe it was time to change the locks. If Mekhi came through for me, I wouldn't be seeing Greg anymore anyway.

"*I still love you, Sammie.*" I smiled thinking about those words. They warmed my heart. Made my stomach flutter.

I called out to him as I moved through the condo. I reached into the refrigerator for a bottle of water, opened it, and downed half of it before I realized he hadn't answered me.

"Greg?" I called, entering the bedroom. I found him sitting there, but I also found a mess. My belongings, clothes, shoes, books, were strewn all over the floor. Everything had been completely ransacked. Papers were everywhere. Even my mattress looked like it had been moved. It seriously looked like a criminal investigation team had been in here looking for evidence.

"What the—?"

He stood from the club chair in the corner. I could tell he was angry, and at that second I realized—*he knew.* I dropped my water and turned to run, but Greg was faster. He leapt across the room and grabbed me by the back of my scrub shirt so tight that the collar became a noose around my neck. I gagged and choked, but he wouldn't let me go. When he did, he shoved me down on the bed like he was trying to break my back.

"Who are you?" Greg looked at me as if he were repulsed.

I was trying to catch my wind, trying to get my voice when he kicked at my feet. "I asked you a question, and I'm not going to ask again."

I was still struggling to get my voice back when Greg reached down and pulled me up by my shirt with a clenched fist. "You better talk to me now."

"What do you mean?" I wasn't sure how much he knew, and as long as he wasn't beating me, I wasn't going to play my hand against his bluff.

He dropped me on the bed again, removed a newspaper from his pocket and smacked the folded item across my face. It really stung. So much for not hitting me. I was sure to have a welt. I took the paper that had become a weapon and opened it. The *Roswell Weekly*. The paper I thought I'd avoided. There I was next to Angelina near the registration table. The photographer must have snapped that one coming in the door.

"That's me at a health fair." I shrugged, nonchalantly. "I'm a nurse."

Greg smoothed his hand over his head like he was losing patience. "You're a nurse." He chuckled, and then he leaned in real close to my face. "It seems, Samaria, you're a lot more than that." He stepped back, slowly, deliberately. The man looked like he was trying to decide what he was going to do with me. I couldn't be sure murder wasn't on the list.

"Why did you wreck my place?" I asked, still trying to play like it wasn't that serious that I was in the picture with his wife. I had to see what he really knew.

"Because." He reached into his pocket again. I threw my hands up this time to protect my face. "I wanted to make sure I knew your real name, and I was looking for something like this." He tossed a picture. I recognized it as the one Angelina had given me the night we spent at the hospital when my mother had been sick.

I was busted. I didn't say anything. I was trying like the devil to come up with a plausible reason why I would be in a picture with his wife.

"I asked my wife who the woman was in the paper this morning, and she told me Rae Burns." Greg clenched his fist. "She told me Rae was a friend from the church. A new one. One of her mentees." He moved around the room sort of pacing, but not in a back and forth fashion. I could tell his brain was racing, trying to figure it out, trying to figure me out. "When I got to my office, I watched the video of the newscast she emailed to me." He chuckled like it was funny. "The one I made the mistake of not caring about."

"Yeah, well you're certainly not going to win any husband of the year awards," I said, getting up the nerve to stand.

"Don't get smart with me." He pointed a stiff finger at my face. "I could break your neck."

"If you were going to break my neck you would have done it already."

"Don't be so sure." Greg was looking crazy. I mean sure 'nuff crazy like a rat trapped in a cage. That wasn't a good look for a man twice my size who was pissed with me, but I continued to try and work my way out of this with just the welt on my face. This place was soundproof, and I didn't know what he was capable of. But I realized I had something I could work with, Angelina didn't know anything, otherwise he wouldn't be over here trying to be sure of who I was.

I crossed my arms over themselves. "Look, I'm tired. It's been a long night."

"You think I'm playing with you?"

"No, but I know I got your trifling, cheating behind where I want it." I moved farther away from him. "I'm not going to be a problem for you, Greg. I'll leave your wife alone, but it's going to cost you."

He snatched his head back. "Going to cost me?"

"Yes, we have a money arrangement that's been a little in-sufficient to meet my needs, so I think we'll need to double your monthly checks."

The look in his eyes told me he thought I was out of my mind. He actually laughed.

"But there's one little thing," I continued. "No more booty. You can leave your key on the way out."

He laughed again. "As if I would touch your psycho . . ." He stopped. "You think you're going to blackmail me? Is that what all this little Rae Burns stuff was about?"

I crossed my arms over my chest. I wasn't giving up any details.

Greg smirked. "Look, I don't know what kind of money you had in mind, but you're not going to be able to blackmail me, because I'm telling Angelina about you."

It was me who laughed now. "You must think I'm stupid if you expect me to believe that."

Greg grabbed me by the arm and squeezed hard. "Actually, you're far stupider than I ever thought you were. And I'm not going to keep the fact that she's been stalked by my psy-chotic, obsessed piece on the side." He pushed me down on the bed, and I was glad he let my arm go. "You're not hurting my wife."

"Hurt her?" I massaged my aching elbow. "What are you talking about?"

"I listened to your message. I heard the guy talking about Angelina." He picked up the picture of me and Angelina off the bed and put it in his pocket.

What message? What was he talking about? I slid to the side of the bed and pushed the button on my machine for the one message that was there and heard Mekhi's voice.

"Hey, Sammie. Look I got somebody checking out that

woman for you, but I need to make sure you ain't got a brother involved in a murder for hire or something like that." Mekhi laughed. "Ring me back when you get in. It was good to see you today. I been missing—" I pushed the button to stop it. I'd heard enough. *Nadine. Greg thinks this is about Angelina.* "Wait a minute, Greg. That's not what you think."

Greg's face was a mask of steel, like the message had dredged up some anger he'd managed to contain. "I don't know if you're a fatal attraction or something worse, but I'm telling Angelina about you." He walked out of the bedroom.

He wouldn't tell her, would he?

"Greg," I called. "You're not going to tell her. There's no reason for that."

"Oh yeah, there is. Mr. Murder for Hire on the tape there. I'm also going to tell the police, so I can get a restraining order to keep you away from us."

He reached the door and I slid in front of it. "Wait," I said. "This is about money. Not obsession. I was trying to get paid."

"I don't want to hear anything you have to say. You're a lunatic, and this is how people get killed." Greg reached around my shoulder and peeled me off the door. He opened it, and I followed him outside.

"I'll go away, but don't tell her about us. I promise I'll never go to the church. I'll never call her again. I'll disappear." My heart pounded through every word.

I could tell he was thinking about it for a second. I knew he'd like to save his skin. He shook his head. "I can't risk it."

I grabbed his arm. "Don't tell her."

He shook his head and pushed me away.

"I'll disappear. You know how to keep a secret. You've done a pretty good job of keeping us from her."

Greg turned back and looked at me. "That's sex, not stalking." He pulled his BlackBerry out of his pocket. "I recorded the message to my phone for evidence. You stay away from my wife, or I swear, I'll see you and that thug on the phone locked up." He took the stairs two at a time, jogged to his car, got in it, and sped away.

Chapter 35

In the seventeen years that Angelina had known him, Greg rarely looked undone. Angelina wanted to get in his case about him walking in the house at darn near midnight, but she didn't even have the energy tonight. The evening, including this very moment, had been too bizarre. Greg had played with her at dinner. Hadn't consented to having a baby. Hadn't done anything really, but look crazy. He'd told her how much he loved her over and over again and ate his food. She could have gone to Bible Study for all they'd talked about. The dinner, the *I love yous*, had left the hairs standing up on the back of her neck. She sensed there was more to it all, and that same foreboding was a bell ringing in her mind's eye now. Greg looked like he'd been in a fight. Greg looked scared.

"I have to tell you something," he said. She couldn't remember the last time she'd seen him look so serious. It had been years. Hadn't been since Danielle's death that he'd looked so uncomfortable, so not himself as tonight. He left the house a few hours ago without an explanation for where he was going. Now he was standing in front of her, looking like he'd been beat down. Something or someone had shaken him up. She pulled the sheet back and threw her feet over the side of the bed. "What's going on?"

Greg dropped his body on the bed. Angelina could see beads of perspiration on his forehead. Her stomach clenched, and she clutched her hands together. "Greg," she pleaded. This time the fear she felt carried her voice to a higher octave.

"I—I don't know how to say this." He closed his eyes and moved his head in circles like he was trying to relieve tension.

Angelina didn't care about his stress. She jumped to her feet. His eyes startled open. "Say it. Whatever it is, just tell me."

He loosened his tie and avoided looking her in the eye. "I've been having an affair."

She immediately regretted pushing him. He could have saved these words for another time. Another day. Another life. Angelina felt all the air leave her body. He wouldn't have winded her more if he'd punched her in the stomach. She sat back down on the bed, Greg reached for her, and she pushed his hand away.

"It's been a few months, I mean, maybe a little more."

Hot tears filled her eyes, and Angelina felt like she wanted to throw up. *Had he said maybe more, like he wasn't sure?*

"I'm sorry. It's wrong. I've been wrong. I don't even know what I was doing, but I want you to know it didn't have anything to do with you."

She looked at him now, long and hard, before whispering, "Really?"

"It didn't. It was a thing that happened, and I didn't stop it. I let it get out of hand."

The tears were falling now. She closed her eyes tight and tried to stop the stabbing pain she felt in her heart.

"Baby, I'm so sorry. If I could go back and erase the last six months I would."

"So it's been six months." She looked at him. She showed him the pain in her eyes before reaching for a tissue on the nightstand.

Greg stood and nodded his head. "Something like that, but it's over."

Angelina suddenly felt confused. *It was over, and she hadn't caught him, so why was he—*"Why are you telling me?" she asked. "Why are you telling me now?"

Greg was silent. Way too quiet. This was bad. Really bad, and Angelina could only think of two things that would have him stupefied. Two things that would make him tell her this way.

"Have you given me some disease? Is she—is she pregnant?" The words came out in a croaked whisper. They hurt her throat as much as her heart.

Greg shook his head. "Disease? Pregnant? No, baby. I—you know I wouldn't do that."

"I know?" She chuckled. "What, are you kidding? What do I know? I don't know anything."

"Lena." He pleaded with his eyes. He was desperate and that was scary.

"Tell me why you're telling me!"

"Because, she did something—she's not who I thought she was."

"They never are." Angelina said the words slowly, venomously.

"She's not who you thought she was either." Greg's words hung in the air for a moment. Words that were so mysterious and telling at the same time, Angelina was certain this was about to get worse. *Not who I thought she was.* Sarcasm had left the building. "What are you talking about?"

"That woman in the paper this morning. Rae Burns. Her name is not Rae."

Angelina shook her head. "What are you talking about? I thought you didn't know—" And then she remembered the way he looked when she handed him the paper. How he'd seemed sick. How he'd suddenly lost his appetite. *No.*

"She's the woman I've been—" His voice broke. "She's the woman I've been involved with."

Angelina ran into the bathroom. She grabbed the toilet bowl and wretched the late night ice cream she'd eaten into the water. She felt Greg standing behind her. He touched her shoulder, attempted to comfort her, but she reached back a free hand and smacked at his legs. He grabbed her arm and pulled her to her feet. She wiped her mouth. "You low down—"

"Lena. I didn't know she was coming to the church. I didn't know you knew her. I didn't know any of this."

"So, what are you saying? She's stalking me?"

"When I saw the paper I . . . the world isn't this small. I knew something had to be going on. And the name. I know her as Samaria. Samaria Jacobs."

Angelina tried to let it sink in, but what he was telling her was the stuff B movies were made of. Then she remembered that night at the hospital. The nurse had called, "The family of Winnie Jacobs." She'd assumed Rae and her mother had different last names, for whatever reason, but an imposter? This kind of drama wasn't real. People didn't do this in real life. "Are you telling me what I'm thinking? That she sought me out. She came to the church looking for me?"

"I think so, but I don't know."

"You haven't talked to her?"

"I have."

"That's where you've been tonight? With her?" She flung a fist at him.

Greg took the blow. "I had to wait until she came home tonight from work. I checked her place to see if see if I could find anything that looked like she had ill intentions."

"You let yourself in her home? You have a key?"

Greg took a deep breath and washed his face with his hand. "I did. I did have a key. I don't have one now."

Anger was boiling. Hurt was the steam. The more she knew,

the more they both grew, but she couldn't stop now. It all had to come out tonight. "So what did she tell you she wanted?"

Greg shook his head.

Angelina rushed out of the bathroom, reached the nightstand and picked up her phone.

"What are you doing?" he asked.

"I'm calling that—"

"No." Greg took the phone from her. "Don't. I'm going to the police to get a restraining order first thing in the morning."

Angelina reached for her phone. He put it behind his back, and with all the strength she had in her body, she raised her hand and smacked him across the face. Hard. "You don't have the right to tell me not to call her. You're not the only one she betrayed!"

Greg put the phone on the bed. Angelina wanted to reach for it again, but her hand was stinging like it was on fire.

"I deserved that." He raised a hand to his reddening cheek. "But this is not about her. This is about me. Me not being faithful to you. You wouldn't have known her if it weren't for me."

Angelina shook her head. He was right.

"I don't think she's stable. She can't be, and I want you to stay away from her."

Angelina let out a sour chuckle. "There's nothing wrong with Rae except that she's as conniving—" She stopped herself. "I've spent time with her. I've talked to her."

"I have too, and I didn't see this."

Angelina sucked in her breath. "That might be because you were—" She shook her head. "You were a little busy, Greg."

He continued to stroke his red cheek. "She's turned into some kind of fatal attraction, and I'm asking you to stay away from her until I can get a restraining order, please."

Angelina sat on the bed. Greg reached for her, and she pulled away. "Stop trying to touch me," she said. "I want you to get out. Now."

Greg nodded. "I'll sleep in the guest bedroom."

"Tonight," Angelina stood to her feet. "Tomorrow I want you out of this house." She heard Greg's intake of breath, heard him say her name as she walked out of the bedroom, down the stairs, and into the powder room in the foyer. She grabbed a wad of tissues just as the first tear fell. She groaned and swallowed a knot of pain that almost choked her going down. *He was cheating. Greg was always cheating her or maybe it was life.* First her father, then Danielle, now her marriage. What had she done to deserve this stab in the back? This betrayal?

Rae had been smiling in her face, working at the church, pretending to be her mentee, and studying the Bible with her. How could that woman be so cold, so calculating, and black-hearted? And Greg; she'd held out a sliver of hope in her heart that she was wrong. That he wasn't doing this to her. But she knew better. If she'd been honest with herself, she knew when it began.

Angelina had no idea how many hours she cried. She vaguely remembered waking in the arms of her husband. Him saying how sorry he was as he carried her up the stairs, laid her in their bed, pulled the comforter over her body, and darkened the room before he left. She remembered more tears erupting from a soul that she was sure was empty of them.

She rolled over in her bed and cried some more. She cried until restless sleep came, when exhaustion pushed out the awful video that played over and over again in her mind like clips from an X-rated film. The movie featuring her husband and Rae Burns, making love.

Chapter 36

I didn't slept all night worrying about this mess I'd made. Greg was going to tell Angelina. I wanted to believe he didn't have the nerve, but the look in his eyes told me he did. My only hope was that he would punk out, decide to save himself like any man in his position would. But I knew the message from Mekhi and his joke about a murder for hire had tipped the scales some. I'd have to wait to see what happened, but I couldn't stop thinking about it. I hated that I cared so much. These people shouldn't have even mattered to me, but they did. Or at least she did.

I hated the idea of her knowing I had betrayed her that way. I hated the thought of her being hurt that I was sleeping with her husband. That anyone was. She deserved better than that. Angelina was a good person.

The locksmith I'd called handed me a key, and I practiced making sure it worked in the lock before I held a check out to him. Greg had left his key, but no telling if he'd had more than one. The last thing I wanted was to find that man waiting in my bedroom again because depending on what his wife said when he told her, he might be coming back to choke me for real.

"I appreciate the quick service."

The jaggedly older man walked through the door. "No problem. Let us know if we can service you again." He winked and closed the door behind him. I turned the lock and went to get dressed for work.

I'd done my best to clean up the mess Greg made before I lay in the bed last night. I had to admit I was a little scared to close my eyes with him being so angry. Plus I kept seeing Angelina's face. Her reactions—would she want to come over here and beat me down, or would she get on her knees and pray for me? Who knew with her? She was so holy, but I was thinking her knees weren't where she'd be going with this bit of information. It bothered me that at this very moment she might hate me because for the first time in my life, I wanted a woman to respect me. Or maybe it wasn't the first time. Maybe it was the first time I was admitting it to myself, and for the first time I'd actually had it. Her opinion really mattered.

I turned my new lock, jogged down the steps, and out to my car. Just as I turned onto the interstate, my phone rang. Mama and Mekhi's calls came within minutes of each other. Hers to say she needed some pills and to cuss me out about telling Mekhi her problem; and Mekhi's to say he was in New York getting a supply for her. I wondered why he couldn't buy the stuff here, but he said he couldn't answer that on the phone. All he would say was everything was cheaper in bulk and closer to the source. So I had to conclude that meant they made oxycontin up north, and it didn't cost as much. I was impressed that the man had gotten on a plane for me. I was worried about how he would get it back to Atlanta.

We talked for the entire ride from Roswell to the hospital in downtown. Talked until my phone darn near ran out of battery. Hearing his voice made me feel giddy, like a stupid teenager in love. Like the stupid teenager I was once upon a time.

Mekhi said he wasn't going to be back until late tomorrow, which meant I was going to have to steal one more time because Mama would be climbing the walls and roaming the streets by midday tomorrow. Since I was temporarily back to

being her supplier, I had to get her at least two more pills to
tide her over.

When I arrived at work, I found I was in luck. Nadine and
I were the only RNs on the floor until seven P.M., and she
preferred to do patient care rather than pass meds. We had
four new admissions from surgery. All taking OX. I reached
into my pocket and felt around for the aspirin I'd brought
with me. Since Nadine liked to see pills go in the sink, I had
some to substitute for the drugs I was going to steal. I smiled
to myself. This one last time would be a breeze.

My phone had an insistent beep. I looked and found I'd
had seven missed calls from Mekhi and one from Angelina.
Just as I was getting onto the elevator it rang again. It showed
Mekhi's number, so I answered. "Hey, you really trying to get
me—"

He cut me off. "You got anything on you?"

The elevator doors closed and the signal became really bad.

"Sammie—" Crackle, crackle. "If you got anything on you,
get rid—"

I couldn't make out what he was saying. "Mekhi, let me
call you when I get to the car. I need to plug my phone in the
charger."

"No, Sammie—Nadine—wait!" I heard him yell right before
my battery went dead. The hairs on the back of my neck stood
up. He'd said Nadine. I guess his friend had found something
out about her. I couldn't wait to get to the car and call him
back to find out what.

The elevator stopped at the lower level. When they opened
things seemed to be happening in slow motion. Nadine and
two men with jackets that had the letters G.A. DEA on
them were standing at the opening. I cursed and tried to push

the close door button, but Nadine put her body against the elevator sensor and stepped inside. One of the men grabbed my hand and Nadine grabbed the other. Nadine removed handcuffs from her jacket. She smiled the most sinister and satisfied grin I'd seen in a long time. She slapped the cuffs on my wrist and said, "Samaria Jacobs, you are under arrest for felony theft."

Chapter 37

Slam! The bars closed, and another woman stepped into the hole that had become my home. Girlfriend didn't have that deer caught in the headlights look in her eye. She didn't even do the customary scan of the occupants of the cell, which meant she was familiar with this joint. I gathered from the tacky way she was dressed, her frequent visits were for prostitution.

The only seat that was available was next to me, so down she plopped, bringing with her a stench that was dying to wash down a drain somewhere. I let out a deep breath and scooted away from her. *Lord, if I don't get out of here soon, I'm going to lose my mind.*

It had been almost sixteen hours since they'd bought me in. I had a bail hearing facilitated by the ridiculously stupid public defender. I winced at the thought that I would be headed to the county lockup in another few hours if I didn't make bail, and winced again because I knew there was no hope of that. Mekhi was in New Jersey. Ebony was judgmental and broke. My mama was broker and out of drugs. There was no one else in my world. Not anyone that really cared about me.

Tears stung like tiny chards of glass behind my eyelids. I was twenty-seven years old, and honestly I had no one who would get me out of jail. It was a good thing I had reconnected with Mekhi, otherwise I'd be locked up until my court date. He'd come get me. *Wouldn't he?* I pushed out the voice in my head that said he would not. Mekhi was older, wiser, and his butt wasn't on the line this time. He'd come through. My stomach flipped. I felt sick and stupid. What was I doing? Having faith? Hoping? Believing in a man again? Was that what I was supposed to do? Oh God, what was I even supposed to be thinking? I was so confused. I didn't know.

I looked across the cell at the other two nurses who'd been arrested last night. We three were the last of the group still in jail. There had been six of us, easy to pick out because we were dressed in scrubs from our night's work. Two had been bailed out, and one had been taken to medical for a fake asthma or panic attack; some crap she did to get out of central holding. In any event, that had been earlier this morning, and the drama queen hadn't come back. My eyes locked with one of them, and she quickly cut hers away. We had no solidarity. I'm sure we were stealing for different reasons, mainly because she looked like a user. I wondered if she would be charged with the same thing as I would since my drug test had come back clean.

"I don't think a negative drug test is a good thing in this type of case," my lawyer said blowing his scarlet red nose. "I'll have to look it up, but I'm certain being addicted to the medicine lends itself toward some leniency. With no history of abuse, you appear to be another drug dealer."

Drug dealer? I wasn't selling anything. I made no profit from my theft, but drug enforcement saw it different. I was actually going to be charged with a crime I hadn't committed.

Nadine was a Georgia DEA agent in the diversion control unit. Those were the folks that came after doctors, nurses, and pharmacists. I was sure that's what Mekhi was trying to tell me in the seconds when I'd heard him yell her name. I'd walked right into her trap. My instincts had tried to warn me who she was.

The story of the arrest played on the guard's television in the hall at least four times throughout the day. With each broadcast, they announced the names of the five nurses who'd been arrested by the undercover team who'd busted up a ring of drug thieves on one of the floors of the hospital. The sixth nurse, Samaria Jacobs had been a bonus. "We were about to make arrest in the other cases when pharmacy alerted us of a high amount of waste on one of the other floors. So we delayed those arrests in order to continue our investigation," a representative from the DEA was saying. It wasn't Nadine, but I could imagine that bucked tooth heifer sitting around somewhere enjoying her success; enjoying looking at the pictures of all of us that were no doubt shown each time they read the list of our names.

Greg, Angelina, my neighbors, and everyone in White Gardens knew I was locked down. Last weekend, I was on the news being celebrated as Rae Burns. Now I was being laughed at as Samaria Jacobs. People probably thought I was addicted to the stuff. Not the folks in White Gardens, but Angelina, Greg, my coworkers, and neighbors. The people in White Gardens knew I was stealing for June. Once they stopped pointing fingers and saying, "Dang that's messed up," some of them might actually appreciate the fact that I was trying to do the right thing. In the hood, all you had was family and taking care of your own brought much respect. That respect, however, only reached as far as the broke down gates. It wasn't going to help me now.

I let my head fall back against the concrete wall and fought to keep tears from falling. I was out of a job, definitely wouldn't have a nursing license, and would probably eventually be going to jail. All this crap over a few oxycontin pills. If I weren't so cheap, I could have bought the things on the street or even doctor shopped for a prescription like most addicts did. I hadn't made time. Stealing was easier and faster. Stealing came second nature to me.

"Jacobs, you made bail." A guard yelled through the bars.

I jumped up. My arm was still sore from the brawl I'd had with another woman they called Big Tina. Last night Big Tina wanted my seat. I preferred not to sit on the floor. Big Tina had won.

I was never so glad to see a set of keys as the ones the guard pulled out to open the lock. I stepped through, and although I knew I was in the same space, the air that had been choking me suddenly felt clean and fresh.

"This way," he grunted, and I followed close enough to count the razor bumps on the back of his neck. He led me to a desk, offered my name to the sergeant behind it, and made the slow stroll back to the cage he'd taken me from.

I looked to the left and right, but I didn't see my mother, or anyone else I knew. "Who paid my bail?" The sergeant at the desk returned my personal items to me and had me sign for them. "My bail, who paid it?"

He didn't answer. Just nodded toward the entrance that was now to be my exit. I took a deep breath, pushed the revolving door, stepped in, and did the twirl around. I was momentarily blinded by the sunlight's reflection off a copper Lexus that was parked in a lot across from the station.

"I drove as fast as I could." His voice came from the left of me. "I know I'm about eight years late."

I turned and looked at Mekhi, the only man I'd ever loved, the only one who'd ever loved me. "You have no idea how on time you are." I walked toward him, reached up and put a hand on the side of his face.

"I was young. I should have been there for you years ago.

If you don't want to be with me, I can accept that, but I need you to forgive me. I mean, we been shorties since we were eight, I don't want the past—"

I put my finger against his lips. "Do you have my mother's stuff?"

"Yeah, that's why I had to drive—"

"Then you came through." I pulled his head down and he drew my body to his. Pain shot through my arm before our lips met, and I pulled away. "Ouch," I winced.

Mekhi's eyes asked the question.

"Don't ask 'cause I'm too embarrassed to tell you how I got my butt beat last night."

Mekhi rubbed my arm where it was sore. "Some big girl whupped ya' behind. Dang, baby, I didn't think you'd get a beat down so fast." He chuckled. "I got a suite up at the Ritz. Thought you might need the luxury after being in holding. I already hooked up ya' moms so we can go straight there."

I shook my head. Greg and countless other men had taken me to the Ritz Carlton. I didn't want to be reminded of that. "Is it too late to cancel it?"

Mekhi looked confused.

"You spent a bunch of money on my mother's stuff. You bailed me out of jail. Now I don't know what you doing to make your money—"

"Ask me," Mekhi said. His eyes burrowed into mine with an intensity that almost knocked me back a few steps. "I've been waiting for you to care about what I do."

I hesitated. I'd been fighting the caring. I swallowed and let fear hit the bottom of my empty stomach. "How do you make your money, Khi?"

Those dimples I loved and missed so much stretched down both sides of this face. "Music, baby. I've got my own record label. I signed Benxi a few months ago and got a great distribution deal because of her."

"Record label." I was having a hard time taking in what he was saying. "Benxi with three Grammy's Benxi? What—how did you get her?"

"She likes my music. I write, produce—I do it all. I pitched her at the airport in Miami after a party Coco Records held last year." Mekhi smiled. "Little did she know I followed her to the airport. I didn't have no plane to catch. I paid nine hundred dollars for that ticket to Atlanta just to get those five minutes with her." I nodded. I was impressed, but not surprised. Mekhi could sell shoes to somebody with no feet. "Anyway, she fell out with Coco about the direction her music was going. She wanted something different and called me." Mekhi stroked his chin. "I was making good money selling my CDs underground, but not the kind of money I'm going to be making now. Airamas Productions is running with the big boys. My CDs are going to be in all the stores."

"Airamas." I didn't like it. "Where did you get that?"

Mekhi chuckled. "I named it after this hot shortie I been digging."

I raised an eyebrow and he laughed. "It's Samaria spelled backward, girl."

My heart thumped.

"I'll tell you more about it when we get to the Ritz."

I shook my head. "I don't want to go to the Ritz, Khi. I've got a paid for bed right up the highway, so cancel the room and let's go to my place."

Mekhi was shocked, noticeably. "But the Jacuzzi."

"I have one of those." I winked, and then I got serious. "I'm not making any promises. I have a lot to think about, Mekhi. We're friends right now."

"That's where we started a long time ago." He nodded. "I'm a patient man. I been waiting for that kiss I almost got for eight years. A little more time ain't gonna kill me. "

I blinked against tears. He had been waiting for me for eight years. Maybe not alone all the time, but in his heart, he'd wanted me. The real me. That felt good. I smiled, slipped my hand into his, and we walked to his car. I couldn't wait to hear more about Airamas Productions.

Chapter 38

"I told you that wretched woman was a low life." Angelina thought the satisfaction in Carol's voice was almost palatable, even over the telephone. "And to think she was using a phony name. I wonder what she was planning to steal from the church."

Angelina reached across the bed to her nightstand and picked up the juice she'd let grow warm. Her head was pounding. The aspirin she'd taken an hour ago had done nothing to relieve the pain. This was why she'd stayed in all weekend. Avoided church even. She didn't want to deal with "I told you so."

"What do you think?"

"I'm really upset about Rae or Samaria. Whatever her name is. I don't want to speculate or gossip about it. So if you don't mind."

"Oh, come on. Don't go getting all holier-than-thou on me. You were wrong about her, and now it's time to admit it," Carol said. "I tried to tell you she was a hoochie."

Angelina laughed bitterly. Not because anything was funny, but because Carol only knew half the story. She knew she was a fraud, and a thief, possibly a drug addict or dealer, but she had no idea how deep it all went.

Angelina heard her cell phone vibrate. She hoped it wasn't another text message or plea from Greg because she was sick of him already. She picked up the phone and saw that it was a local DYFS phone number on the LCD screen.

"Carol, I have to go." Angelina hung up without saying good-bye. Then she pushed talk on her cell. "Hello, Angelina Preston."

"Hi, Angelina. This is Debbie Burgess, Katrice's case manager. I called the office and was advised you were out on sick leave today, but you told me to keep you posted on Katrice."

Unconsciously, she sat up. The pain in her head intensified with the jolt. "What's wrong?"

"Her foster mother, Mrs. Henry, was in a car accident today. She's in the hospital. She'll probably be there for a few days. The husband is feeling overwhelmed about having to care for his own children, so I have to take Katrice into respite care."

"No, don't." Angelina said the words so fast she wasn't sure they'd come out of her mouth. When the caseworker didn't respond on the other end, she repeated herself. "I . . . I'll take her. I don't want her to have to adjust to a new home. She won't understand that it's temporary."

"Okay . . . if you're sure?"

"I'm positive. Is she at daycare?"

"Yes," Debbie said. In that one word, Angelina recognized joy in the woman's voice. She was probably relieved she didn't have to find a respite home.

"Call and let them know I'll be picking her up. It'll give me a few hours to rest a little."

"Will do," Debbie replied. "And Angelina, thanks. That's one less child I have to worry about tonight. Feel better."

They said their good-byes and Angelina lay back on the pillow. She felt guilty. Her first thought was the case worker wouldn't want the work involved in moving Katrice, and here the woman was concerned about the child. Like she should be. Maybe there was hope for the agency after all.

She closed her eyelids and whispered a prayer to shake the

headache. If she weren't emotionally together, she wanted to at least be physically ready for her new houseguest. She pulled the comforter around herself, turned the television and her cell phone off. She'd sleep a few hours without the intrusion of text messages from Greg. She'd also sleep a few hours without seeing Rae's face plastered all over the television news. She hoped she'd sleep a few hours without imagining them together in bed.

"Ms. Angelina!" Katrice ran to her, smiling and arms opened. She latched onto Angelina's leg and squeezed like she was holding on to a tree during a twister.

"Hi, baby." Angelina reached down and picked her up. The daycare teacher handed her a jacket and bid them both a goodnight.

Angelina fastened Katrice in the staff car seat and climbed in the front of the SUV. Although her headache was only slightly less intense, she was feeling better just having the ray of sunshine that was Katrice's spirit in her presence. Katrice would fill her home with giggles. Katrice would fill her time. Katrice would help her to not feel sorry for herself. She needed Katrice more than Katrice needed her.

"I hungry," Katrice announced.

"Okay, we're going to get pizza."

"Yeah! Pizza! Pizza!" Katrice's screams echoed in the space between them. She began to sing the word pizza in a song.

Angelina pulled the car out of the driveway and reached for her cell phone. Felesia was back in the country and joining them for dinner, but she'd told Angelina she couldn't walk out of her office a second before necessary because of a huge mess at one of the plants, so Angelina was to call her when they were fairly close to the restaurant.

Angelina dialed and waited until she heard the line stop ringing. Felesia spoke before she could say hello. "Girl, I'm sorry. Got a last minute call from my boss. You know he's in the Dominican working through our manufacturing problems. I have to hang around in case he needs some information from the files."

"That's fine." Angelina maneuvered the vehicle though traffic. Stop by the house if you feel like it later. I'm sure we'll be up.

"Greg still calling?" Felesia's disgust was apparent in the rapid fire with which the words came out.

"No, he hasn't since this morning. I'm sure he's trying to let me cool off."

"Yeah," Felesia said. "Take your time. Do what's best for you, and uh, I hate to bring this up, but you might need to get an STD test. You never know what that woman might have been into with this drug thing. And you know how stupid men are about condoms."

Angelina nodded. That hadn't occurred to her. But of course, Felesia was right.

"I don't mean to add to the stress. Just loving you, okay?"

"Okay, thanks."

"We'll talk later."

They ended the call. Some of the stress Katrice's smile had taken away had returned. Angelina hadn't even thought about the possibility of disease. She was really, really going to let Greg have it the next time she talked to him. Men. Always thinking with the wrong head. He could have picked up more from that tramp than he'd planned on getting and given it to her.

She and Katrice entered the house a little after seven P.M.

They'd had to stop at the mall because Angelina realized she didn't have anything for the child to sleep in or wear tomorrow. They hit the *Disney Store* and *The Children's Place*, and Angelina shopped until she'd purchased the girl an entire new wardrobe. She even bought some toys and movies. The more she spent on Katrice, the smaller the hole in her heart became. At least until she re-entered her home, then memories of Greg and his betrayal came rushing back.

"TV," Katrice pointed to the flat screen in the family room.

"Let's take a bath first," Angelina replied, reaching for the bag that included sleepwear. She hated the idea of putting pajamas on her without washing them first, but it was late, Katrice's bedtime was around the corner, and she was worn out herself.

They ascended the stairs, and Angelina ran a tub of water while Katrice undressed.

"Where's Mr. Greg?" Katrice asked, putting her clothes in the hamper that was in the corner of the bathroom. It always amazed and saddened Angelina how mature foster children could be. At three, Katrice knew to not leave her things on the floor. Neatness was expected from them when foster parents wouldn't always demand it of their own children.

"Mr. Greg," she paused, thinking of the best thing to tell her. "He'll be working for a few days. I don't think you'll see him this time."

The child seemed to understand. She climbed her small body over the side of the tub and slid down into the bubble bath Angelina had run with strawberry scented bath gel she'd picked up at one of the stores. Angelina let her play in the water until her heart was content. Then she dried her, moisturized her skin, and took the sleepy child into the guest bedroom. Two books later, Katrice she fell off to sleep. Angelina held the girl for a long time before she laid her down. She thought about how alone in the world Katrice was. She had a drug addict for a mother, an unknown father, no grandparents, and a deceased sister. So sad. Angelina's heart broke for her.

Then she considered the fact that the hospital drug bust story had its upside. It was a bigger scandal than the child death. The bigger, better story she'd been waiting to come along had finally broken. Angelina hated that it had to hit so close to home. "Be careful what you wish for," she whispered, and Katrice stirred.

She stood, placed the girl in the bed and left the door open so the light from the hall would enter in case Katrice was afraid of the dark. She'd have to remember to get a night light tomorrow. Maybe she'd redecorate the entire room and make it fit for the princess who slept in it. So what if it were temporary, it was only money. Greg's money. If he could spend it on his tramp, she could certainly spend it on Katrice. She descended the stairs and reached the bottom just as the doorbell rang.

She ignored it, surmising it had to be Greg, and if she didn't answer, he would use his key. Change the locks; that was another thing she'd have to do tomorrow. When the door didn't open and her cell phone rang showing Felesia's number, she realized with great relief that it was her friend. She rushed to open the door.

"Hey, Mami." Felesia reached for her neck and gave her a tight hug. She raised a small gold paper bag and jiggled it. "I got Godiva. We gonna chase those blues away."

Angelina smiled.

"It looks like you broke the bank getting Katrice settled in." They'd made cups of tea and settled on the sofa in the family room. Katrice's new toys and movies were still in bags, but anyone could see it was going to feel like Christmas in the morning. "How long is she going to be here?"

Angelina took a sip from her mug. She deemed it too hot and placed it on the coaster in front of her. "A week, maybe more if her foster mother needs more time."

Felesia nodded. "This is a first."

"What?"

"You've never brought a child home before. You've been in this business a long time."

"She's special."

"I gather that," Felesia replied. She took a tentative sip from her mug. "Why is she special?"

Angelina took a deep breath and released it. "The truth?"

Felesia's look said the words, "of course" without her having to open her mouth.

Angelina didn't avoid her friend's eyes when she said, "She reminds me of Danielle. In a good way. I want to treat her the way I'd want someone to treat my baby if she were motherless."

Felesia nodded and continued to blow and sip. "You're sure this is okay, right? I mean, the way you feel about her isn't unhealthy?"

"I'm fine." Angelina gave her friend a reassuring smile and patted her knee. "Besides, maybe I'll keep her."

Felesia's eyes bugged and Angelina laughed. "Girl, I'm kidding. Right now anyway. All I know is she needed a place to go, and I need the distraction." She slid down on the floor and pulled a bag open to remove a Barbie Dollhouse. "This is going to take some putting together."

"I hate doing that stuff." Felesia grimaced. "You want me to send my handyman over tomorrow? He's good at working on houses."

Angelina chuckled and stood the dollhouse box upright. "I think I can handle it."

"You want me to hang out over here a few days?" Felesia's voice had taken on a serious tone.

"No. You're busy at work. I'll be fine. Trust me, a little one can be great company."

"Let me know. I'll get my gear and get in one of those overdone rooms upstairs." They both laughed.

"Speaking of which, I think I'm going to redecorate Katrice's room tomorrow while she's at daycare."

A cloud of concern spread over Felesia's face again.

"I'm not going to change it into Cinderella's castle or anything. I'm going to lighten up the colors and get rid of the Baroque. That room is so grown up. I want to make her comfortable. I'm surprised she didn't have nightmares in there with all those tassels hanging down around her.

"I suppose the Knights of Arabia could be tough on a kid."

Angelina laughed. "Plus it felt good to shop today. It anesthetized some pain. I needed the pain killer."

"I'm so angry with that Greg. I can't believe he would do this. And that woman. What a low down, sneaky thing to come up in the church like that. What did she have planned?"

"I don't know." Angelina pulled at the sides and popped open the box.

"You might need to get a restraining order. I mean, is she crazy?"

"I think she's in jail."

"She's probably got men all over town. Somebody is going to bail her out. Watch your back."

"Girl, if I see Rae . . . I mean, Samaria, the only person that's going to need help is her. I've got a New Jersey butt whuppin' with her name all over it."

"I know that's right." Felesia laughed. The two women fist bumped. "I wish we could whup that trick together."

Angelina gasped. "You did not say trick?"

"Yes, I did, and I meant it. That's what women like her are."

Angelina shook her head. "I don't know; I mean, what she did was bizarre, really over the top. I want to be angrier at her, but I can't even think about her right now. I'm too mad at Greg. I've known Rae or Samaria for a less than two months. I've been married to Greg for almost fourteen years."

"Aye, chica." Felesia nodded. "I know what you mean. You know, I know. My ex still can't keep his pants up."

They sat there not speaking until they finished their tea. Felesia broke the silence. "I can almost hear those wheels turning in your head. What you thinking about doing?"

Angelina fought to keep tears from coming to her eyes again. She swallowed and looked Felesia in the eyes. "I think I want a divorce."

Felesia nodded. "It's early yet. Maybe you guys can go do counseling. You never really did get over Danielle."

Angelina snatched her head back. "What do you mean I never got over Danielle? You don't get over losing a child."

"I don't mean you. I mean your marriage, Mami. As a couple. You guys didn't get any help. You need to heal the damage to the marriage. You have to do that together."

Angelina couldn't imagine doing anything with Greg right now. Not counseling. Not talking. Not even looking at him. "I don't know, Fee. It might be too late."

"It's never too late with Jesus," Felesia said. "And He shows up in the nick of time to fix things that need fixing, right? If you guys didn't need something supernatural, then you wouldn't need God."

Angelina nodded, absorbed the words, but didn't respond.

"It's a test, Mami. We all have them. Just try not to lean to your own understanding, okay?"

Angelina nodded, but she wasn't sure if she even heard Felesia. Greg and Samaria in bed for six months. Greg was greedy. Not like he'd even stopped making love with her. *How could he. How could he do that?*

"Angelina," Felesia's voice broke through. "You hear me, chica. Don't act hasty. You guys try counseling. I have a feeling Greg will be willing to do anything you want at this point."

Maybe, she thought, but she also thought it was too late. Any effort he'd make to reconcile would be too little and too late for her. He'd gone too far this time, and she couldn't see trusting him with her heart anymore.

Chapter 39

Greg stood in the foyer. He hung his head like the beat dog he was. The strong angle of the jaw that she'd always loved, always thought added to his masculinity, was now a part of the sorrowful frown that encapsulated this handsome face.

"I asked you to give me time," Angelina said in response to his question. The one she'd been avoiding hearing. *Baby, when are you going to let me come home?* "This is not what I call time."

"It's been weeks," he begged. "I miss you. Please, Lena. Let me make this up to you."

She shook her head. Shook away the image of Samaria and him in bed. "I don't know that you can."

"Thirteen years. We have too much history to let Samaria come between us."

"You put her between us."

"I know, and please don't think I'll ever forgive myself, but honey, I love you. I don't even know what I was doing with her."

Angelina held up a hand to stop his words. "You were having sex. Probably good sex. I'm thinking better sex than you have with your wife, or it wouldn't have gone on so long." It hurt to say that. It was like she'd stabbed herself with a knife, but she wanted to get in every jab that she could. She wanted him to know what she was thinking. What she was feeling.

"Don't do that." Greg's voice changed. It was deeper now.

She could hear his pain. "Don't compare yourself to her. Please don't." He hung his head again.

Angelina dropped her arms to her side. She opened her hands and closed them into fists over and over again. All the pain she'd been trying to hold in was coming out now. Coming out of her pores and her ears and her mouth. Every orifice in her body was leaking the anguish she'd bottled up in her busyness. Busy with Katrice, busy at work, and even busy at church. She hadn't stopped to think about the pain she'd been pushing deep into her belly until she looked into her husband's eyes. They were tired, swollen eyes. Eyes she hadn't seen since their daughter died. *Had he been crying?*

"I don't know what's going to happen with us." Tears fell down her cheeks. "But I know nothing's going to happen right now."

Greg reached for her. She pushed him away. He reached again, this time grabbing her and pulling her closer to him. "Please, Lena. I swear to God, I love you." His voice was hoarse, raspy, and desperate. "Let me come home. I'll spend the rest of my life making it up to you. I'll go see Dr. Luke. I'll do whatever you want to do."

She allowed him to hold her as she cried. She alternated between holding him tight and pummeling him with angry fists as the visions of him and Samaria moved in and out of her mind. She wanted to forgive him. She wanted to so badly, but the pain was too fresh. The hurt was too great. Still she felt something tingle inside of her. *Desire.* She wanted him to make love to her. To prove she was more woman than Samaria. That was crazy. Angered by her attraction to him, she pushed her body away from his and wiped her face with the back of her hand. It took her a minute to pull herself together. When she spoke her voice cracked. "Get out."

"Lena."

"Get out," she repeated the words louder this time. "Just get out."

He moved away from her, slowly making backward steps to the door. He stopped, turned, and stood at it for a long time. Like he wasn't sure how to leave. Angelina looked away from his back. She fought the voice in her spirit that wanted to tell him, *It's okay. Stay. Love me.* She fought the simmering in her blood that wanted him to take her upstairs and make her forget the entire world. Greg was capable, when motivated. She knew that. She swallowed her uncertainty. Samaria's face in her mind helped with that. "Get out," she whispered.

He reached for the door knob, looked back and faced her like he was going to say one more thing. Angelina closed her eyes, turned on her heels and headed toward the powder room. She yelled over her shoulder, "Lock it on the way out." She closed the door, turned on the faucet and splashed cold water on her swollen face. It took awhile, minutes she was certain, but then she heard the unmistakable click of the dead bolt in the distance.

Chapter 40

Angelina wouldn't take my calls, and the selfish girl that I was—I wanted closure. For some reason I thought I deserved it. So I sat on a bench at the bus-stop outside of *Shine and Swing Hair Salon* waiting for her to come out. Waiting for her, because she was never ever going to return one of my calls.

I knew this crap was risky, because true to his word, Greg had gotten a restraining order. If I broke the law, my bail would be revoked, and I'd go back to jail. So even though I knew this wasn't a good idea, I had to talk to her. It was like I couldn't go another day without getting some things off my chest.

This obsession of mine was riskier still, because although I grew up in the hood, and I've had a fight or three or four in my life, I could get a beat down. Real anger trumps experience any day of the week. Even Mike Tyson knew that. Angelina Preston was the angry one in this situation, so I was at a disadvantage.

I noted expensive shoes clicking on the pavement before I heard a voice and turned to see Angelina and Katrice. I looked into Angelina's eyes. Then I looked into Katrice's. "Your hair is pretty," I said to the little girl. Katrice blushed and pressed her body against Angelina's leg. Shirley Temple curls bounced as she moved.

Angelina took Katrice's hand, walked to her SUV, and put the girl in the car seat. After she let the windows down, she returned to where I was sitting, where I had held a sixty second prayer vigil that she wouldn't get in the car and drive away.

"Still stalking me?" Angelina asked, approaching the bench. Her hair was freshly laid, her attire, casual. That was a look I'd rarely seen on Angelina. Even her casual wear was designer—I recognized the outfit as Betsey Johnson. With everything she was going through, she was a fashion force to be reckoned with. Not that I expected she wouldn't be. I'd underestimated her from the beginning. I'd been way out of my league. You don't win against a woman like Angelina.

"You still have her." I nodded in the direction of the SUV.

"She's staying with me," Angelina replied. "I'm her permanent foster mother. I want to adopt her."

I nodded. That was great news. News I might have celebrated with her if it had been before everything happened. I noticed she hadn't said "we" want to adopt her. I didn't have the nerve to ask about Greg. I swallowed a knot of emotion in my throat. "I saw on the news that the investigation into her sister's death is complete. They're saying DFYS is ready to settle the lawsuit out of court."

Angelina's lips formed a tight thin line. "You have something to tell me that I don't already know?"

I let out a breath. This was the moment I'd been waiting for. My last chance to have my say. "I need to explain." I slid to the far end of the bench, hoped and prayed she'd sit down. To my surprise she did. I raised my eyes to hers. I opened my mouth to speak, but before I could get the words out, she asked me a question.

"Were you planning to hurt me?"

"No." I shook my head. "I wanted Greg's money, so I was scheming on you. I wasn't even really expecting to get that close when I came to the church, but then you had that mentor thing."

"And it worked right in with your plan." She cocked her head to side, and the length of her hair billowed in the breeze.

I nodded. "I expected to find someone I wouldn't like. Someone I wouldn't feel guilty about ruining. I didn't expect you to be so good to me."

Angelina didn't say anything. She just stared at me, her anger not abating, not for a second.

"I've never had a friend before." My voice cracked. It sounded so small. "Never." I shook my head like the addicts I'd seen in White Gardens when they were trying to hustle up money. They moved too fast. They were too desperate for you to listen. I was desperate. I wanted her to hear me. "My whole life women haven't trusted me. Didn't want to be around me."

"Well, Samaria, look at me. I trusted you. You're your own self-fulfilling prophecy."

She was right about that. I didn't have words to combat it, so I kept going with the words in my heart. "Growing up in the hood with a mother like mine can be hard on your self-esteem. I've always felt like I was less than, you know. Like people saw me as this low-life because of where I came from. But you—you were different. You treated me better, even when your friends at the church were turning their noses up."

My eyes burned with tears. I tried to keep them from coming out because I didn't think she'd want to see them. I didn't want her to think I was putting on an act, but I couldn't keep them back. I wiped the salt off my mouth and kept speaking. "I have loved talking to you. Learning about the Bible from you. Having you treat me like an equal. Like I was good enough to be around you."

"But even after that you continued to sleep with my husband."

Her words sliced me in half. "Not really."

Angelina tilted her head. "Not really?"

I was so ashamed. Ashamed especially of that last night with Greg. I could have said no. Larger tears spilled down my cheeks. "I mean—I didn't really want to, but I didn't have a plan B."

Angelina stood. She shook her head and looked up at the sky.

"About Greg." The words came out just above a whisper.

Angelina looked down at me now. Looked like she couldn't believe I was going there. I knew I didn't have the right to, but I owed her. "You remember that night at the hospital when you talked to me about Mekhi. You said you knew that he hurt me, but he loved me and maybe I should try to forgive him."

She didn't say anything. Didn't move. She was taut like stretched rubber band, waiting for my next words. "He never talked about you. I mean . . . Greg isn't the first married man I've been with," I said with shame. "And they all kind of talk, even if it's a little; they complain about their wives. He never did that." I shook my head and swallowed. "Never. So what I'm trying to say is, I don't know why he was with me, but I think maybe it had nothing to do with me and nothing to do with you. I don't know a whole lot about relationships, but I think Greg really loves you. Just remember what you told me about Mekhi."

Angelina stood there for a long time. Maybe a minute just staring at nothing in particular. The light breeze gently moved her hair in a cascade of ribbon. Her makeup was flawless, her clothes, her stance. She was the woman I wanted to be when I grew up. I realized looking at her in that moment that *who* she was wasn't about money and it wasn't about clothes. It wasn't about who she was married to. It was about who she was on the inside. I wanted to say something. I wanted to tell her that I appreciated all the things she'd taught me. I had been too choked up to find words, and just when I was getting it together to speak, Angelina came out of her trance. She had some words for me, and she let me have them.

"Rae—Samaria, whatever your name is. You are a home-wrecking, backstabbing, tramp. I'm not going to make you feel better about what you've done. I'm not going to tell you I forgive you, and I'm not going to tell you any of it is okay." She walked to her car.

I heard the words. Felt them prick my heart, but I still couldn't let her leave this way. "Wait," I yelled and followed.

She pulled the car door open, looked at Katrice, then at me. "What do you want?" Her teeth were grit so tight, I thought I might get my butt whop after all. She had run out of patience.

"I want you to understand." I made a fist and banged it on the passenger side door. Angelina's eyes cut to Katrice, and then back at me. "I'm sorry," I whispered.

Angelina shook her head incredulously. "I do understand, Samaria. I understand that I was wrong about you. Now I never want to see you again. Please don't make me involve the police. I believe you're already in enough trouble." She climbed in, started the vehicle, and pulled away.

I returned to the bench and stayed there a long time; thinking about my life. Thinking about my choices. It wasn't Angelina who needed to understand. It was me. I didn't get it. Mekhi warned me that I might do something that I needed to be forgiven for. He was trying to warn me about the karma or the cycle of what comes around, goes around, and I hadn't heard him. I hadn't thought I'd ever love anyone enough to care, but I was wrong. I'd never been more wrong in my life. That woman had been my friend. I'd hurt her in the worst way possible, and I wanted her to forgive me.

Chapter 41

Angelina climbed into her bed and turned off the lamp on the bedside table. She lay flat staring at the ceiling above her. She refused to look at Greg's empty side of the bed, because she wasn't going to cry tonight. She wasn't going to let her mess of a marriage ruin the happiness she felt over today's events. She closed her eyes, rolled over on her right side, and pretended his space wasn't behind her.

Today had been a good day. The lawsuit against the DYFS had been settled out of court. The agency had taken the first steps toward severing the rights of Katrice's mother. It would be an easy termination. The woman had already told the caseworker she didn't want the girl. Although Angelina had not attended the settlement meeting today, she could just imagine Katrice's mother walking out of the director's office with her lawyers and her big check. Robin had been dead for months now, and she'd had one visit with Katrice. That alone would help with the termination of parental rights petition.

"Her loss, my gain," Angelina whispered in the darkness. That wonderful child that God had bought into her life would be hers to love, and she needed that. God knew she needed to love and be loved by someone.

She'd be a better mother than a drug addict could ever be. Too bad she wasn't offering the child a two-parent home. She thought about Greg. Thought about the meeting she'd been sitting in when media was snapping pictures of Katrice's mother. The meeting with a different type of attorney, where she'd uttered words she'd never thought she'd say. "I want a divorce from my husband."

She pulled the comforter tighter and pressed her head into the pillow beneath her. She refused to let the tears she was fighting come forth. She wasn't going to grieve over her marriage one more night.

"*Angelina, I love you.*" Those were the lone words Greg had left as a message on her voicemail this evening. Those words had been moving through her soul for weeks.

The telephone rang, and the digital caller ID showed Greg's cell phone number. *Talk about timing*, she mused. He was thinking about her too. She didn't believe in karma, but she couldn't deny the timing of his call felt like some type of divine connection, so instead of ignoring the phone, she reached for it.

Greg didn't say hello. He didn't start off asking her how she was and follow with a homily about how he missed her. He asked her one question. One that surprised her because it was the question she'd asked herself just today. "If it weren't Samaria, if it hadn't been someone you'd known—could we work past this?" Greg's voice was huskier than normal. She recognized pain in its tenor.

Angelina sat up, looked at his side of the bed. She let her loss envelope her for a few seconds, then she swallowed and spoke. "It was Samaria. I don't know how to think about it another way."

"Try, Lena," he whispered. "I'm sorry it was someone you knew. I'm sorry it was someone at all, but please try to move past her." He paused for a moment before saying the words she knew were coming next. "I love you."

She shook her head. Gasped for her breath and pushed the END button on the phone. *I love you.* The words reverberated in her mind and in her soul, but Angelina didn't want to receive them. She didn't trust that he meant them. Greg had cheated on her before. What kind of fool would forgive him again? The marriage was over. She closed her heart, closed her spirit, closed her eyes, and fell asleep.

Chapter 42

I walked up the center aisle of *New Mercies Christian Church* with one goal in mind. I was going to give my wretched life to Christ. I didn't know what drove me here. Why I'd chosen this tiny little storefront church with mismatched chairs that was badly in need of new carpet. I got dressed this morning and drove until something in my heart said stop. I also didn't know if I was really converted, or if I were here out of fear and humiliation. Fear that I was going to go to prison. Fear that my mother was going to kill herself with those drugs, or fear that Mekhi would let me down again.

I had to be honest with myself if I were ever going to be honest with God. Angelina said He knew everything anyway. So that meant the Lord already knew my motivation for taking these steps. Based on what I read in the Bible, I didn't know if it even mattered to Him as long as my heart was in it. But I did know one thing for sure, I wanted to change. I didn't know anyplace else to make that happen, but the altar. It had been calling me all night.

Although it was difficult I ignored the stares of the congregates around me. Once again, I was the center of attention in a church, but this time, not because I was dressed sexily. Today was quite the opposite. I wore a two-piece sweater set and modest heels. Last night I cut every piece of weave out of my hair, relaxed it and pulled it back into a simple ponytail. No makeup adorned my face. I was surprised. I actually thought what I saw in the mirror this morning wouldn't have been so bad if I didn't hear the word tramp reverberating in my mind, but that didn't matter now. All that mattered was this moment.

Angelina had told me the story of the Samaritan women who'd had five husbands and was currently involved with a married man. God had forgiven her. I'd done some of my own study last night and found Mary Magdalene. Actually read about her. I'd always heard her named referred to as the tramp in the Bible, but tramp though she may have been, Jesus had loved her too. If He could love these women, He could love me.

"What is your name, sister?" the pastor asked, taking my hand.

Tears streamed down my face. The emotion that was heavy in my soul made it difficult for me to answer. "Samaria," I replied, feeling proud of who the Samaritan woman had become, of who I could become.

The pastor's lips split into a warm, genuine smile that embraced me. "Samaria, praise God. Welcome to *New Mercies*. Are you coming under Christian experience or to give your life to Christ?" he whispered for my ears only.

"I've come to give my life to Christ." I used my free hand to wipe my tears. An usher stepped up and handed me a tissue. I took it and swiped beneath my eyes. The pastor was looking at me. His gaze held sincere concern over the weeping that wouldn't stop. I smiled through my pain and said, "I need salvation."

He nodded understanding. "You're in the right place." Then he took my hand and turned me to face the members, who up until now, had been looking at my back. "*New Mercies* family, I present to you Sister Samaria. She's come to give her life to Christ."

A raucous roar of applause sounded from the small congregation. I also thought I heard the angels celebrating in heaven. . . . Celebrating for a sheep that had been lost, but was now found.

Reading Group Discussion Questions

1. Should it matter how a Christian woman dresses? Why or why not?

2. At the end of Chapter 4, Angelina reflects on how Danielle's death had been God's will. Do you agree with that statement? Why or why not?

3. Why do you think Samaria preferred married men?

4. Like most of us, Samaria made lots of choices based on the values that were imparted to her by her mother. There are several places in the book where her mother's opinion heavily influences bad decisions. At the end of the book she blames her mother for her low self-esteem. How much of who we are as adults can we lie at the feet of our parents?

5. How do you think Angelina's heartbreak over her father's desertion affected her?

6. At the end of Chapter 15, Samaria declares she's going to bust up Angelina's marriage if it's the last thing she does. Do you believe Samaria busted up Angelina's marriage? Why or why not?

7. In your opinion, can Angelina and Greg's marriage be saved? Why or why not?

Reader Discussion Questions

8. Samaria takes on the burden of supplying her mother with drugs. In Chapter 37, she talks about the people in White Garden respecting her for doing the right thing. Do you agree that trying to save her mother was her responsibility? What were some alternatives to the choices she made?

9. How could Angelina have better structured Mentor-a-Sister to protect herself from what happened?

10. How do you feel about the outcome for the characters? What would you have liked to see happen differently?

About the Author

Rhonda McKnight is the owner of Legacy Editing, a free-lance editing service for fiction writers and Urban Christian Fiction Today (www.urbanchristianfictiontoday.com), a popular Internet site that highlights African American Christian fiction. She's the vice president of Faith Based Fiction Writers of Atlanta. When she's not editing projects, teaching workshops about writing, or penning her next novel, she spends time with her family. Originally from a small, coastal town in New Jersey, she's called Atlanta, Georgia home for thirteen years. *An Inconvenient Friend* is her second novel. Readers may contact her at her website at www.rhondamcknight.net or at www.3sistersbooks.com.

Coming Soon

In the sequel to *An Inconvenient Friend:*

Angelina Preston is about to learn a broken heart doesn't have to be a bitter one.

What Kind of Fool

Rhonda McKnight

Chapter 1

"I can't ever trust you again," Angelina Preston said, sliding divorce papers across the table. "It's over, Greg, just sign them."

She watched her husband sit back and slump in his chair. "But—" he began.

"Don't say it." Angelina waved a hand to cut him off. "It won't matter."

"But I do," Greg continued, "I love you. I want to work this out."

Their waitress crept past them. Angelina and Greg's menus were still open, so she continued to the next table. Angelina supposed she'd assumed they still weren't ready to order. Little did she know if any eating was going to happen, Greg would be doing it by himself. She wasn't planning to stay around long enough to dine. She'd just wanted to meet in a public place so she could end the conversation on her terms, and so she wouldn't be weak.

"Angelina, are you listening to me?" Greg asked. The velvety tenor of his voice pulled her from her thoughts. "I feel like this is more about Samaria than it is about me," he said, pushing the papers back in her direction. "If it hadn't been her—"

"It'd still be over."

"I don't believe that."

"Why, because I put up with it before?" Angelina's mind

went back to the other affair, an anesthesiologist. She remembered the pain in her heart, the months it took to stop crying, and what it took to rebuild trust. But nothing had compared to way she felt when she'd found out about Samaria. She'd known there'd been another woman, but not her . . . friend. She closed her eyes to the pain that was still fresh. She then reopened them and met the sad gaze of her husband; soon to be ex-husband. Angelina cut her eyes away from him before his good-looking-ness melted her resolve.

Greg Preston was the most handsome man she'd ever known in her life, better looking than the actors on television. Skin the color of a cocoa bean and hazel eyes that were so sharp in contrast to his complexion that it gave him an exotic look, almost animalistic; like a wolf dipped in chocolate. His looks were the gift of a Creole mother and a dark-skinned Cuban father.

"Talk to me, Lena," he pleaded. It was so unlike Greg to beg for anything. He'd been begging for months. "Punish me, but don't do this. Please, can't you try?"

Angelina released a plume of air from her lungs and forced Samaria's face from her mind. "I wanted to work it out before," she said. "I wanted a baby. I was determined to have one, so I thought if I just put up with you no matter what, I'd eventually get pregnant again. But now, I realize I've been a fool." She shifted her eyes away from him. "For years, I'd been a fool."

"So are you saying you haven't loved me for a long time?"

"No. That's not what I'm saying. I'm saying I compromised because I wanted a baby, but now I have Katrice, and there's no need to settle."

"So you do still love me?"

"Greg," she said sharply, "what part of 'that doesn't matter' don't you understand?"

"Lena, It's not like I knew who she was." He leaned forward, raised his voice a little, and they both looked to the left and right to see if they'd drawn an audience.

True, Greg had not known that Samaria Jacobs, the woman he was sleeping with, was the same woman his wife had befriended and had known as Rae Burns. Greg had not known his mistress was so devious that she'd joined Angelina's church and wormed her way into her life, all with the intention of gleaning enough inside information to wreak havoc on their marriage. But it didn't matter, she'd told herself the first affair was the last affair, and she was standing on that, no matter how much he begged, no matter what her heart said. It was time to use her head.

"But what about my will?" She ignored the voice in her head and slid the papers that had now become a hot potato back across the table.

Greg lowered his head. When he raised his eyes, unshed tears shown in them. "I know—I know I was wrong, but I thought—I thought Christians were supposed to forgive."

It was she who sat back now. Angelina was shocked he'd pulled the Christian card on her. Steam rose in her belly and annoyance that he'd hit a nerve. She'd wrestled with the same thought all week; the thought or the voice that entered her head when she accepted the papers from her attorney.

"Are you sure you don't want me to just have these served?" Mavis Benchly, one of the top divorce lawyers in Atlanta, had asked as she peered suspiciously over her glasses.

"No," Angelina had answered. "He's asked to meet with me this week, so I'll just give them to him myself."

"Don't do it." There was the Holy Spirit again. Angelina felt an uneasy burst of perspiration, and her breath caught in her throat for a moment. But she shook her head, just as she was doing now. She didn't want to hear what that voice was asking her to do.

"Forgive?" Her hand felt unsteady. She returned the glass to the table. "What makes you think I haven't forgiven you?"

Greg's face clouded over with confusion. He didn't really know anything about the doctrine of forgiveness, and he'd just played himself.

"Then if you forgive me, why this?" He let his eyes fall on the papers for a second, and then returned his heated stare to hers.

"Because forgiveness doesn't always mean things will work out the way you want them to. Forgiving doesn't mean a happy ending." Angelina raised her glass and took another sip of water. Her stomach felt like it was in knots, and the same bead of perspiration was forming over her lip.

"I can read you. You still love me."

Angelina hated that those words were true. She hated that she wanted nothing more than to reach for his hand, let him touch her and take her home and make love to her again. She was such a fool for this man. And five months of celibacy wasn't wearing well, not after thirteen years of marriage. She wanted . . . she needed. No, be strong. You have to end this. "I want a divorce," she said, looking him squarely in the eyes, praying her waning confidence didn't allow him to read her.

Greg threw his head back and touched the papers as if her final declaration had made them real. He picked them up for a few seconds and lowered them to the table. He did not meet her gaze when he said, "I need my attorney to look at them."

"I'm not asking you for anything."

That statement got his head up. "What does that mean?"

"I just want the house, and I'm probably going to sell it and buy something smaller."

"That's ridiculous," Greg replied. "I will not agree to give you nothing."

"I thought it would be easier that way. Faster and I'm willing to do anything—"

"To get free of me." He raised his hand and washed his face. "I won't let you walk away without anything. It wouldn't be fair."

Angelina thought of Katrice, her new daughter or soon to be daughter, once the final hearing regarding the child's mother's parental rights had been held. They'd be severed, and then Angelina would be free to adopt her. Having the extra money in the bank would look good on her adoption application, and she could use all the pluses she could find with the divorce pending. Single parents adopted children all the time, but having a strong financial situation could help the application.

"Can you see Les right away?" she asked, knowing he'd give them to his frat brother, who for many years had been their personal attorney.

Greg put the papers inside the manila envelope Angelina had delivered them in. "In a rush?" He closed the metal clasp and let out a long sigh.

"Not really, but it's a good time to put the house on the market," she replied. "And well, I know someone who's interested in buying."

Greg looked down. At what, Angelina had no idea. He seemed to be concentrating hard. His lips were a thin angry line and his eye brows were furrowed, but even through his angry veneer she could see desperation.

"Angelina –"

"Save your breath." She stood. "I'm not going to change my mind." She picked up her handbag. "Just have Les send them to my attorney, and please, come get the rest of your things from the house. They're in the garage." Angelina turned on her heels. She couldn't bring herself to say good-bye, so she didn't. The emotional rollercoaster in her spirit moved her through the restaurant. Once on the street, she did a slow jog to the entrance of the garage and impatiently tapped her foot as she waited for the parking valet. Not wanting to wait even a second for change, she over-tipped him, slid behind the wheel, and gunned the gas. Angelina was running, and she didn't know if it were from her husband, herself, or her God.

ORDER FORM
URBAN BOOKS, LLC
78 E. Industry Ct
Deer Park, NY 11729

Name: (please print):_____

Address: _____

City/State: _____

Zip: _____

QTY	TITLES	PRICE
	A Man's Worth	$14.95
	Abundant Rain	$14.95
	Battle Of Jericho	$14.95
	By The Grace Of God	$14.95
	Dance Into Destiny	$14.95
	Divorcing The Devil	$14.95
	Forsaken	$14.95
	Grace And Mercy	$14.95
	Guilty & Not Guilty Of Love	$14.95
	His Woman, His Wife His Widow	$14.95
	Illusion	$14.95
	The LoveChild	$14.95

Shipping and Handling - add $3.50 for 1st book then $1.75 for each additional book.

Please send a check payable to:

Urban Books, LLC

Please allow 4 - 6 weeks for delivery

ORDER FORM
URBAN BOOKS, LLC
78 E. Industry Ct
Deer Park, NY 11729

Name: (please print): _____

Address: _____

City/State: _____

Zip: _____

QTY	TITLES	PRICE
	16 ½ On The Block	$14.95
	16 On The Block	$14.95
	Betrayal	$14.95
	Both Sides Of The Fence	$14.95
	Cheesecake And Teardrops	$14.95
	Denim Diaries	$14.95
	Happily Ever Now	$14.95
	Hell Has No Fury	$14.95
	If It Isn't love	$14.95
	Last Breath	$14.95
	Loving Dasia	$14.95
	Say It Ain't So	$14.95

Shipping and Handling - add $3.50 for 1st book then $1.75 for each additional book.
Please send a check payable to:
    Urban Books, LLC
Please allow 4 - 6 weeks for delivery

ORDER FORM
URBAN BOOKS, LLC
78 E. Industry Ct
Deer Park, NY 11729

Name:(please print):_____

Address: _____

City/State: _____

Zip: _____

QTY	TITLES	PRICE
	The Cartel	$14.95
	The Cartel#2	$14.95
	The Dopeman's Wife	$14.95
	The Prada Plan	$14.95
	Gunz And Roses	$14.95
	Snow White	$14.95
	A Pimp's Life	$14.95
	Hush	$14.95
	Little Black Girl Lost 1	$14.95
	Little Black Girl Lost 2	$14.95
	Little Black Girl Lost 3	$14.95
	Little Black Girl Lost 4	$14.95

Shipping and Handling - add $3.50 for 1st book then $1.75 for each additional book.
Please send a check payable to:
Urban Books, LLC
Please allow 4 - 6 weeks for delivery

ORDER FORM
URBAN BOOKS, LLC
78 E. Industry Ct
Deer Park, NY 11729

Name: (please print):_____

Address: _____

City/State: _____

Zip: _____

QTY	TITLES	PRICE

Shipping and Handling - add $3.50 for 1st book then $1.75 for each additional book.

Please send a check payable to:

Urban Books, LLC

Please allow 4 - 6 weeks for delivery